I0653988

THE LAST LADY OF ALBESSIND

TALES OF THE RIARDAN
BOOK ONE

Lloyd A. Meeker

WAYFARER PRESS

This is a work of fiction. Names, characters, places, and incidents are either the product of the author's imagination or are used fictitiously, and any resemblance to actual persons living or dead, business establishments, events, or locales, is entirely coincidental.

The Last Lady of Albessind – Tales of Riardan Book One

COPYRIGHT © 2025 by Lloyd A. Meeker

All rights reserved. No part of this book may be used or reproduced in any manner whatsoever without written permission of the author except in the case of brief quotations embedded in critical articles or reviews.

No artificial intelligence was used in the making of this book or any book by this author.

The author expressly refuses consent to any Artificial Intelligence (AI), generative AI, large language model, machine learning, chatbot, or other automated analysis, generative process, or replication program to reproduce, mimic, remix, summarize, train from, or otherwise replicate any part of this creative work, via any means: print, graphic, sculpture, multimedia, audio, or other medium. This applies to all existing AI technology and any that comes into existence in the future.

Contact Information: wayfarerpress@gmail.com

Cover Art and Interior Design by Fablesmithy, © 2025 Fablesmithy

Publishing History

This book was previously published under the title of Blood Royal

Wayfarer Press

Print ISBN 978-1-939092-12-0

Digital ISBN 978-1-939092-13-7

Tales of Riardan, Book One

Published in the United States of America

Acknowledgements

Heartfelt thanks to all who helped
bring this story to publication—so many!
Especially
To Susan, Mattie, Susan, Sandy, Helen, Nancy Rose,
Patsy, Lily, Martha, Sue, Clare and Michael
for their creative feedback;
Fablesmithy for this great cover art and book design;
storytellers throughout time,
who have nourished our souls
with stories like Isolde and Tristan,
which is the kernel of this one;
and always, deepest affection and gratitude
to my very resilient husband Bob.

Dedication

To my mother Kathleen,
whose brief and noble life shone with
her courage, her music, her generosity, and her beauty.
After all these years, I still wish
I could have had more time with you.
You still inspire me.

Chapter One

Unlike the large, perfect fruit shown in the flyer, the Granny Smiths at Budget Foods were small and beaten up—yet another disappointing triumph of reality over promise. Eva Milaras gazed at the poor things as she tore off the coupon and stuffed the rest of the pages back into her bag. Everything got bruised, one way or another.

Still, she was sure she could find half a dozen decent ones in the stack. She'd get some yams and put them together in a casserole—a tasty and inexpensive declaration that she was now back in charge of her life in spite of being broke.

She'd tough this out with what little cash she had in her purse until the gallery could figure out what was causing the mysterious delay in her payment. They owed her for two large paintings, and that money would be more than enough to get her back on her feet again. It was just a matter of time. She yanked a plastic bag from the dispenser and began picking through the apples.

She refused to think about losing her little studio. It had great light, decent ventilation, and was within walking distance of most everything she needed. So what if she had to maneuver around her bed to get to the tiny kitchen? With Derek gone, it was all the room she needed for her easel and canvases. She'd loved it, but the rent was due in two weeks and...well, she'd go to the gallery this afternoon, see what Leslie had to say.

She found two more unbruised apples and took them as a sign of better times coming. She really would take charge of her life—simplify, concentrate on her work, and avoid complications like an unemployed boyfriend.

"Pardon, Serenissima." A strong, warm voice from behind pulled her from her reverie.

Turning, she saw a man, early thirties probably, tall and well-built, dressed completely in black. Who wore such an expensive silk shirt and slacks to Budget Foods on a Saturday morning? They had to be club clothes, but he didn't look like he'd been out partying all night. And what a great face to paint! A delicious olive tone to his skin, deep eyes, strong angular face-planes, so... compelling, framed by black hair that fell unbound, thick and dangerously sexy, past his shoulders. Great shoulders. Lean waist. Yes, he'd make a terrific model. She found herself smiling at him, realizing too late that it probably wasn't a good idea. He was already standing uncomfortably close.

"Are you talking to me?" She backed away and tilted her head at the apples. "I'm afraid I've picked through these already. Good luck finding more decent ones."

"Forgive my abruptness," the man said, reaching toward her, "but you must leave this place with me immediately. You are in gravest danger. Please—we must leave this instant to avoid disaster."

Suspicion chilled the spark of interest she'd felt. "Look, I came here just for apples." She slid one hand into her purse, locating her pepper spray. "Leave me alone, please, or I'll call store security."

She hoped this guy didn't know that Howard—the entire security staff of Budget Foods currently on duty—was in his seventies and would never be able to stand up to someone like this man, who carried himself with the smooth precision of a dancer or a martial artist. But at least Howard had a radio.

The man dipped his head and upper body in an odd, twisting bow. "Milady," he said, his voice tight and urgent. "Please, I beg you. Your life is in real danger. You must trust me in this. I will explain later, but first we must flee."

Flee? Eva looked around at the worn ordinariness of Budget Foods, with shoppers inching their carts along the aisles. There was nothing here to flee from, except boredom.

Her finger found the directional notch on the tiny canister in her bag. "Look, I don't know you, what you're on, or what your deal is, but you're scaring me." She pulled out the spray and held it up. "This is nasty stuff, and I'll use it on you if you don't back off—right now." She backed away from him again and bumped into the stacked apples. Several of them tumbled to the floor—even more bruises, she thought, as if they didn't have enough already. She kept her eyes on the stranger, wincing as the apples thumped and rolled on the scarred wooden floor.

In a single fluid motion, the man flicked the can out of her hands and wrapped his arms around her, pushing her toward the floor, covering her with his body. Before she could scream for help, an explosion ripped away all sound. In a strange, time-suspended clarity on the way to the floor, Eva could feel the muscles of his torso flex and twist, pushing hot against her in a symphony of coordinated physical power.

How the heck did he know this was going to happen? Her back hit the floor, and her breath whooshed out in a grunt. She looked up into his face. His eyes bored into hers, fierce as a breaking storm. Blue gray, she thought. No, slate. He was heavier than he looked, and she needed to breathe. Her body had forgotten how. He had great eyes.

Then she remembered how, pulled in air. "Get off me!" She pushed against him, and he rolled away without protest.

She sat up. She couldn't think. Her ears hurt. The store—or what was left of it—was a mess. She could see two, no, three shoppers on the floor, not moving. In fact, nothing moved, and the stillness was horrible.

A soft groan floated through the smoke from somewhere. Still in its pink sweatshirt sleeve, an arm without an owner lay on the floor. And blood. Lots of it. This was so wrong. Oh, my god. She swallowed several times against a wave of nausea. What on earth had happened?

Then there was movement. All around her, shards of glass began to twitch and shift, becoming dark red scorpions scuttling toward them—dozens of them, different sizes, all the same. Glass shouldn't do that, she was certain of it.

"Do not move, Serenissima," the stranger commanded, his voice icy. He turned his back to her, putting himself between her and the scorpions. She stared at his back. He'd been hit by several pieces of glass—two of which stuck partway out of his flesh. All of those would have hit her if he hadn't thrown himself over her. What the hell was going on?

His hands glowed, and pale fire flowed from his fingers in dancing streams—first carving a circle around them, then striking out at each scorpion. As his fire hit each one, the creature sparked into smoke and dropped, again becoming an inert piece of glass.

What did he just do? Eva looked around, trying to locate her pepper spray, but couldn't see where it had rolled. She needed to get out of here. But her body was too heavy, felt too far away to respond.

"I don't know how," the man growled, "but your enemies have discovered who you are, milady. Now you will have no peace until you reach your Ceremony or they have destroyed us both, for I swear I will not outlive you."

He stood, bending down. His hair tumbled forward, as if reaching to touch her. "I apologize, Highness, but I have no choice but to carry you to safety. With or without your permission."

Why was he calling her these strange names? As he reached for her, Eva saw another shard of glass sticking out of his arm. Blood drenched his shirt down to the cuff. His hand dripped red, but he seemed oblivious of the injury. Still dazed, she felt him reach under her shoulders and knees and pick her up as if she weighed nothing.

He was kidnapping her. "Stop!" she screamed. "Put me down! Help!" She twisted against his iron-hard grip and grabbed a coconut from an end display as they passed. Eva pounded it against his chest and face, but he didn't even look at her as he strode through the carnage to the rear of the store, kicked open the warehouse doors, and jumped off the loading dock to the ground.

On the other side of the alley sat a sleek limousine with darkened windows. As they approached, a passenger door swung open. The man deposited her inside, wrested the coconut from her, and tossed it away. He climbed in opposite her and pulled the door shut, wincing at the reach. The limo began to roll.

Chapter Two

P anic electrified every nerve—she was trapped in a stranger's car. "You can't do this!" This was so not good.

She forced herself to deepen her breathing, get grounded in her body again. She needed to get out of this car and looked for anything she could use as a weapon. There was nothing but smooth luxury all around her.

Eva rubbed her arms as she scanned the compartment, grateful for the comfort of her own touch. Her hands were ice-cold against her skin, but still reassuring. *Maybe he left the door unlocked!*

She lunged for the door and pushed it open, prepared to leap. But the city of Roanoke was hundreds of feet below them. Inexplicably, they were airborne. The river was a sparkling blue ribbon wandering past the rail yards. This was really wrong.

The man scowled at her and gestured at the door. It swung shut against all the resistance she could muster.

"You can't fly in this thing, there'll be radar—" Eva realized she had no idea what she was talking about. "Or something. Homeland Security... You'll be tracked down." Maybe she could bargain with him. "Take me back now, and I promise not to file a complaint."

The man grunted, his face a pain-filled grimace as he unbuttoned his bloody shirt. "No one saw us on the ground, or since, milady. We are enshrouded in magic which makes us invisible to others."

What the hell did that mean, enshrouded in magic?

This wasn't supposed to happen when someone walked two blocks over to Budget Foods to buy apples. But it had. She wanted this to be a dream but knew it wasn't. She'd left butter on the counter at home. In this heat it would be a puddle by the time she got back. If she got back.

The man smiled at her—or maybe it was a wince—as he used his uninjured arm to peel his sodden shirt from his back. He obviously worked out. A lot.

So this is what cognitive dissonance felt like. "You know how serious a crime kidnapping is, don't you? Besides, I'm broke. I have nothing for you to demand in ransom. I'm not the one you want. You've made a huge mistake."

The man's smile was grim as he shook his head, saying nothing as he dropped his bloody shirt on the seat beside him. It made a heavy wet plop against the leather.

"Answer me!" she shouted. "What the hell is going on here, and where are you taking me?"

"I take you to safety, Serenissima," the man said with an apologetic dip of his head. "I ask for your forgiveness, but a longer explanation, which you most certainly deserve, must wait while I attend to my injuries. They require my most urgent concentration."

Eva watched as he arched his back and reached behind him. He's flexible enough to hold a difficult pose, she thought, and then laughed aloud at herself in disbelief. This man had probably saved her life, kidnapped her, shoved her into an invisible flying limousine going gods knew where, and now sat half-naked across from her, bleeding all over the cream leather, and all she could think about was how good a model he might be. But he really would make a terrific model.

Then there was the whole scorpions-from-glass thing. Maybe she'd been drugged and was hallucinating. Maybe. That would be the best answer possible, but this felt horribly real.

The man let out a sharp grunt. When she could see his hand again, it held a red-stained shard of glass, which he tossed into a corner on the limousine floor.

He blew onto the tips of his bloody fingers and murmured words she didn't understand. His fingertips glowed again, just like in the store. This time the air filled with the scent of lilacs, or maybe honeycomb—yes, honeycomb. He reached behind him again, and there was a sharp hiss.

Her kidnapper took a deep breath, arched, and reached behind him again. He scowled, and this time his hand returned empty.

"Forgive me, milady, but would you be willing to draw a piece of glass from my back? I would be most grateful." He lifted his shirt to his mouth, bit down on the torn sleeve, and ripped away a small strip. He offered it to her. "If you grasp the glass with this, you can get a better grip."

"You want me to help you? Oh, right!" She glowered at him. "There's nothing to stop me from pushing it in the rest of the way, is there?"

"Nothing at all." The man smiled, affable and grim. "And I might die. But whether I live or die, this car's course is already set, and it will take you to its destination. Without me to protect you when you arrive, you most certainly would die as soon as your presence was discovered. Quite unpleasantly."

He dipped his head, as if apologizing. "So, as distasteful as it may be to you, I represent your very best chance of survival." Again he proffered the scrap of cloth.

She was in a flying car and had no idea where she was or where she was going. So not in control of her life, just when she'd sworn to take charge and never give it up again. Hallucinating or not, survival sounded good to Eva.

"Damn." She took the scrap from him. It was the thickest, richest silk she had ever felt. "I have to tell you I don't do well with blood."

"Most grateful, Highness. But I beg you, please pull straight out, rather than up or downward. It is in a delicate place. I can reach it, but I cannot pull it straight out." He turned sideways. The shard stuck out of his right trapezius, she noted with an artist's anatomical eye, between the thoracic spine and scapula.

When she pulled that thing out, there was going to be more blood. It would come spilling out of the wound and... She fought down her squeamishness and folded the cloth between her thumb and forefinger. "Brace yourself," she said, talking more to herself than to him. "This is likely going to hurt."

"Pain does not matter. I am certain you will succeed beautifully. Just pull straight out, if you please."

Just as she grasped the shard, the limo lurched. "Sorry!"

"You are not at fault, Serenissima," he said through a clenched jaw. "We have crossed the threshold."

"I wish you'd stop calling me those names. It makes me nervous." Again she squeezed the glass and pulled. As it slid out, she saw it was much longer than she'd expected, and curved like a small exotic dagger. It was a miracle that it hadn't killed him. A thick rivulet of blood sprang from the wound. Nausea pushed up her throat and she tasted salt, but she'd be damned if she was going to throw up in front of her captor.

She dropped the bloody glass on the floor. She tried to look away, but couldn't. "It's bleeding—a lot," she said, holding the scrap of shirt against his flesh. "I'm supposed to press on the wound, but I don't think I can."

"I am indebted to you forever, milady," he said, his voice tight. Eva watched him blow onto his fingers, muttering the strange words again. Again his fingers glowed, making a nimbus of blue light, and he reached behind him to touch the wound. There was another sharp hiss, and Eva watched the flow of blood stop as the heavy fragrance of honeycomb swirled around her. The gash sealed to a thin white line.

Even through the blood drying on his back, Eva could see that it was not the only such scar. There were easily half a dozen others, some much larger than the new one. Who had scars like this? A soldier? No wonder he was so calm about it all. But regular people didn't do what he'd done.

The man was occupied with his wounds—this was her chance. She lunged forward to get to the controls of the car.

There weren't any.

Where a steering wheel and dashboard should have been, there was nothing but elegant wood-burl paneling and leather. How the hell did this thing work, and how was she supposed turn it off? Eva grabbed the seat back facing her, dizzy and frantic. This was all so horribly real, but surreal, as if she had been forced into someone else's life. Something had gone terribly wrong. These events had to belong to someone else.

She sagged back into the soft leather of her seat, calming her stomach, and studied her captor. She couldn't help it—with his intense eyes and sexy angular face, he really would make an incredible subject. She pushed the thought away—not the time for Stockholm syndrome. He was her captor.

"Okay. I need answers now." She scowled, hoping she looked fierce. "Who are you, what's happening, and why do you keep calling me 'Highness' and 'Serenissima'?" She focused again on his face. "Start with you—who are you?"

"My name, milady, is Talak." He smiled, looking apologetic. "There is no need for you to attempt my family names, as you would find them tediously long and hard to pronounce. I am your guardian."

Eva sagged in relief. She laughed, giddy and gloating. "I knew you had the wrong person! I don't have a guardian—both my parents are still alive. You've screwed up big-time, mister, so take me back right now."

"Not legal guardian as you know the meaning." He gazed at her, his eyes patient. "I am quite certain that you have strange dreams sometimes, perhaps often, as if you are in a completely different world. A beautiful world, with rather dangerous undertones."

Eva stopped breathing. How could he possibly know about those? She'd never told anyone of her dream world, even though it was where she often drew inspiration for her paintings. Against her will, she nodded slightly, breathing again, but already feeling cornered.

"They are not just dreams. The world you dream of is as real as the one you are familiar with, Highness. Two worlds occupy the same

11

physical space, this same planet, if you will. Although they occupy the same space, they are for the most part separate, joined only at particular threshold points. One world you know well. The other world is mine—and yours, if you wish it."

Perspiration tickled her neck. This was going to get worse, she could feel it coming.

Talak knelt before her on the limousine carpet, lifting his hands, palms upward. "That other world is a realm of magic, developed and practiced just as widely as lesser technology is in yours. Although the practice of magical craft is everywhere in that world, all the nations are ruled by members of a single royal bloodline who for some genetic reason are impervious to magical spell-work. They are an imperfect lot, our royals, and given to their own deadly intrigues, but they provide our only check against chaos. They maintain an order that could not be sustained in a realm of ungoverned magic."

Eva's head spun. The man kneeling in front of her, this Talak, had to be insane. But then there was the scorpion thing and the healing thing. To say nothing of the fact that they were in a flying limo with no steering wheel. This had to be a dream, and it was a doozy. On the flying highway to crazy.

She tried not to believe him, and failed. He knew about her dreams—that was more frightening than anything else. "Even if what you say is true, what does all that have to do with me?"

Talak bowed his head toward the floor, and his voice floated up from the stained carpet, past his dark hair and a shoulder crusted maroon-black with dried blood. "Years ago, one of the Clans Royal crossed a threshold to choose a breeding partner. Once every other generation, they do this to avoid the dangers of inbreeding, for the royals mate only with themselves in order to keep the purity of their blood line, to preserve their immunity to magic. In this particular case, she chose your father to sire her child. You, milady, are of the blood royal."

"What? My parents would surely have told us something about this if it were true."

"No. They would never have known. Or at least remembered. Your parents would have been ensorcelled. The royal who bore you would have been accompanied by a magician of great skill who would have bound them in spells of unknowing. The man and woman you think of as your parents would have believed completely that you were their own progeny, just like your two siblings. But the woman you think of as your mother never bore you. Your real mother came from the world you are now entering."

Eva fought vertigo. "Maggie and Johnny, too? All three of us? And get off the floor."

"Thank you, Highness." Talak rose and sat again on the seat opposite Eva. "You are the only one. Your older siblings are not of your mother. Even if they were, the genetic condition is not always predictable, which is why those who carry the royal immunity are so important to us. You—and your offspring to come—are essential to the survival of our realm and our way of life."

He smiled apologetically. "I am mortified to cause you such distress and confusion. I did not intend that you should learn these things so suddenly, without any preparation. I expected to have more time."

"Well, I expected to buy apples and then paint all afternoon."

Talak looked out the window as if he could see through what seemed to be fog. "I expected you to do that, too. Your identity as a royal was supposed to be kept secret until you could be properly educated and protected by your Ceremony of Recognition. I was assigned by our queen to be your guardian four years ago, when...when something terrible happened to your blood mother. But your identity is known now."

He made a face as if he had just tasted something rotten. "At the grocery store, you were the target of an assassination attempt, most likely mounted by some of your more unscrupulous and ambitious clan relatives. I have no doubt some of them see you as unwelcome competition for position and power."

"Well, they can have it all. I'm not interested."

"They would never believe you. It's all that matters to them."

A wave of helplessness washed over Eva. She shouldn't be in this limousine and this shouldn't be happening to her, but she couldn't find any rational way out. "Where are we going? And why can't I see anything through the windows?"

"There is nothing to see outside at present, Serenissima. We are between the worlds. We travel to your Ceremony of Recognition." Talak smiled, and Eva was sure he meant it to be encouragement. It felt like sadness. "After your Ceremony you will be safe." He lifted his shoulders, apologetic. "Well—safer, at least."

Chapter Three

E va glowered at the opaque windows of her flying jail, then at Talak. "You said this magic world was mine if I wanted it. Well, I don't. I've got money from a gallery to track down, so take me back home right now. I want out of your damn limo and out of your whole damn world."

"That is not possible, milady."

She wheeled on him, pounding her fists into the seat. "So you were lying when you said I get to choose? Lying about everything else, too, no doubt. Damn, you're smooth. I almost believed you."

"It is difficult for you to understand, milady, but——"

"But what?" She could hear her voice getting shrill. "I can't understand that I'm your prisoner and I don't want to be? What part of that do you think I have trouble understanding?"

Talak shook his head. "You do have the right to choose. It's just that you can't choose right now. Not until after your Recognition."

"So you say."

Talak shrugged. "It's our law."

For a moment Eva was so frustrated she couldn't speak. The man was reasonable as a stone wall. "Your law, not mine. Not mine! Now turn this thing around and take me home."

"No." Talak returned her glare, his voice flat and steel-hard. "For two reasons. First, if I returned you to your world as you ask, you would be dead within a week. Even I cannot protect you from the pack of assassins that would hunt you down now that your identity is known. Second, our law requires you to be Recognized before you are entitled to choose what you want to do, and where you will live."

"And I'm supposed to believe you."

"Eva—" Talak's face turned red, as if the tender tone of his voice startled and embarrassed him. He pressed his lips into a thin line. When he spoke again, he'd regained his polished formality. "Milady, I am more sorry than you can imagine that I have had to abduct you to safety, but I had no choice." He smiled in apology. "So you have no choice, either. Not yet."

Eva fumed. "What if I refuse this precious ceremony of yours?"

This time Talak's smile was a joyless thin line. "I will take you, willing or not, to our queen, and you will have your Ceremony of Recognition. To refuse would bring your immediate execution. I doubt you consider that an attractive choice."

He leaned forward to open what looked like a liquor cabinet between the two seats. "We will arrive soon, and you must prepare. Royals love formality and ostentation and will expect you to arrive in an appropriate manner." He drew out a large towel and several pieces of dark green cloth, precisely folded.

"You don't like them either, do you?"

Talak shrugged. "I am a magician, a lower caste, a servant in their—your—world. For the most part, they are no worse or better than anyone who grows accustomed to power and privilege." His face brightened. "But what can I do? I am part of their kingdom. It is in my blood to serve them. You."

"You serve me?"

He looked up, a strange fire burning in his eyes. "Never doubt it, milady." He took a deep breath. "You are about to be plunged into a world strange to you, full of dangers, things that aren't what they seem. One thing you must never doubt—I will gladly give my life protecting you. I told you I will not outlive you. That remains absolute. At first it was true only because of my commission to protect you. Professional pride, if you will. Now it is true"—he stopped and looked away—"for other reasons, also."

"Well, if you serve me, take me back home."

His face hardened. "So in a few days I can die trying to protect you from your enemies, knowing that you will die mere moments later? What kind of service would that be? No. You deserve better than that."

Eva shivered at the vision before trying to banish it. It wouldn't leave. She sat up stiffly in a posture she hoped looked royal. "I don't believe you. I order you to take me back."

He shrugged. "Order the sun not to rise, if you wish." He pointed to the stack of items on the seat. "We will arrive soon at a place where you can bathe and make yourself ready."

She crossed her arms in defiance. "I'm not getting ready for anything."

"That is, of course, your choice. More than one royal has arrived at their Recognition bound hand and foot." Talak smiled, looking resigned. "At court, elegance and decorum are valued. It would be to your advantage if you do not arrive as a badly dressed and unwashed prisoner, but one way or another, Highness, you will arrive."

The limo's windows cleared as it settled on the ground with a gentle thud. They were in some kind of park. Near them a large pond nestled against clusters of weeping willows, with rolling meadows and groves of trees stretching as far as Eva could see. Several swans swam on the glassy water, their wakes rippling out behind them. She turned back to Talak. "Where are we?"

"Welcome to my home—my most treasured and beloved place in this world, Serenissima. My sanctuary."

The car door clicked and swung open without her touching it, and Eva stepped out onto tufted grass and moss. The air was warm and rich with something sweet, like magnolias and jasmine. "Where's your house?"

"Not far. But we must save that for another time."

"Why?"

"The fewer who know you are here, the safer you will be. My house is always watched, by both friend and foe."

Talak led her to a stone bench facing the water under the willows. Beside a low fountain pouring into the pond, smooth flat stones led into the water. "Please feel free to bathe. The jar contains a cleanser that will nourish life in the water once you have rinsed it away. I will bring you fresh clothing and then wait at the car. I guarantee you will have complete safety and privacy."

"Says the guy who just kidnapped me."

Talak stiffened. "I am not a barbarian, milady. I understand and honor my duty. Better than you presently know."

Eva felt herself blush. That had been unkind and unfair of her. But she had a right to be, dammit! "Well, I need more privacy than this." The park's tranquility whispered to her, and she softened. "It's a beautiful spot, really, but I'm not a fan of bathing al fresco."

"Of course, milady. Give me but a moment." Talak strode to the trunk of the nearest willow and knelt with one hand on the grass and the other on the tree. He murmured something Eva couldn't hear. The fountain's jets rose higher, splashing their bright music against the stones.

The trees bent closer to each other, and their hanging branches wove together—forming a grotto walled off by a thick curtain of green. Ropes of green-black vines rose from the water and tangled with the hanging branches. From the vines, white blooms like water lilies flowered open all around. As they spread, they became luminous and released a voluptuous scent. Talak stood and bowed. "I hope this will suffice, as it is the best I can do under the circumstances."

"Wow." The grotto's soft, welcoming light and the sound of the splashing fountain charmed her. "Yes, it will. I don't suppose I need to understand what you just did."

Talak smiled and shrugged. "I have had a very long time to build a relationship with the land and water of this place. We are old friends, owing each other many favors." He loped to the car and returned with the folded green cloths. "I believe you will find these fit you perfectly, milady."

Eva couldn't think of anything to say, so she took the clothing and placed it on a stone just outside the grotto. She pushed aside the willow curtain and let it swing shut behind her. She crossed quickly to the other side and tried to slip out. The wall had become solid. She tried the area where she had entered. She couldn't part the branches.

"Escape is impossible, Highness." Talak's voice floated gently to her. "Besides, where would you escape to? You are in a world that presently offers you no path except to the queen, and that is precisely where I will take you."

Eva turned back to the fountain and stood still, her heart racing. Her prison had gotten smaller still. It should have been a relief to be alone for the moment, listening to the play of the fountain, bathed in the glow of lavender and cream blossoms, breathing in their luscious scent. But Eva felt numb. She was in someone else's dream—not in control, not knowing what anything meant, even though this part of the dream was as idyllic as any Maxfield Parrish painting.

She gave up. For the moment, at least.

Eva took off her clothes, noticing for the first time how much blood was on them. Talak's blood. She didn't want to think about him right now. She just wanted to wash away this fog of strangeness, the shock of having been yanked into a reality that earlier today she didn't even know existed.

She reminded herself that one of her strengths was resilience. She'd always made the best of a situation, and she'd learn how to do that in this one, too—she'd play along, at least long enough to find a way home.

Standing on the smooth stones at the water's edge, she let the fountain splash over her. The water was surprisingly warm, and soothing. She reached for the jar and opened it. An intoxicating fragrance rose from the pale yellow cream inside—complex, rich. And it felt delicious on her skin.

As she bent to rinse out her hair, she noticed minnows had gathered at the edge of the stones in the pond, clustered around where the cleanser formed milky fingers reaching out into the water. The pattern of the bright fish and the multi-shaded water captivated her, and she found herself memorizing the composition. It would make a great start for painting something abstract. She laughed in spite of herself.

After drying off with the wonderfully soft towel, she reached through the branches, which now parted without resistance, for the clothing. The dress was made from the same kind of thick silk as Talak's shirt. Sumptuous. Even without a mirror, she could tell the simple full-length gown and matching cloak fit perfectly, as did the soft green leather shoes.

When Eva emerged from the grotto, the car was gone. In its place was what looked like an open sleigh without horses. It sat as if plucked from some carnival's genteel water ride and deposited on the grass. The low door was open, and Talak sat on the red plush seat with one booted leg resting on the step. He'd cleaned up and donned fresh clothing as well. Still all in black. His eyes told her she looked good before he spoke.

"You are magnificent, milady. Magnificent." He lifted a flat brown box from his lap and stepped onto the grass. He presented the box with both hands, making the same odd bow he'd used introducing himself in the store. "These belonged to your real mother. It would be a good idea for you to wear them. Your clan will expect it."

"My mother...I don't know anything about her. She's dead, isn't she?"

"Yes, milady," Talak answered, his voice heavy with sadness. "Perhaps after your Ceremony..."

As she took the box, her fingers brushed his, and the jolt of attraction made her gasp. She looked up, surprised. Talak looked away.

The box was covered in butter-soft leather. Inside lay a necklace and matching earrings, made of elaborately looped and woven gold wire, set with what looked like garnets and amber. They had to be worth a small fortune.

She might be rich. No more food coupons. For the first time the possibility that she really did belong to some noble clan registered in her body. It was a strange but rather pleasant sensation. She put on the earrings. She loved the delicate brush of the dangles against her neck.

"Yes," Talak murmured his approval. "Allow me to fasten the necklace for you, Highness. Its clasp is unusual and may be difficult for you at first."

Eva held up her hair and tried not to shiver when his fingers grazed her skin. The warmth of him standing close behind her made her uneasy. She ignored it and let her falling hair push his hands away.

He returned to stand before her, nodding approval. "You are truly breathtaking, Serenissima." He gestured toward the sleigh door. "If you please. Your new life awaits."

Chapter Four

"What happened to the limo?" Eva stepped in the sleigh and sat down.

Talak closed the cutaway door. "This will be our carriage here," he said, walking around to the other side, "and we do call them carriages. In this world, your familiar technology is considered unacceptably crude. Abhorrent, even. Anything powered by combustion or electricity is dismissed as especially disgusting. Wherever your world would use such technology we use magic."

He sat back in the seat, raising one hand, palm up. The carriage rose, floating a few feet above the ground. "Although your bloodline rules, milady, we magicians make the realm work."

Talak's smile was at once playful and proud. "We who are especially adept are highly prized members of any royal retinue. Indeed, sometimes we become objects of bidding wars, symbols of status. I trust your Highness appreciates the services I can render." He gestured again, and the carriage flew forward across the meadow.

"So you wouldn't need roads." Eva thought about some of the other implications, intrigued. "What a strange place. I've got no one else to rely on but you for information about it, and frankly, that makes me a little uncomfortable. Good-looking men have lied to me way too often." Instantly she regretted calling him that.

If Talak was insulted, he didn't allow it to show. He seemed focused on the flight of the carriage toward a large lake. "You may choose to disbelieve me at any time, Highness, or consult others as you please. I have no claim upon you but through my steadfast service."

Eva thought his tone sounded a little too nonchalant.

"But please bear in mind," he continued, "it is most likely that members of your own clan were behind this attempt on your life." His face darkened. "In fact, I think it certain. Your Confirmation—and the potential for royal offspring it will bring—means a demotion for them in the order of succession, and therefore a loss of power and prestige for those who gained from your mother's death."

She hadn't thought of that. "Is the kingdom really so full of intrigue and danger as that?"

Talak turned to face her, his eyes flat as death, and his lips pressed into a tight, joyless line. "Highness, the deadly games of power and succession played at court make your Borgias and de Medicis look like half-witted stable-boys. I beg you, never forget that. If we can arrive at your Ceremony without another attempt on your life, I will consider that a small victory."

The lake had disappeared behind them, Eva hadn't really noticed when. The terrain they were crossing now had become rocky and harsh. Looking behind her she saw that they had also been climbing in altitude along a mountainous slope. "How much farther?"

"Not far, milady. I am reluctant to stop unless you need to. Our stealth and speed are our best protection until you enter the formal sanctuary of the Court. You will then be protected by law until after your Recognition."

A ripple of fear swept through her. "What is that, exactly?"

"Forgive me, but I'm prevented from disclosing its nature."

"In spite of all your steadfast service, I think you called it, you're not being very helpful."

He shrugged without taking his eyes off the terrain ahead. "I will always give you all I can, milady. Always." Talak hunched forward. "We must go faster over this last stretch. Castle Riardan is just ahead, and we have now become visible to all who may care to look."

The carriage raced between stark boulders and through wisps of cloud, as if they approached a mountain summit. Grimy snow lay in crusts between boulders and along gullies. Then the rocky slope fell away beneath them. They were over the mountain peak, which Eva now saw was actually the lip of a vast volcanic cone, many miles across. Its floor was verdant, dotted with lakes. Canals, each lined with clusters of buildings and gardens, formed spokes of an enormous wheel. At its hub rose the towers and turrets of a spectacular castle. The carriage dipped into the crater and sped toward it.

"Oh!" Eva felt a rush of wonder, excited—before a chill of fear took her. Suddenly this seemed uncomfortably familiar. Yes, she'd seen the castle before, in her dreams. She pretended that didn't bother her. "It's straight out of a fairy tale."

"It is a great edifice, to be sure, milady." Talak's voice was solemn. "But unlike fairy tales, where the castle is never attacked, siege has been laid against this one several times, twice in my own lifetime. It has never fallen. Queen Rhianna has ruled for a very long time."

He brought the carriage to a stop at the castle gate, and they disembarked onto a cobblestone plaza. There were no guards, no challenge, but as they approached, the massive doors swung silently open.

"You must enter before me, Highness," he whispered. "I will walk at your left side, slightly behind. Once inside, do not stop. I will whisper directions to enter the throne room. Prepare yourself—there will be an assembly of your new allies and enemies, all gathered to witness your Ceremony."

"So they knew we were coming."

"Before we crossed the mountain rim. If you please, milady."

Gathering herself, Eva took a deep breath and let it out. The air was sweet with the scent of gardens and fountains. She shivered, even though the sun was warm on her skin.

Well, there was no point in just standing there. If she had to go through this ceremony before she could get back to her real life, then that's what she'd do. She touched the necklace, warm at her throat, squared her shoulders, and marched forward.

"To the large closed doors directly across from us, milady." Talak's voice was a subtle murmur, no louder than a breeze. "The queen will ask you if you claim membership in your clan. You must answer yes."

"Must?"

"You must answer yes, or die. I beg you to say yes."

Goosebumps prickled her arms, but Eva refused to rub them. The soft tap of their steps on the marble floor echoed like an enormous clock ticking as she looked straight ahead and crossed the cavernous atrium. The air thrummed with power, thick with silent whispers and unseen forces. Every nuance of their movement seemed to rise, curl along the soaring vaults above them, and shimmer down the stone walls on every side. Eva shivered, certain they were being watched.

They neared carved wooden doors which opened unattended, swinging silently toward them, revealing a vast hall full of people parted to either side of a central path carpeted in scarlet. On a raised dais at its far end was an enormous gold throne. On it sat a dark-haired woman dressed in white. The light and color dazzled Eva, but the motionless silence of the assembly was like a physical blow. Every eye was trained on them.

"Directly to the throne, milady. Do not look at the queen until invited. Kneel on your right knee only and bow your head only. I will make your introduction."

Encouraged by Talak's quiet instruction, Eva stepped onto the scarlet carpet, keeping her eyes lowered. As soon as the first step of the dais came into view, she stopped and knelt as instructed, lowering her head until her chin brushed her mother's necklace. Reassurance flowed from it, giving her strength. She belonged here, it said.

"Most Serene Majesty," Talak declared with the effortless authority of a trumpet. "It is my privilege to present to you Eva bryl Madris, daughter of Madris bryl Hova, Peer of the Realm, heir to House Albessind, of the noble Clan Athat. She presents herself before you and this court to claim her rightful station."

The thick silence returned as Talak's voice reverberated against the stone walls and tapestries until it was no more than a breath. Eva wanted to look up. Instead she stared at her knee resting on the carpet and waited. The silence lengthened. Eva tried not to think about waiting, but waiting filled her and held her still. A musical, silver voice floated down from above her. "Whence comes this Claimant?"

"From the Seeding of Madris bryl Hova in the Lower World a generation past, in the country of United States, Virginia. The city of Roanoke."

"Who has held safe the Records of Proof?"

"I have kept and protected them, Majesty, according to your commission."

A doubt pricked Eva before she understood its question. How could Talak have kept the proof of her lineage? He would have been only a boy when she was conceived. She heard a soft rustle of clothing, which got louder, then ceased. "Eva bryl Madris, welcome." The silver voice sounded happy, perhaps even amused. "Rise."

Eva stood and raised her head to meet the queen's gaze. Eva gasped. She had seen that face, those ice-clear eyes in her dreams. Often.

The queen smiled, as if understanding Eva's shock of recognition. "Do you claim right to the seat of House Albessind, Clan Athat, as declared?"

Disoriented, Eva lost track of her instructions. She stepped back and dropped again to her knee, head lowered. "Majesty—my queen, I do."

"Rise, child." Eva stood and looked up. Queen Rhianna raised her hand, smiling. Her voice sounded pleased, on the edge of laughter. "Then I grant you a Ceremony of Recognition."

The hall vibrated to a susurrus of hushed voices until the queen addressed the assemblage. Her voice was no longer kind, but icy, commanding. "I summon six Space-Holders, two Referees, and three Assassins."

Assassins? Eva felt a clench of fear. She looked around for Talak. His eyes met hers, steady, but his face remained an expressionless mask as he stepped back, joining the courtiers. Eva's chest tightened, and she forced herself to breathe deeply. She stood alone in a widening circle in front of the throne.

"Those who have served in the last nine ceremonies, draw back. Those willing to serve, step forward."

There was a discreet shuffle as some men and women moved toward the walls. From all around the circle, two dozen courtiers stepped forward and bowed. Eva counted eleven as the queen assigned the roles. Those not chosen melted back into the crowd.

The Space-Holders formed a large circle around Eva, pushing the crowd back further. They motioned for her to move to the circle's center. With a gesture the referees floated upward, hovering a dozen feet above the stone floor. The assassins entered the circle and faced her. The hall fell silent. Eva kept her eyes on one of the assassins, a graceful red-haired woman whose smile was so sweet it felt predatory. Something awful was going to happen, she could feel it.

Would Talak have saved her life to deliberately put her in a situation where she might again become a victim? He'd seemed so concerned about getting her here safely. Was it just so she could die here instead of in Budget Foods? She decided it was unlikely, but what did she know? Maybe that was a part of the ceremony he'd refused to divulge.

She touched her mother's necklace, and again she took comfort from it. At the upper edge of her vision, she could see the dark orange shoes of one of the airborne referees. Whatever the rules of this event might be, she hoped the referees would enforce them.

"Are the space-holders ready to contain Our Ceremony?" the queen asked from the dais. The six around the circle spread their arms.

Eva shivered, as some force swirled around her. Everything beyond the circle seemed to ripple and warp, as though she viewed it through distorting Plexiglas.

The queen sat. "Begin," she commanded.

The red-haired woman raised her hand. Fire sprang from it and arced its way to Eva. It seemed to hit her, but she felt nothing. Her dress rippled, but she remained untouched. The fire turned to a stream of what looked like small silver blades. Each one struck her body and shattered. Then, reaching from behind, a dark claw of oily-looking smoke tore at her chest, blunting and fading as it struck. Relief washed through her in a warm tide. They were trying to kill her, but she was still alive.

Eva noticed the crowd beyond the circle applauding as if they were watching circus performers. They seemed far more interested in what the assassins were doing than what effect they might be having on her. A soft push against her back made her turn to see the third assassin, mouth open wide in a grotesque snarl. Eva could feel pulsing not-quite-sound flowing around her, vibrating across the circle. Like a worm crawling across her skin, Eva felt a tickle of queasiness—then it was gone.

The referees descended to the floor, and the shimmering dome that had isolated Eva and the assassins melted away. For a moment the hall was absolutely silent.

Then the queen stood, and her silver voice filled the air. "Eva bryl Madris, daughter of Madris bryl Hova, I welcome you to this court as a Peer of the Realm, and acknowledge your rightful place in the noble house of Clan Athat."

Applause burst from the crowd, and some kind of cheer that Eva didn't understand went up all around her. She shivered, giddy and tingling with relief—and to her surprise, pride. Then Talak was at her side, murmuring in her ear. "Approach the throne again, and kneel as before. Wait for the queen's command."

Excitement surged through her like music as Eva set her eyes on the scarlet carpet at her feet. With the applause echoing around her she walked slowly to the foot of the dais and knelt. Eventually the queen's jeweled slippers appeared in Eva's field of vision and stopped in front of her. She felt a touch on her right shoulder.

"Rise, Daughter of the Realm, and welcome to Our Court. Rise."

Eva stood, still looking down until the queen's cool fingers lifted her chin. She stared into the face she had seen so often in her dreams, the strange, happy, merciless gaze of her ruler, who touched her cheek and smiled. "Welcome, child. Your new life begins. May it be long, and full of wise service to Our sovereign glory." Everyone bowed as she turned and strode from the hall, disappearing through a door behind the throne.

Again Talak's quiet voice guided her. "You will now have an audience with Clan Athat's Ambassador to the Throne. Go out the way we entered. I will be right behind you."

The sun had descended below the mountain's rim by the time Eva finished the long train of introductions conducted by the ambassador, as well as receiving dozens of informal congratulations and social invitations. Talak had never been far away—accompanying her at a discreet distance from one interaction to the next, deferential, alert. Eva had relied on the ambassador for guidance during the introductions, but it was Talak's presence, his occasional tiny nod, that had made her feel like she was doing this right. She'd weaned herself of men's approval long ago, but there she'd been, enjoying his. He was an intriguing man.

Even now, as he guided their carriage along a peaceful canal in the twilight, Talak seemed on high alert. Reflected lights sparkled on the water everywhere in the soft evening as they passed mansion after mansion. Eventually they came to the front of an especially imposing three-story house, almost Victorian gothic in design, set by itself in the midst of an expansive park. A row of ornate iron lanterns showed a stone path leading from the canal to its entrance. Brighter light streamed from the tall windows, casting soft shadows in the garden surrounding the carriage.

"I feel like we've parked on the lawn like drunk teenagers."

Talak laughed softly as he opened Eva's door. "There is nowhere else to leave our carriage." His nose wrinkled from a deep frown. "And you will never encounter the stinking scab of asphalt here."

He gestured to the house. "As the ambassador said, your clan will provide you with a house appropriate to your station. But that will take a few days to get ready. In the meantime you will stay here as a guest of the queen. I will remain at your service—as protector and assistant—until you have fully established your own household." He turned to Eva, and his voice softened. "Longer, if you wish."

The soft light played across the angles of his face, and shadows turned his body into a lithe mystery of chiaroscuro maleness. Eva felt an inconvenient tingle spread through her.

"When am I allowed to decide whether to stay here or go back home?"

Talak shrugged, a small, cautious gesture. "You are entitled to decide now. You can announce your decision at court tomorrow, and I will take you back immediately." He paused. "But you don't yet know what you would be giving up. Give this life a chance. Please." His voice was earnest as he leaned toward her, and his hair fell across his cheek. She wanted to stroke it back behind his ear. "Let me help you see what life here might be like."

"But I've got friends...business..."

Talak smiled and shook his head. "I've taken care of everything. Your rent is paid ahead for six months, your checks from the gallery are deposited, your parents and friends have a message from you that you've taken some time off to travel and make sketches. You have no urgent reason to return right away."

Shock, then anger burned along Eva's spine. "How did you..." She couldn't finish, so she started again. "You've no right..." Then she realized the implications. "You've made me disappear! How dare you?" she said, her voice rising. "What else have you so thoughtfully arranged without consulting me?"

Talak looked over his shoulder, as if they might be overheard. "We should not discuss this out here. You have more enemies than you know, milady, and at this point, very few friends. We should go where our argument will be less public." He gestured toward the house.

"We're not arguing! You're treating me like a child, and I'm objecting. You're making decisions for me that only I have a right to make. Worse—not like a child, like your prisoner!" Eva marched to the door without waiting for him and tried to open it. It was locked. She stared at the door until he came up behind her.

He passed his hand over the lock, and Eva heard a bolt slide. "I'm sorry you are offended, Highness, but I will never apologize for taking care of you," he said quietly as the door swung open before them, and Eva stomped into the atrium.

The place smelled of quiet luxury—a mix of wood polish, lilies, and roses, of meticulous care from generations of devoted servants. Lamplight shone through lavishly wrought crystal and gold. Carved paneling and balustrades, all made of some coffee-black wood and oiled to luminosity, glowed against the red-cream marble of the floor. Her eye followed wide curved stairs leading into the amber light of an upper floor. She refused to be impressed.

"Well, I don't want whatever heavy-handed management you call care. I want to go back to my own life." She tilted her head at the foyer. "I may not live like this, but at least I'll be making my own decisions and depositing my own checks. That's far more important to me than luxury."

Talak was silent for a moment, his face tight, guarded. He bowed, formal and deep. "With your permission..." He clamped his mouth shut, as if holding back words he wanted to say. "I will arrange an audience in the morning. You must make your declaration before the queen and the court, which can probably take place tomorrow. In that case you will be in your familiar home by evening."

"Good." Eva wheeled away but realized she had no idea where she should go. "You've no doubt decided where I should sleep," she snapped without turning back. "Show me where it is, and then go away."

Talak passed her to mount the stairs, then turned to face her, his lips flat in a thin smile. He gestured toward the upper floor. "Your rooms are chosen by the queen, milady." His words were clipped, dry. "I regret I will not be able to follow your instructions to go away, however. My responsibility is to attend and protect you. I will do so as long as it pleases the queen, even if it does not please you."

The wood of the banister was warm and perfectly smooth under her hand. "I'm sure she'll understand when she hears of my decision."

"It is you who do not understand!" Talak's anger startled Eva, making her flinch. Her foot froze to the first step. "You thrash around like a spoiled child without understanding anything, without the slightest idea of what you are about to throw away, what kind of life lies ahead of you!"

His voice became quiet, but remained hard. "Regardless of the life you live, or where you live it, there will always be forces beyond your control at work—making certain decisions for you. It is the essence of civilized life to recognize what is not yours to decide and then to accept those necessities with at least a hint of adult grace."

The last bit stung, because Eva knew there was truth in it. Even so, she stuck out her chin and ignored the petulance in her voice. "It's my decision to choose where I live, and I've made it."

Talak bowed his head. "Indeed you have, milady, and I ask forgiveness for my outburst." To Eva he sounded resigned rather than apologetic as he started up the stairs. "Your decision will shape the rest of your life, and the lives of your children."

He turned his head to look down at Eva, his smile full of sorrow. "Tonight, however, you are a prisoner of my care, as you describe it, and you can do nothing about that." He gestured again to the floor above, and his voice floated back to Eva over his shoulder as he started up the stairs. "By tomorrow night you will be free to live however you please."

At the head of the stairs, Talak opened a door of carved wood with inlay—it looked like ivory, or maybe seashell—making an intricate vine pattern that rose from a thick root at the base into dozens of flowering branches twining symmetrically as they spread. Whimsical birds perched on the branches or flew nearby.

Eva knew enough about inlay to be impressed. It was masterful work. But it was nothing compared to the room beyond the threshold. A sitting room filled with graceful furniture upholstered in soft greens and gold glowed in lamplight. Giant tapestries depicting noble families picnicking in manicured landscapes adorned the walls. Forest green and cream rugs, so beautiful that Eva hesitated to step on the first one, covered the dark wood floor. The combined effect was of intimidating wealth and comfort.

"Impressive. Where do I sleep?"

"In the bedroom beyond. Through the double doors. Staff will assist you."

"Will you be in here?"

"No. I will occupy a chair in the hall."

"How can you sleep like that?" That sounded far too kind, Eva decided. "Not that I care." Gods. She really was behaving like a spoiled child.

"I will not sleep tonight, milady. Please rest in my protection one more night." Talak bowed and disappeared behind the closing door.

As soon as the door clicked shut, two older women in white aprons appeared from the bedroom. "Will milady bathe this evening?" asked one.

"No. Thanks." Eva felt a little dizzy. "In the morning, please." One of the women turned and disappeared. Silently, the one remaining lifted a flowing white gown from the back of a chair and made it clear she intended to help Eva change. Absentmindedly, Eva let her, even though it felt wrong, then watched as the maid turned down the enormous bed.

Tomorrow, she told herself, I will be home and this bizarre nightmare will be over. I will live the life I want, the way I choose.

Chapter Five

E va woke to the efficient bustle of the two maids opening drapes and setting a table next to a bay window. Strange, she'd slept like the dead. She stretched as a pleasant anticipation rose in her. By tonight she would be free, and Talak would be gone from her life.

Mysteriously sexy as he was, he was also controlling, arrogant, and infuriating. She'd be well rid of him and his exotic, pompous world. Tonight she would be back in her own little apartment and could get on with her real life. Full of delicious triumph, she arched her back, pushing against the thick linens of the bed, making them rustle and twist.

She sat up, but before her feet touched the floor, both servants stood waiting before her. With only a few murmured and deferential words, they guided her first through a luxurious toilette, and then to the table by the window where breakfast had appeared, waiting for her in crystal bowls and silver chafing dishes more delicate and graceful than anything she'd ever seen. The food was unfamiliar but delicious, and the coffee perfect.

As she set her napkin down, there was a knock at the door, which Eva knew would be Talak. At least he waited for one of the maids to let him in. He was dressed in black—again or still, Eva didn't care. She just wanted to finish this.

He looked good, though. She would never have a chance to use him as a model, but that was a small price to pay for her freedom.

He bowed. "We must return to Riardan for your audience, milady."

Eva nodded and stood. She thanked the servants, who seemed shocked to be acknowledged, and followed Talak down the stairs to the carriage outside. She tried to beat him to the carriage door, but somehow he got there first, and opened it for her with what Eva thought was sarcastic courtliness, as if he were making a point. The ride to the castle was silent.

Once again the doors swung open unattended, and as they had done only yesterday, Eva walked across the cavernous entry with Talak just behind her.

Once again Talak whispered in her ear. "This time I cannot announce you. When the doors open, you must stop as soon as you are inside the hall and kneel. You must wait for the queen's summons to approach the throne. Then you will approach the throne with your head down and kneel at the foot of the dais just as you did before. The queen will give you permission to rise. At that time you must declare that you renounce your claim to succession and petition to leave the kingdom, never to return. Use those exact words if you can. She will ask you a number of questions, and you must answer each. Then she will release you to return safely to your former life."

Eva gave a short nod and picked up her pace, impatient now at the imminent prospect of going home. The doors swung open before her. Again, the intensity of color and light of the throne room was a blow to her senses. She stepped across the threshold and knelt.

Head down, she listened for any sound of movement. An uneasy silence swirled around her. Only now did it occur to Eva that in sharp contrast to her arrival at court yesterday, this time her purpose in presenting herself before the queen was unclear to most, and once revealed would be considered madness by nearly everyone present. She didn't care. They were welcome to their world of magic, luxury, and political intrigue—all of them. She just wanted to go home. To her family. Her little studio. A life she knew how to live.

"Rise, Daughter of the Realm, and approach the throne." The cool silver voice of the queen floated serene in the restless air.

Eva rose and, as before, walked to the base of the dais and knelt again.

"Rise and speak your matter before Our court."

Eva stood. "Your Majesty, I renounce all my claim to succession, and want"—she corrected herself—"petition to leave this realm immediately, never to return."

Surprise rippled through the assemblage, a buzz of whispers, laughter, coughs, even a suppressed guffaw. It seemed to take hours to subside, leaving a silence more tense than before.

The queen remained motionless and without a flicker of expression, but it felt as if the temperature in the room had plummeted. Goosebumps rose on Eva's arms and a chill prickled up her neck. Taut silence stretched across the room, as if holding all breathable air far away.

"Do you hereby renounce for all time your lineage of Clan Athat, with its rights and responsibilities henceforth, for yourself and all your offspring?"

Eva squared her shoulders. "I do. I want to go home."

"Do you renounce all right to present yourself at Our court?"

"I do." Eva thought she heard a note of regret in the queen's voice, but whether it was real or imagined, it didn't matter. She was going home.

"Do you hereby sever all relationship with this realm and its affairs?"

"Yes." Would this tiresome formality drag on forever?

The courtiers around her stirred and whispered, but Eva kept her eyes locked on the motionless queen. Again tense silence spread and seemed to paralyze everything around her.

"Very well." The queen's voice rang louder, again serene. "We have heard your petition, and deny it. You may not leave."

The words were a punch to Eva's stomach. Her breath caught, and she clenched her fists. "What?" she shouted before she could think, "I have a right—"

The queen's slender hand flicked up like a pale knife, a small gesture, but it stopped Eva in mid-sentence.

"You have the rights I afford you, child—no more and no less." The queen's voice, now cold and hard, cut through the air. "I could have you executed where you stand for your insolence. Because you are unschooled in Our customs and the conduct appropriate to Our court, I pardon you instead. But do not test Our clemency again with such contempt for Our sovereign honor."

She stood, and everyone in the room dropped to one knee. "Let all now be witness to Our solemn decree: Eva bryl Madris of Clan Athat, daughter of Madris bryl Hova, shall remain a beloved subject here with Us, with all her honors, properties, rights, and duties to the realm intact. She shall not depart—on pain of death. A traitor's death

41

awaits any who would contrive or conspire for her return to the Lower World. She is a Daughter of the Realm, and shall remain so." The queen descended the dais and strode from the room.

Stunned, Eva stood motionless. She was trapped, a prisoner. Helpless. Her blood pounded in her ears, nausea churned her insides as she watched the courtiers rise and gather in small groups.

Then Talak was at her side, his face a stony mask. Eva hated to admit it, but she was grateful to see him. "Now what?"

"Now we get out of here before the wolves have a chance to gather."

As the carriage glided silently along the canal back to the queen's guest house, Eva alternately fumed and fought tears, determined not to let Talak see her cry. He drove in stone-faced silence.

In spite of her effort at self-control, her hands wouldn't stay still, as if their motion could somehow spring her free of the trap she was in. It was a luxurious trap, to be sure, but every bit as much a prison as if it were a dungeon cell. Her frustration blossomed into fury.

As the carriage stopped on the grass in front of the house, Eva turned to Talak and grabbed his forearm. "Okay." She pulled away because her hand had begun to shake, sending uncontrollable tremors up her arm to the rest of her body. She hugged her shoulders to hide the shaking. "Did you sabotage my chance at departure? Just one more thing you arranged for me because you already know what's best for me?"

"Milady—"

"And I'll know if you're lying."

Talak shook his head. "I can understand how you might suspect that, but I did not." He stared into Eva's eyes with alarming intensity. "I will never lie to you. I...never." He stared at Eva until she looked away. She believed him.

He came around to open her door. "I fully expected a different outcome and was as startled by the queen's decision as you." He smiled, looking apologetic. "Although probably not quite as disappointed."

He wanted her here? What was his agenda? But maybe there was still a chance... Eva got out of the carriage and looked up at him, standing so close she could feel his body heat. "I'm going to hold you to your promise not to lie to me. Ever." She put a hand on his chest, feeling the hard curve of his muscles through the black silk, feeling him tense at her touch. "You're attracted to me, aren't you?"

Talak stepped back, and Eva let her fingers brush downward over the ridges of his stomach as he moved away.

"You have to tell me the truth. You said you would."

Talak shook his head, looking vulnerable. It was a very satisfying look on him. "I promised not to lie to you, milady, and I will not. You must decide for yourself what my silence might mean."

Ah... she might be able to use this. She stepped forward, closing the space between them again, and stroked his jaw, his throat. "I think it means you are," she murmured. She licked her lips. "If you were to sneak me back home, I would be especially...incredibly grateful."

Talak flushed. His breath caught, and his voice sounded trapped in his throat. "We must go inside. Now, milady!"

As the door slammed behind them, Eva expected him to grab her in an embrace. Instead he turned away, pacing the length of the foyer and back, his hands on his head. He stopped in front of Eva, breathing as if he'd just run a long distance. "Let me tell you how this is—I neither lie nor exaggerate." He gestured to a chair covered in thick brocade. "Please sit. I will pace.

"What you just said is treason, and death to both of us. If I were not..." he bit off his words and massaged his forehead, "...your ally, I would report it. You would then be used and eventually executed."

"Used?"

"Yes, used." He knelt beside her chair and stared up at her with desperation burning in his eyes. "You must understand, finally, that the rules here are different from the ones you are familiar with. If you were to attempt an escape, here is what would happen." He rose and began to pace again. "You would become a nonperson, a mere chattel of your clan."

He whirled to face her. "Your principal value here is your ability to continue the bloodline. You would be used for that purpose." He grimaced, as if smelling a dead animal. "Bred. By whomever your clan might choose as the sire of your babies. Maybe several different men. After you had given birth to two, maybe three healthy children, however many the clan decided, you would be executed. In public. Your children would be raised by an appointee of the clan and taught to despise your memory." He stopped, his face flushed. "I doubt you consider that a desirable fate, but that's what would happen if what you just said to me ever reached the court."

He knelt next to her again, his eyes begging. "Please. Understand that you are not going to escape until the queen allows you to go." He paused. "If the queen allows."

Talak reached to touch her hand, but stopped short. "I beg you, turn your attention now to making the best of your situation, since you cannot presently change it."

He walked to the foot of the stairs and spread his arms in appeal. "I am completely at your service to help you do that, if you will but let me."

Chapter Six

The blended fragrance of numberless blossoms in the queen's walled garden drifted around Talak in the warm evening air as he knelt on marble pavement inside an ornate iron gate.

"Rise, loyal friend." The queen's voice was welcoming and gentle. "Come sit here with me."

"Thank you, Majesty." Talak rose and approached, tension a fist in his gut. It could be dangerous to ask for an audience like this, depending on the queen's mood. So far, her disposition seemed benign. "I know the hour is late and do not wish to intrude too deeply into your solitude."

"After your long service to Our throne and dynastic reign?" The queen's laugh sparkled like a fountain in sunlight. "Your presence is not an intrusion. Besides, We expected your request for an audience after Our decree this morning concerning your young ward's petition to renounce."

Again she patted the long marble bench she sat on. "I love this garden. It's where my aunt Estelle was slain. So many unintended consequences... Her murderers never intended to put me on the throne, which I didn't expect or want either. But that was the outcome—after a great deal of bloodshed."

She sighed, looking out on the walled garden's perfect green formality of low hedges, marble pools and fountains, and carefully placed statuary. "Their ambition put me here against my will. The ambitions of others may remove and destroy me at any time. This place gives me good perspective."

Talak knelt again before sitting on the farthest corner of the bench. "I also seek good perspective on unintended consequences."

"Your ward's petition touches a complex situation."

He relaxed a little, still cautious. "It does, Majesty. In my recollection a petition to renounce has not been denied in over two hundred years. It is your right to refuse, and of course I have no right to ask your reasons."

"But I will tell you anyway." The queen's voice hardened. "My reason is simple. I can't afford not to have her here. Her presence as an eligible bride is my best tool to expose certain alliances which plot my demise."

"Certainly, Majesty. But Eva is—"

"Eva? My concern is not for her at the moment, except that she stay alive and is able to breed. My concern is keeping my enemies as weak as possible. She's the last of this most recent seeding in the Lower World, and therefore a great prize. That I denied her renunciation has clearly marked her significance to me, and I'm sure those clans who know I suspect them assume that their suitors have no chance at her. For all those reasons, she will be sought by many and targeted for death by others—perhaps clumsily enough to expose their threat to me. Your job is to keep the girl alive, and see she's readied for royal life quickly. She must marry someone loyal. Soon. I will have her at court as quickly as it is possible to arrange. Even before she is married."

At court before being married? The queen must indeed have significant plans for Eva—and imminent. Talak took a deep breath and held it for a moment. It was time to confess what had gone wrong. "Majesty, concerning Eva, there is something else...another unintended consequence..."

The queen's frame stiffened, before she slowly turned and studied Talak with an appraising stare. "You are besotted with her. Well, have your fling, if she invites you to touch her, but make sure you don't interfere with my plans. On pain of death, Talak. Even for you."

Talak knelt in front of the bench. "There is more, Majesty."

He pulled in a breath, pushing against the tightness in his chest. "This is not infatuation. I...I love her. I know it is hopeless, and against all our custom, but I cannot extinguish it. In over three hundred years I have not loved like this."

Prepared for the queen's rage, he waited. Rhianna remained silent for a long time. When she spoke, her voice had retreated to regal formality.

"An unintended consequence, most certainly. We sent you to be her guardian after Madris's death because We knew We could trust you. We would never have imagined a magician of your powers, your standing, loyalty, and experience might fall in love with a woman of royal blood—whom you could never even think to approach, let alone wed."

Talak expected to feel shame at his failure, but found none. He waited.

The queen shook her head, gazing out over the twilit garden. "We are glad those of Our blood cannot have their lives extended by magic.

We do not think We could bear making such a stupid mistake, jeopardizing everything built during four hundred years of flawless service."

She sighed, and it sounded like resignation. "Well, at least you are invested in her well-being. That is what counts at the moment."

The queen stood, luminous and hard as marble in the twilight. "By the oath that binds you to Us and Our throne, Talak, keep her alive. Get her educated and married well. Never forget she belongs to Us, and to Our realm."

"Yes, Majesty."

"Leave Us now."

For a long time Rhianna pondered Talak's disturbing news. Astute as she was in assessing dangers and subterfuge, she could never have imagined or anticipated this. Over and over—even during just her reign—he had proven his unquestioning loyalty, his complete trustworthiness. He had fulfilled every mission with efficient obedience.

Now his loyalty had divided, and she could no longer rely on him as she had. He had been blind as a stone lion in his honor and duty, and she had always been able to manipulate him easily with it. If his sense of duty and honor should ever drift elsewhere... He would never admit it, but she knew love made men do stupid things without the slightest notice, and she couldn't afford that. Not now.

She sighed, regretting the prospect of losing such an effective weapon. Perhaps there was another way... No. She couldn't afford to let him live. He knew far too much about how she had maintained her crown. If he was ever forced to make a choice, his own sense of honor might turn him against her. She couldn't afford that uncertainty.

The problem was that she needed him a while longer, at least until Eva bryl Madris's courtship had flushed her enemies into the open. She would have to be patient. And very careful.

Late that night Queen Rhianna received another visitor, ushered through a secret door into the dim chamber where she sat. He was wrapped in robes that obscured his identity from even the guards who escorted him.

"It appears," she said, without waiting for him to rise from his knee, "an opportunity is at hand for you to advance your clan's status at court and at the same time have your long-sought revenge against your old enemy."

"My queen is most gracious," a muffled voice replied.

"Yes, remember this favor. Make certain your clan puts forward a suitor for Madris's daughter, and be ready to act swiftly when Talak becomes vulnerable. You will not touch him until We send word, and then act only in the manner We dictate. Is that understood?" The cloaked figure nodded and knelt again. "Yes, Majesty. Most grateful, Majesty. You can count on me."

"By your life, We do count on you. You may go."

Chapter Seven

T he next few days passed in an unhappy fog for Eva. Garthius, Ambassador for Clan Athat to the Court of Queen Rhianna, asked her to choose between two homes, and Talak escorted her to view both. In fact Talak was always near—supporting, advising, relaying her instructions to workers, making her tasks as easy as possible.

She chose the smaller of the two houses, which had only forty rooms, because it had larger and more beautiful gardens. It was a far cry from her tiny studio apartment back home, and Eva felt embarrassed, even intimidated at the prospect of occupying such a huge house. What would she do with forty rooms? She had no idea. Her learning curve looked like a wall.

While her house was being readied, another message came from the ambassador. It was time, he said, for her to visit the lands of Athat and her mother's estate, which now belonged to Eva. She owed the estate and its people a visit. Would she like him to arrange an official party to accompany her? No, she replied, still too numb to object to another obligation she didn't want or understand. She would rather go on her own, and she would have Talak accompany her.

She'd often joked with friends about owning an estate on the Mediterranean one day, but now the prospect of being a wealthy landowner seemed much less attractive. What did one actually do with an estate? She didn't need it, and it didn't need her. It had obviously been running since her mother's death without anyone at the helm—other than some manager, no doubt. And a staff. She thought about a group of servants—no, people—and their families, running a house and a farm or whatever made up the estate for years, repairing, planting and harvesting, caring for livestock, gardening, living their own lives, just carrying on, until the owner showed up.

As far as they were concerned, she was the new mistress. The idea made her feel obligated to them and even more helpless. This was way more responsibility than she wanted. Living her own kind of life now seemed more than ever an unattainable fantasy.

"We head west, milady," said Talak as he gestured the carriage into motion. "Athat is a beautiful province, with an abundance of scenes you may wish to paint one day. It is rich in agriculture and has many fine artisans. Achthon, one of the great rivers of the realm, runs through it, making it strong in commerce and trade. Your estate lies on its banks in a particularly pleasant spot." He smiled knowingly, adding, "And a strategic one, also."

Eva nodded, feeling daunted but determined to cope as best she could. She recalled the map of Athat and its surrounding provinces Talak had shown her last night at the queen's residence. She'd taken note of the river he'd pointed out on the map, which ran from near the foot of Riardan to empty into a vast body of water. She couldn't remember the name.

Her estate. A place she was connected to by blood, but built by forebears she knew nothing about, inhabited by a series of strangers, full of a history she had never learned. So intimate, so alien.

"So what about my mother? You were going to tell me about her."

"What do you want to know?" Talak sounded cautious.

"Everything. Anything. What kind of a person was she?"

He shifted in his seat. "She was beautiful, smart, kind." Talak turned to Eva. "A gifted amateur artist, a sculptor. You come by your artistic gift through her, I think."

"What happened to her?"

"She was betrayed. Murdered by political enemies."

"But what happened?"

Talak shook his head. "You don't want to know, milady. For your own sake. At least until you understand your new world better."

Eva stiffened. "Stop telling me what's best for me," she snapped. "I deserve to know how she died."

"My job is to protect you, and I must make decisions to do my job," he said bluntly. "There are conflicting versions of what happened. You can hear them all from other sources whenever you wish, but I refuse to contribute to your confusion. You're already under pressure to learn far more in a short time than is fair."

Eva was surprised at the sadness in his voice.

"Please," he continued, his voice softer. "It is better that you learn more of her life, before focusing on her death. I'm sure you'll become more familiar with her at Albessind."

Was he just being her controlling jailor, or was he giving good advice? Eva tried to hold on to her anger, but the grief in Talak's voice had somehow taken it away. Maybe she really didn't want to know everything, at least right now. And he was probably right, there'd be as much of her legacy as she could absorb when they landed. But she'd learn the truth about her mother's death sometime soon, one way or another. Of that, Eva would make certain.

Past the rocky headwaters of the river, the landscape below them softened, opening to a rolling, fertile expanse. Farms, forests, and small villages shaped the landscape into a picturesque quilt with their fields and fences and, to her surprise, tree-lined roads with the occasional animal-drawn wagon.

"Why do they have roads here? I would have thought they weren't needed with magic."

"No roads in Riardan," Talak acknowledged. "But here most rural folk can't afford magic to transport them. Even on the wealthy estates such as yours, you'll see that magic is seldom used on the convenience of serfs and mixed-blood sharecroppers." He brought the carriage lower, until they were only a dozen feet above the water.

Eva listened to the occasional sounds of livestock and farm life drifting to them as they passed, and the low voice of the river itself. It seemed unfair to her that the hardest physical tasks should go unassisted. "But why not?"

Talak shrugged. "A gifted magician will head to Riardan to train, then seek well-paid employment there. That leaves only relatively unskilled magicians here in the countryside, maybe a nature witch or two. The reality is more complex than that, because it also shows the disregard of the privileged for the welfare of those they control." He looked away. "It could easily be much improved, if anyone cared to address it. But most of the elite, both magician and royal, care only about what happens in Riardan."

She squirmed slightly, feeling guilty by association. "Can't you do anything about it?"

"I myself am no more than a servant, albeit a privileged and wealthy one. Those of our caste have no right to initiate anything. Moreover, I am bound in service to the queen. Her primary concern is to hold on to her throne, which she does with..." Talak stopped, as if selecting the best words, before continuing, "fierce singleness of purpose."

He shook his head. "She has no time or interest in disturbing a long-standing inequity that most others take for granted." Talak smiled at Eva. "She directs my efforts elsewhere."

His words chilled her. As powerful a magician as he was, Talak was no more than a servant, belonging to a lower class than hers. "But if magicians make everything work, why don't you run the realm, too?"

"That was tried, long ago. As bad as our present system may seem, history teaches that magician rule was far worse." He barked a grim laugh. "Magicians can take power easily, but generally make very bad monarchs once they have it." He shrugged, apparently at peace with the status quo.

They followed Achthon's banks in silence, traveling until the gaunt cone of Riardan was only a gray shape on the horizon. From here there was no visible hint it contained the capital city, or that the kingdom's wealth and power were so concentrated inside it. A comfortable relaxation spread through Eva. How far away it seemed.

Hours later, they rounded a bend in the river and a substantial manor, built of warm tan stone and set on a hill, came into view. Below it on either side of the river lay several farms dotted around a modest village. On the near side of the river, the village was dominated by a tall brick building set right on its bank, half out over the water. Several barges were tied up to its wharf.

"Albessind, milady. Your ancestral home." Talak pointed the carriage toward the terraced grounds of the manor. "Welcome, and long may you enjoy it."

They were met by Mirren, the house manager, a slender gray-haired woman with high cheekbones and the crisp, caring manner of a head nurse. She introduced her staff of eight, the groundskeeper and his two assistants, then the farm manager with his field laborers and stable boys clustered at a respectful distance. All seemed eager and anxious—proud to have the Mistress in residence, but unsure of what kind of mistress she might prove to be.

Eva introduced Talak, whom they acknowledged with more reserve and, to her surprise, fear. She watched him converse with each of the managers with respect and interest, and watched them warm to him. She smiled to herself as she mounted the steps to her ancestral home. He would charm them all in no time, she had no doubt. He always knew just what to do and what to say.

Dinner was much simpler than what Eva had eaten at the queen's residence, but unquestionably more fresh—and delicious. "Farm-raised lamb, milady, and vegetables taken from the garden this afternoon," murmured Cook, who asked to be called by title rather than name. Eva had summoned her to receive the diners' compliments, so she stood just inside the door to the kitchen, wiping her glowing forehead with a sleeve and beaming nervously before bustling back into her domain with a curtsy.

Eva's apartment occupied half the top floor. The front offered a spectacular vista of the river, fields, and village. At the back, the windows looked out onto a large patio and garden, a large walled garden with rows of vegetables and fruit trees. Beyond the wall stretched dense woods.

The calm, rich power of the land was comforting, something she had not felt in Riardan. She slept soundly in the heavy four-poster bed, and awoke only when one of the maids drew back the curtains to reveal a sun well above the horizon.

Eva hurried through breakfast and found Talak and Stoich, the farm manager, standing by the carriage. Stoich was almost as tall as Talak, and lean as a rail. He pointed at fields across the river as he spoke, his lined, weathered face probably as animated as it ever got. As she approached, Talak turned and bowed and Stoich immediately did the same. They planned to tour the farms on the far side of the river first, then work their way in a rough circle back through the village, across the river to the mill, the near farms, and home again.

Stoich climbed into the back, while Talak assisted Eva, then pointed the carriage toward the river. They descended in an arc gentler than the slope of the manor's hill.

A kaleidoscope of scenes and information followed, all of which was interesting but more than Eva could absorb. These fields raised only this grain, others grew a variety of crops in rotation. She felt humbled to learn some families had been tenant farmers here for more generations than records went back.

People greeted Eva with a mixture of respect, fear, curiosity, and hope. For her part, she hoped her questions and comments came across as she felt them—warm, genuine, and unpretentious. Not at all knowledgeable, of course, but interested.

In the village they stopped at the mayor's office for Eva to sign the Albessind genealogy maintained there. He bowed and pressed Eva's fingers to his forehead, then brought the book out of its vault with trembling hands and opened it to the last entry.

Above the space where she was to sign, Eva saw her mother's name printed, and a signature. It was the first time she'd seen her mother's handwriting—a strong and sensual signature. In a column to the left of the signature were four names, including her own. Madris's children. The other three names—like their mother's—had a line drawn through them, each with a date adjacent. Without asking, she knew her siblings were dead. She was the only one left. Eva shivered as she picked up the pen.

Next they crossed the river to what Stoich had called the mill, the large building extending out over the river. Most of the grain raised in the entire region, he said with quiet pride, was milled here. It provided a significant income for the estate, and relieved many other landed families of the need to construct and maintain such a facility—a good arrangement for everyone. The barges came and went all year long. The mill needed constant maintenance, which was a burden, and occasionally the flow of the river was too low to turn the driver wheel, but those times were rare and short-lived.

The last visit of the afternoon was to her stud farm, boasting acclaimed bloodlines, even one with several show champions. She listened attentively to the manager describe the traits of the breed, known for its combination of speed, strength, grace, and endurance—considered to be the finest for a quality carriage horse. Buyers came from all over the kingdom to augment their stables.

Eva hadn't seen horses used at all in Riardan, but was assured they were a part of most ceremonial events and processions, and outside of Riardan, carriages were the fastest form of transport for all except those who had access to hired magic.

The sun hung just above the horizon when they arrived back at the manor. The house was already lit in welcome, and another delicious meal was brought steaming to the table. Tomorrow Eva would tour the house and grounds, then visit artisans and business folk in the village. But this evening it was all she could do to finish the meal gracefully, retire, bathe, and collapse into bed.

Again she slept deeply, with dreams of land, river, and forest—gentle and resonant as a cello's melody in her bones.

She awoke on her own and drew the curtains to watch the sunrise. When the room was bright, she rang for the maid, ready to take on another day of learning. But first she needed some breakfast—she was ravenous.

The tour of the house began. It was larger than it looked, with more gardens than she'd seen from her apartment windows. The entire third floor was closed up, with everything draped in dustcovers. There were huge cellars full of wine, cheese, and preserved foods; armories full of weapons; storage rooms of unused furniture and chests of memorabilia. There was also a complete wardrobe, belonging to her mother, which would require minimal adjustment to fit her.

"What was she like, Mirren?" Eva asked, fingering the sleeve of a russet satin dress.

"Your mother, milady?"

"Yes. I want to know about her."

"She was the finest mistress I've ever known." Mirren sighed. "I watched her grow from a wee one," she announced with obvious pride and tenderness. "She was so smart and happy as a child. And beautiful."

Mirren blushed. "I'm afraid I'm not very objective about her, milady. My happiest years were spent serving her." She looked squarely at Eva, her eyes brimming with tears. "Four years gone and I still miss my mistress. She made this place come alive, so warm."

A shadow passed over the house manager's face, and she dropped into a curtsy. "And I'm sure you'll do the same, milady," she said quickly.

"I can only hope," Eva said, trying to soothe Mirren's concern. "Thank you. Is there a portrait of her somewhere?"

"The truest one is in the library. When you're done inspecting the house, we'll go there for the accounts. You'll see her then." Mirren wiped her cheek and closed the doors to the dressing room.

"And all her other children, my siblings," Eva murmured, "dead, too."

"Gone before her, milady," Mirren whispered. "Picked off one by one in the year before she...went."

She faced Eva, her face anguished. "The last killing changed her. Broke her heart, it did. She told me there was one more—you—in the Lower World, but she kept it a close secret."

The cold reality of her mother's loss settled on Eva. "A parent's worst nightmare, to outlive your children."

60

Again, Mirren wiped her cheeks dry, but her eyes burned with intensity. "Aye, milady. Lady Madris took great comfort knowing you were safe. Please take care of yourself—for all our sakes."

Eva smiled, pretending she didn't feel like someone had painted a large target on her back. "I will, Mirren. Thank you."

All the other rooms were appointed with fine furniture, sculpture, paintings—including a display case of Eva's own early drawings. With a jolt she realized they must have been stolen from her childhood home and brought here to a mother who couldn't visit her daughter without endangering both their lives. Now they were a bitter confirmation of why she was here, and that the family story she'd grown up believing was a lie. It didn't matter much that everyone had sincerely and even lovingly believed the lie—it was still a lie.

Eva shivered when Mirren pulled open the carved double doors to the library, as if she were about to meet her mother in person, not knowing whether Madris would approve of how her daughter had turned out. The room smelled of oiled wood, books, and countless hours of undisturbed silence. Sunlight flowed through the tall windows, but somehow the room still seemed dim.

And there she was, framed in gold—Madris bryl Hova. Her mother. A strong, intelligent face looked down at Eva—inquisitive, noble, but kind. Her dark hair, swept up into a formal coiffure adorned with a rainbow of gems set in gold. A strong but full mouth, with a hint of humor gracing the lips. Filled with the loss of never having known her, Eva tried to stretch across the gulf of time to connect, and almost reached her. Eva had the strongest urge to call out to her but stopped just in time. She'd only look silly.

The artist had admired his subject. The brushwork, although imperfect, highlighted her mother's beauty, vigor, and warmth. Madris's graceful hands were folded in her lap, resting on the voluminous folds of her forest-green dress. Eva recognized her own chin in the portrait, and it made her chest hurt. She was drawn again to the eyes—wide-set and knowing, somewhat sad, wise—as if she wanted to say something, too, she thought. She wished she could hear what it was.

Eva became aware of others sitting quietly at a long table, waiting for her. She didn't care. She leaned forward, let her mother flow into her, and felt something change, maybe even complete, in her body. She took a deep breath, as if receiving it from her mother's exhalation, and breathed it back to her. Their bond was sealed. Her mother had given her this place, and would watch over it with her.

Slowly she turned to those waiting at the table. "Thank you for waiting for me. That's the first time I've seen her." She wiped her eyes and sat as Mirren took the top leather-bound book from a stack on the table and placed it before Eva, opening it to a place marked by a black ribbon.

Going through the finances of the estate was overwhelming. The farms, the grain mill, horse breeding, lumber, a fleet of barges, the ferry between the two halves of the village, various leases—all had been profitable for decades. All this was hers now—more wealth than she had ever imagined having.

After lunch, she and Talak returned to the village. They walked through the market square, where vendors were closing up their stalls for the day. They visited the tiny schoolhouse, presently lacking a teacher, weavers using local wool on their looms, artisans making bright ceramics and metal jewelry, the village doctor, the blacksmith, and even an instrument maker.

Later, as they sat down to dinner, Eva felt already nourished by the textures of interconnectedness, depth, and beauty of what she'd seen. She'd never lived in a small village before, and she was awed by its grounded, determined, fragile life. Sure, that interconnectedness could be a knife that cut both ways, but even so, it was such a welcome contrast to the court intrigues that Talak kept talking about.

She put her fork down and looked up at Talak. "I was wondering. Could you use your magic or your connections to help these people? They work hard and yet have so little. And I have plenty to fund the efforts. It seems silly to have the means and not use it to help the people here."

A smile warmed Talak's face. "What sort of help would you suggest?"

"Finding a good teacher for the school, for a start." Eva shivered, remembering the empty building, and its promise of a cruder life for the whole village as long as it remained empty.

"I'll pay the salary, or at least most of it, depending. Someone the villagers approve of, someone who's likely to stay and become part of the community."

She gazed at the wholesome food on her plate, remembering how often her fridge back home had been nearly empty. How different tonight's meal would look in the rooms above the shops, or in the little stone house the ferryman lived in.

"It would help everyone if we could provide the doctor with more supplies, and more skill, if you can do that." She looked up at Talak

63

and smiled. "I saw you do that blue-fingered healing thing on the ferryman's arthritic hands. Did it take? I understand sometimes on mixed-bloods it doesn't."

Talak grinned. "I thought I was being subtle, but yes, the blue-fingered healing thing helped. I'll check in the morning to see if I can do more. I expect you'll be fully occupied here."

"Good. Then if I'm making a wish list I'd add reducing maintenance at the mill, and making it more efficient with the water we've got. Also repairing that farmhouse that needed attention—the second farm we saw yesterday. And its hay shed, too."

He lifted his wineglass to her. "All very observant and generous choices, milady. Let me see what I can do in the next few days. And if not this visit, then next. I will report to you on my progress."

Chapter Eight

Five days later Eva stood in the middle of her new house in Riardan, arranging her mother's possessions that had been shipped up from Albessind. The array of wealth and furnishings inherited from a woman she had never known proved to be mysterious and disorienting. Even the smallest ornament had a story behind it. Eva could feel it in everything she touched, a history no one alive could tell her. Stories of an intimate stranger.

Earlier that morning Talak had brought her a small wooden box—remarkably plain in design. Inside were a few shells and rough agates that looked like they had been collected on a beach, and a heavy silver ring set with a single carved stone that resembled malachite.

"It's your mother's signet—Seal of the House of Albessind, milady. Now yours," Talak said quietly. "You will wear it nobly, I have no doubt."

It felt clumsy on her index finger. She was unused to its weight or bulk, and she did not feel particularly noble at the moment. Standing in the midst of her new house, with servants moving here and there unpacking, arranging, and preparing, a sudden rage took her, blurring her vision and making her shake. She was being walled in by every artifact, as if comfort was supposed to make her captivity acceptable.

She'd been kidnapped from her life, but nobody at all seemed to care. In fact, everyone seemed to think it not only perfectly normal, but cause for congratulations. Inevitable and appropriate. And no one would risk a traitor's execution to help her get home. Why would they? As far as they were concerned, she belonged here.

Eva focused on the ring, heavy on her hand, channeling her anger into the dark green stone. Talak had been right. If she couldn't escape this world, she would focus on making a success of being a prisoner here. She would learn to survive, no matter what. She would learn to play her captors' games, and master them. Inside this fancy prison, she would create a life that suited her.

As a small start, she'd set up one hell of a studio in her house, and she'd make Talak sit as a model for her.

Chapter Nine

E ven before the furniture had settled in her new home, Eva began receiving invitations to attend social events, meet potential
suitor families, or join special interest groups. Her newly appointed
tutor and advisor in matters of protocol, a thin, rather academic man
named Hulvis—who seemed to come alive only when talking about
the intricacies of royal society—explained the significance of each invitation, and the advantages and risks of accepting or declining it. Who
she aligned herself with in these early days, he said, would have great
bearing on what her social and political landscape would look like in
the future.

Only a few days after her return from Albessind, an invitation from
Ambassador Garthius arrived by lone courier without any fanfare—in
sharp contrast to many of the others—to attend a celebration welcoming her to her seat on the Clan Council.

Accepting this invitation was not optional, Hulvis had said, his
eyes sparkling with excitement as he reviewed it. Which clan members
had also been invited would indicate what the ambassador might have
in mind for her political career—an extremely important first step.
Hulvis began to quiver with a puppy's excitement when he saw the
list of those attending. It was clear, he said in a rising voice that made

Eva want to stop him before he made a puddle, that the ambassador intended to include Eva at the highest levels of political function. It had required several appreciative but increasingly firm remarks to curb his effusiveness. Now, preparing for the ambassador's dinner, Eva sat as still as possible while Celine worked her hair into a woven sweep—to be held in place with a delicate web of silver and pearls, her maid had promised cheerfully. It was a traditional design for un-married women of her clan, and perfectly appropriate for tonight's event.

Eva wasn't used to having to sit so still, even though she'd always demanded it from her models. And she still wasn't used to having a staff of servants hovering around her. It felt a little immoral, but she had to admit it was more enjoyable than she'd thought it would be.

Celine's movements were deft as she finished her work. Eva really liked Celine's warm, ample-bodied energy. Her thick, gray hair was always drawn into a tight bun at the nape of her neck, and she always dressed in a plain gray smock with a white apron. As befitting her station, she'd said without a trace of embarrassment when Eva had asked if she wanted more variety in clothing.

Celine didn't converse, really, although she would quickly re-spond to any question or instruction. Mostly she nattered steadily in a cheerful monologue that meandered through a maze of domestic news and musings connected by the freest—and sometimes star-tling—associations. At first Eva imagined Celine's chatter would quickly become annoying, but it hadn't. Instead it was comforting, as well as informative. Motherly, even, Eva thought with a pang. She'd never see her parents again, or Maggie and Johnny. Ever. She choked on a sob.

Celine's hands stopped. "I know it's hard, my lady. A shock, really, to be dropped into a new life." She gave Eva's shoulder an affectionate pat. "We'll all help."

Eva gazed at Celine's kind face in the mirror. She was mixed-blood, she'd informed Eva with the same cheerful practicality that she might use in announcing she was right-handed, or that the garden was producing the best melons she'd seen in years, even though that single fact had fixed her social station forever as one who served others. Neither adequately magician nor royal clan, her blood had determined her future from the moment of conception, and it seemed she had embraced her destiny with contented enthusiasm.

Some mixed-bloods, she'd said in one of her monologues, were enough royal or enough magician to have special status, but most were "just regular folk." Eva was dismayed at the rigid caste system at the center of their society, but Celine didn't mind at all; in fact, she claimed that she had the advantage. Healing spells usually worked on her and her kind, although not always. One had to be more of magician blood for such magic to be reliable. And she certainly hadn't enough royal blood to hold even the most minor government post. "Lightning never strikes cabbages, milady," she had said, obviously happy to leave such involvement—and its dangers—to others.

Eva admired Celine's handiwork, smiling at her own elegant reflection. Just two weeks ago, or whatever it was, she'd lost track—before Talak and the explosion—she could never have imagined her hair adorned with a small fortune in silver and pearls. She looked good. In spite of its restrictions, this new life did have some benefits.

A discreet but firm tap sounded at the chamber door, and Efron, the house manager, flowed in holding a silver tray. On it rested a piece of cream-colored paper. Eva watched him cross the room. For a heavy-bellied man, he moved with surprising speed, a kind of oily, silent efficiency.

Talak had been furious when she'd chosen Efron from the candidates her clan had recommended. But she'd taken Celine at Talak's recommendation, and she felt obliged to listen to suggestions from members of her clan as well. Eva felt a little uncomfortable around Efron, but he ran the house with quiet precision.

Celine backed away, deferential, head down. Her previous warm enthusiasm had vanished, replaced by the neutrality of an inanimate object.

"Milady," Efron intoned with a soft bow, "the list of tonight's guests, and a note concerning their station and lineage, prepared by your advisor in protocol."

He placed the tray on the bureau in front of Eva and stepped back, his lips pursed in disapproval. "Your magician friend has insisted upon driving your carriage tonight instead of one of your qualified staff."

Efron sighed. "He seems to forget he's just a magician and therefore not indispensable to you. I do wish you would not let him meddle so, but of course, whatever your ladyship desires."

He backed away and bowed again, more deeply. "Is there anything else, milady?"

Eva shook her head, surprised by the snick of dangling pearls colliding behind her ears. "Nothing else, Efron, thank you."

Only after Efron had noiselessly slipped away and closed the door behind him did Celine move, returning to stand behind Eva, patting invisible strands of hair back into place.

"You don't like him much, do you?" Eva asked.

Celine smoothed the net of pearls. "That's not right for me to say, milady."

"I insist."

Her maid looked around the room, as if ensuring Efron was really gone. "It's not because he's a eunuch, I swear, milady," she whispered close to Eva's ear, "but no, I don't like him at all. He's not a friend to you or me, and that's all I've got to say about it."

"You're afraid of him, aren't you?"

Her eyebrows shot up. "Of course I'm afraid of him, milady!" Celine took a deep breath and looked around again. "All of us are. He could ruin my family, my whole life in an hour, if he chose."

A ghost of revulsion curled through Eva. "How do you know he's a eunuch?"

"It was a scandal, many years ago. He is magician pureblood, and once was very powerful. He made advances to a royal—even kissed her—without her permission." Celine shivered, her face a cloud of disgust. "For punishment he was castrated and placed under a geas to prevent him from using magic ever again." She clamped her mouth shut, as if biting off her sentence.

No wonder Talak was so careful in his gestures toward her. "Tell me the rest, please."

Celine hesitated and then bent again toward Eva's ear, her voice barely audible. "He remembers, milady," she whispered, "what he used to be. He's a very angry creature. Cruel, too—a side of him I pray you never see. Please don't trust him too far, for your ladyship's sake. For all of ours, too."

She rubbed her palms against her apron as if wiping away something unpleasant and bustled to an armoire where a lustrous pale blue evening gown hung.

"Now then, milady," she said, loud and cheerful once more. "Let's get you dressed for dinner!"

Eva studied Talak's strong profile as the carriage flew through the warm evening, following a canal lined with ornate lampposts. She'd missed being with him, she realized. He really was striking. She remembered how he'd looked after the bomb-blast, relentless and bleeding, carrying her to the limo while she beat on him with a coconut. "I miss seeing you all the time," she said, surprised at the tenderness in her voice.

"I you also." His jaw twitched as he stared ahead. "You have but to send for me, milady, and I will come to you—no matter what. My opportunities to take initiative in such matters are now severely limited by protocol."

"I'm sorry—I didn't realize..." A ripple of embarrassment washed through her, learning she was responsible for his absence. She was still struggling to absorb the complex but one-sided code governing the interaction of magicians and royals. It seemed a royal could behave however they wanted toward a magician, yet the code governing magician conduct toward a royal was strangely rigid, and penalties for violation seemed disproportionate, often horrifying—as she had just learned in Efron's case. To maintain the purity and safety of the Blood Royal, her tutor had explained. A royal owed no courtesy to those below her, and could never acknowledge any claim to social equality with the ruling class. Nothing could be allowed to jeopardize that prime directive.

She decided to change the subject. "I don't mean to be insulting, but you're sure you don't mind sitting outside with the other chauffeurs tonight?"

Talak smiled enigmatically, or so she thought. "I do not mind in the least, Serenissima. I wanted very much to do this, which is why I offended your house manager by insisting that my offer be delivered to you."

"You don't approve of him, do you?"

"You know I don't, milady. I believe I've already made that quite clear."

"But why?"

"There are many reasons. Principal among them are that I can't trust him to act in your best interest, and that the member of your clan who recommended him may not be your friend."

"I know about him being a eunuch and why it happened."

Talak's laugh was a sharp, cold bark. "I doubt very much you know the whole story, milady. It's one best left unrepeated. But always remember that he served someone else before he came to you."

"But so did you."

Talak stiffened as if she'd spat on him. The carriage stopped, hovering above the water. He swung to face her—pain, pride, and anger turning his eyes to storm clouds.

"I serve the throne," he said, his voice measured and flat, "and always have."

He straightened into a rigid, formal posture. "I serve the throne—bound by an oath forged hundreds of years ago. For far longer than you have drawn breath, that oath has been my life and my honor. I've made no secret of it to anyone and have never violated it. Never!" His voice rose, tightening.

"You defile..." He swallowed hard. Twice. "You do not understand that you heap the most repugnant slander on that oath and on me by comparing me to the treacherous slug you have chosen to manage your household."

Eva sucked in a breath, shocked. She could feel a flush of embarrassment prickle as it rose along her neck and face. What was the rest of Efron's story, that Talak knew and she didn't? And Talak taking offense? Her words obviously had cut deeper than she'd imagined they would. She was embarrassed, paralyzed by their effect. Too embarrassed to apologize.

"Hundreds of years?"

Talak looked away. "This is not the time or place to explain to you the sacred chains of my honor." He bit off each word, his voice icy, bitter. The carriage started forward again, at a much faster clip than before.

Chapter Ten

The vaulted ceiling in the ambassador's dining hall glittered, as did everything below it. Glittered. There was no other word for it, Eva decided, and the sight took her breath away. The vast wood-paneled salon where the clan members gathered for introductions had been spectacular, but this was the most spectacular setting she could imagine. Garthius must employ a staff of utility magicians just to keep the lights blazing and the silver shining, she thought. Her clan was obviously wealthy, even by the extravagant standards of this kingdom.

The ambassador's chair—throne, really—sat on a small but distinct dais, occupying the head of a table that stretched half the length of the hall. Along each side were a dozen place settings, all of which occupied less than half the table's length. At a discreet distance behind his chair, a trio of musicians played graceful, bright music. The lower half of the hall had been set with two dozen seats facing away from the table, arced toward a small stage. It looked like there would be entertainment after dinner. Eva shivered in anticipation. This would be fun!

She was escorted to the place of honor, to the immediate right of the ambassador. Footmen bowed to each guest and stepped back, disappearing into the inanimate opulence of the hall as if merely another ornate fixture.

Following the example of all the other guests, Eva stood behind her chair, her excitement rising, until the ambassador—resplendent in official robes of the court and flanked by two enormous wolfhounds—strode in. Once he had settled on the dais and the dogs lay stretched at his feet, the footmen materialized again and seated everyone amidst genteel chatter.

The first three courses were indescribably delicious. Many of the aromas and flavors—even textures—were new to Eva, adding to the exotic wonder of the evening. Drawing on Hulvis's social coaching and watching other guests, she managed to follow most of the etiquette without any more embarrassment than what provided the basis for light-hearted banter. The wines, strange and captivating, turned her excitement to a warm glow of contentment.

The ambassador's wife, who sat across the table from Eva, and the charming man who sat next to her kept her entertained and engaged throughout the meal. Even the ambassador entered the conversation from time to time, and Eva was encouraged by his polished, avuncular interest in her progress in establishing her new household.

Just as the next course was served there was a scuffle at the hall's main doors, and Talak strode in, arms lifted. "Stop!" he bellowed. "Touch nothing!" His voice was like a sword, beheading all other sound. The musicians halted in mid-phrase, and the eerie silence that followed thundered in Eva's ears.

Armed sentries, looking shaken and disorganized, entered and formed a hasty semicircle behind Talak. He ignored them and approached the dais. The wolfhounds rose to their feet, growling. Eva exhaled. She'd been holding her breath.

Talak continued, his voice a commanding boom. "I apologize for the intrusion, my Lord Ambassador, but an illegal murder is being attempted. As each of you loves life, you must not touch the food in front of you."

"But this is an outrage!" fumed the ambassador, standing between his giant guardians. "How dare you burst in here and disrupt us? This is a clan affair, and even if you are right, you have no authority here! I will see you in chains for this trespass!"

Talak bowed slightly. "On the contrary, your Honor, I do have jurisdiction. This house is provided to you and Athat at the pleasure of the queen. It is her property, and all are guaranteed safety on it. Any clan bloodshed on the queen's property is a violation of the Pact of the Clans. You above all should know this. I present myself in the name of our queen to enforce that agreement."

Nervous murmurs skittered around the table, but nobody touched a fork. The soldiers behind Talak slowly lowered their weapons.

The ambassador huffed. "But this is my residence! No one would attempt a murder here. As you say, this place provides sanctuary for all of us."

"Then give some of the food in front of your guest of honor to one of your beloved dogs, Ambassador."

Stunned silence echoed the length of the hall, and its tension stretched out forever. Nothing and no one moved.

Finally, the ambassador fidgeted with the knotted silk at his throat. "That will not be necessary. I believe you now. We will find and punish the culprit in our own way. You may leave with our thanks."

Talak took another step toward the dais. "I regret the embarrassment, my lord, but that is insufficient. In the name of the queen, I order you to let this assemblage witness how you have failed to provide sanctuary for the members of your clan gathered here. I expect many present will insist on demonstrated proof of my charge before they believe it," he paused. "Unless you wish to taste her food yourself."

The ambassador's face turned scarlet. "Damn you!" he muttered, and signaled to his footman. The servant quickly gathered up Eva's plate, approached the dais, and hesitated.

"But the dog is innocent!" The words were out of Eva's mouth before she knew she had spoken. Every head swung to regard her—most looked astonished, some even amused.

Talak turned to her, stone-faced. "Then milady can choose something—or someone—else in this room to taste her food."

She stared at the circle in the tablecloth where her plate had been, her face burning.

Her host made a curt, impatient gesture and looked away. The footman picked up a small morsel with a spoon and fed it to the dog. In a heartbeat it yelped once and collapsed, twitching.

Eva gagged, fighting to keep down her dinner. Horrified murmurs filled the hall and evaporated into a confused silence that seemed to wait for some sign from the ambassador, who himself seemed paralyzed. She tried not to turn her head as she looked down the table. She felt as though everyone was staring in accusation at her, even though she was the one who had nearly eaten the deadly food.

The tense silence was broken by a cough from one of the footmen standing behind Eva. She turned to see him fall to the floor in convulsions. Two of the guards rushed to the fallen servant and made to carry him out, but Talak took command again, stopping them with a lifted hand. "Place him on the floor behind the ambassador," he ordered, "we will examine him in a moment. Well, ambassador?"

Without even a glance at his wife, Garthius wheeled away, cursing, and strode from the hall with his remaining hound trotting at heel.

As if nothing at all had gone awry, Talak approached the ambassador's wife and drew back her chair. With skirts rustling she scurried unceremoniously after her husband. One by one, the guests stood and silently departed without looking back.

Eva was the only guest remaining. The glitter of the hall now seemed garish, made ugly by death. She rose, staring across the table at Talak, unsure of what to do.

"Are you ready to return to your house, milady?" he asked in a gentle voice, as bland as if he had asked if she was enjoying the weather.

She scanned the empty hall, trying to comprehend what had happened. "You just saved my life. Again."

Talak grinned and tilted his head. "With the greatest of pleasure." However his smile faded, replaced by a scowl. "I think you are still unaware of how perilous your existence here is, milady. I propose that after you have gathered yourself we review this evening's events as a lesson in survival. We can either do that at your house, or we can travel quickly to mine, where I can ensure your complete safety."

The room began to spin. Eva grabbed the back of her chair to steady herself, and Talak was immediately by her side, solicitous, gentle, protective. She could feel his body heat caressing her bare shoulder.

She wanted to let go, to collapse into him, to have him hold and comfort her. Instead she focused on the family ring as her fingertips followed carved crevices and shapes in the chair-back in front of her.

For the first time since arriving in this world, she was truly afraid and unsure of what to do. Although she hated her cowardice, she wanted to hide. "I'd like to go wherever I am safest, please," she said quietly.

"Then it will be my pleasure to offer you my hospitality, milady. Allow me to escort you to your carriage. Soon you will be completely safe in my home."

Chapter Eleven

The canals and houses of the city slipped past them in a blur as they flew through the warm night. The carriage swept up the slope of the great crater of Riardan and sped down the other side. As her adrenaline jitters subsided, Eva noticed her white-knuckled grip on the side of the low door. She forced her hand open. As her breathing calmed and the terrain below them softened into rolling countryside, she turned to Talak. "Help me understand. What happened tonight? How did you know my food was poisoned?"

"Tonight you learned that you have more enemies close at hand than you know. Your enemies are keenly aware how serious a prize you are. One or more of them—think if they can't win your hand, or at least win an alliance with you—are willing to violate highest law to get rid of you so their rivals can't have you either."

Eva didn't even try to hide her irritation. "I asked for help understanding. I don't need yet another condescending lecture from you to remind me that I don't know anything."

"I apologize, milady." Talak dipped his head but kept his eyes on the fields ahead. "I didn't intend... It's just that this is so important, and I don't know how else to convey it to you. Your very survival demands that you make profound shifts in your outlook—socially, in particular. This is not Roanoke, where murdering one's rivals is usually frowned upon."

He sounded sincere, but Eva still smarted. "I know murder is legal among royals. I do know that much."

"Murder, yes—but not under every circumstance and most specifically not on Crown holdings."

Her anger deflated. This was the kind of knowledge that other royals would have grown up learning a piece at a time. She envisioned layer upon layer of condition and implication, creating an intricate code for acceptable murders. A code she knew almost nothing about, and yet she'd been a target twice. Tonight she'd almost died before learning the most basic rules governing her survival.

"So how did you know my food had been poisoned?"

Talak's slight pause spoke his agreement to change subject. "I noticed an unusual command spell—directed not at an inanimate object but at a person. In order to be effective, someone must already be under a compulsion spell. Enslaved, if you like. The difference was very subtle but important. Forgive me if I sound self-congratulatory, but I doubt that many magicians would have noticed." He turned in his seat, scanning the night.

"But to me it was a sign that something was terribly wrong," he continued. "I scanned the house for connected spells and found one. A concealment spell and what it concealed was poison. I traced it to your plate and the pocket of the ensorcelled servant who delivered it. Whoever cast these spells was of superior skill, most certainly working for one of your relatives, who himself was probably seated at that table. Or herself.

"In a setting where no one would have expected magic and poison to be used, I expect it would have gone undetected until too late." A grim smile darkened Talak's face. "I forced myself upon your festivities before that could happen."

Eva shivered in the warm air. "But was it the ambassador? It was his house."

"No, most unlikely. It would be too obvious and too dangerous. Too many risks for him if you, a clan member, were killed in his home, since the ambassador's right to commit murder is suspended for as long as he holds office. He may have been behind the bomb blast in the Lower World, but he would never attempt your murder in his own house."

Talak shifted toward Eva, apology filling his face. "This may sound condescending, but I have to say it. This attempt on your life has levels of cause and effect, appearance and reality. To analyze it you must first think of who in your clan might benefit most from having you die, and especially having you die under the ambassador's nose to discredit or weaken him. Then we must think of who might benefit most from your death in the ambassador's house if an innocent person could be framed as the perpetrator of a disgraceful and illegal assassination."

"Wow. That's really disgusting." Eva shook her head, chilled by the vicious subtlety of the intrigue. "I'm glad you're on my side."

"Never doubt my devotion to your welfare, milady. But also do not doubt that someone at your table tonight wanted you dead. Probably more than one, but at least one who was willing to break royal law to get you out of the way before you could become a more serious threat to them."

Talak turned the carriage away from what in the darkness looked like a lake—Eva thought maybe it was the lake where she'd cleaned up only recently—to traverse a broad, rolling field. When he spoke, his voice was tight, pleading.

"I beg you to rely more heavily on my knowledge of this world, at least until you can navigate it on your own. To do that, you must believe that behind whatever actions seem arbitrary or condescending is my...my deepest concern for your welfare." He fell silent, although by the way he pressed his lips together Eva could tell he wanted to say more. They traveled in silence as a full moon lifted slowly from the hills forming the dark horizon.

The carriage entered a thick stand of what looked like old-growth fir and cedar. Their massive quiet enveloped them, and Eva breathed in, relishing their pungent scent flowing around them.

Talak smiled at her sigh. "Some of my sentinels," he said. "They like you." Then the forest gave way to a vast meadow. On the far side of it Eva could see a large house built against what looked like a much older tower, set next to another lake. "Welcome again to my home, Serenissima—this time to my house."

As they sped across the meadow, Eva watched the windows in Talak's home light up, ready to receive them.

Talak bowed deeply as Eva entered. "You honor my home, milady. It is a privilege to provide you safe refuge tonight."

She stood in the atrium of Talak's house, astonished. It was a breathtaking combination of the simple, almost rough textures of natural stone walls and sophisticated artwork perfectly displayed—uncluttered, almost austere, full of meticulous beauty. He had an artist's eye, no question.

The stone walls glowed in soft warm light that came from...she didn't see where. It didn't matter. She soaked up the peace of his home. "Impressive," she murmured. "And beautiful."

Talak dipped his head. "Thank you. I am fortunate enough that I can afford whatever artwork I desire, so I must take the greatest care in selecting what actually belongs here."

Looking wistful, he caressed a black torch-shaped sculpture that gleamed like obsidian in the soft light. "Often it takes time to find out. After over twenty years, I have realized that this beautiful piece needs a new home now." Then his face relaxed. "Later, perhaps tomorrow, I will show you some of my latest acquisitions. But first, allow me to show you to your rooms."

"I'd like to see the rest of the house, too."

He nodded in agreement. "Of course. But we should probably do that tomorrow. A product of my craft, this house is, ah, significantly larger than it looks."

Always something unexpected from this man, and it made Eva nervous every time she was reminded of it. As they walked up a short flight of stairs and down a hall, she realized something else was bothering her. She tried to make a joke of it. "You bought that sculpture back there when you were a kid?"

Talak shrugged. "I'm somewhat older than I look."

Eva froze. "Just how old are you?"

"Does it really matter?"

"Look. At my recognition you said you were the original keeper of my birth records, or something like that. You couldn't have been a child twenty-five years ago. Other times...and now you say you've evaluated a sculpture for twenty years before you decided it doesn't fit. So how old are you?"

Once again, he shrugged, as if giving up. "I'm a little over four hundred years old. Four hundred and thirty-seven, to be exact. The explanation is—complex."

She felt the blood drain from her face, leaving her dizzy. "Oh, no doubt it's complex, all right," she fumed. "How many more of these little surprises do you have up your sleeve? You keep saying I'm supposed to trust you, but I have no idea who—or even what—you are."

As stupid as it sounded, even to her, she had to ask. "You're not some kind of vampire, are you?"

Talak laughed. "No, I'm not a vampire, although given the current literary fashions of your country of origin, I can see how you might wonder."

Eva shivered, ashamed and angry at his apparent amusement.

His face became serious. "But to your question. At the discretion of the Monarch, a magician can be bound in service to the throne and his or her life extended to fulfill that service. It happens rarely."

He stared at Eva, as if looking for some sign of acceptance.

"When I was invited to court as a young magician, the king—Ayax, Queen Rhianna's ancestor—offered that role to me." He straightened, and his voice strengthened with pride. "I accepted, and have served his family's rule ever since."

"Okay. So you're not a vampire, you're just some freak that I'm supposed to trust just because you say I should? Or because the queen assigned you to me?"

Talak stiffened, and his face hardened with irritation. "Milady, for reasons I fail to understand, you continue to feel offended when you discover that things in this world are not what you expect."

He hesitated, then his words erupted, angry and sharp. "What gives you the right to have your expectations met? Why make such...surprises, as you call them, a test of your trust in me? What could it matter how old I am? Or why?" He shook his head in disbelief. "That without a second thought I would give my life protecting yours is what matters."

He drew in a deep breath, and his courtly restraint returned. "If you spent half the energy suspecting the motives of those who actually want to harm you as you do suspecting mine, you would be much, much safer."

He gestured to a door behind him, which swung open at his motion, and bowed.

"I'm sorry."

"This, milady, is your room. You are completely safe here, and I trust you rest well."

"Thank you." She strode past him and started to close the door but paused—defiant, embarrassed, wanting something more. Was it his understanding? Yes. That's exactly what she wanted.

"Maybe you could see this from my point of view for a moment," she pleaded. "I'm snatched from the only life I've known by a stranger who saves me from a bomb attack. Against my will he takes me to a world I don't understand. I find out I don't even know who my blood family is. All I want to do is live my life. My life, not someone else's. In spite of the fact that I want to go home..."

Eva fought tears and her voice broke. "But I can't. I'm a prisoner—a privileged, very rich prisoner that people apparently want either to have or to kill because I'm valuable as some damn royal brood cow."

She realized she was shouting and stopped, angrily swiping the tears from her cheeks. She glared at him and squared her shoulders. "On top of that, I have everyone in Albessind relying on my goodwill and looking to me for some kind of leadership. I'm not used to that kind of responsibility. So cut me some slack if I raise a few objections and doubts now and then. I'm learning as fast as I can, and it's just too bad if that doesn't satisfy your damn expectations. Good night!" she said, slamming the door shut.

Talak's voice came through the door, muffled and contrite. "You are absolutely right, milady. I apologize, and beg your forgiveness." There was a silence, a dozen heartbeats long, before he spoke again. "May tomorrow bring both of us a deeper—and happier—understanding of each other."

There was a quiet noise of movement behind her, and Eva turned to see a maid approaching with a tray. With a small curtsy she asked, "Would milady take some soothing tea before bed?"

"No, thanks. Wait—yes, I'll have some. In a moment." The woman put the tea on a table, curtsied again, and turned to leave. "Oh, and can you help me get this stuff out of my hair? I'll never be able to sleep with it in, and I have no idea how to undo it."

"Of course, milady," the maid said. "I would be honored. If you would sit here..." She pulled a bench from under the dressing table.

"What's your name?"

"Piaggiarelle, milady, but most everyone calls me Page."

As Page worked in silent efficiency, Eva watched a delicate curl of steam rise from the teapot, then for the first time looked around the room. It was beautifully appointed, not as ornate and heavy with luxury as the queen's house where she was staying, but somehow more elegant, and harmonious. It felt good. And it did feel safe. Why did Talak have to be such a pain, even though he kept saving her life? She should be glad she was still alive, that he was doing his job well. But why did he get on her nerves so?

Page lifted the last web of silver and pearls from Eva's hair and laid it carefully on a chest of drawers next to the other two, curtsied, and bustled quietly away.

Eva poured a cup of the tea, and a wonderful fragrance of flowers and spices rose from it. It was delicious. She undressed absentmindedly, pulled on the nightgown laid out on the foot of the bed, and climbed in, sitting against the pillows and sipping tea.

Yet amidst all this comfort, she ached for something familiar—for her cheaply furnished studio, for the gloriously hard work and solitary pleasure of painting, for the constant street noise outside her apartment, for a big plate of macaroni and cheese hot out of the microwave.

She put down the empty teacup, turned down the light, and settled into the soft covers. She was exhausted, and let herself fall into a relaxed fog. It felt like a week ago that Celine had braided those pearls into her hair. She let the fog wrap her up and carry her away.

Chapter Twelve

T alak stared at Eva's door for a long time. This was the second time he'd raised his voice to her. How could he? His angry words returned to him—"What gives you the right to have your expectations met?"

His anger would be far better directed at himself. His expectations, his hope—of finding love again after all this time—had been fulfilled, but with the cruelest twist. He'd found love, but the one he loved was literally untouchable.

He turned from the door and walked slowly down the hall, self-recrimination cutting at his heart with perfectly aimed blades. Both times he'd let his anger out and shouted at Eva, his words had been more applicable to himself than to her.

That first night, after her recognition, she'd announced she wanted to forfeit her life here and return to the Lower World. He'd told her what he himself most needed to hear—that wherever one lived, there would always be forces beyond one's control at work, dictating certain decisions. It was the essence of civilized life to recognize what those forces were and then to accept their necessities with at least a hint of adult grace. What a coward he'd been, to hide his own pain behind anger directed at her.

But could he tell her he loved her so much that it took all his self-control to hide it? No. That would bring Eva only more confusion, and more distrust of him would make her less safe.

He was a magician, and she was of the blood royal. They could never marry, could never build a life together, never raise children. They could never be more than lovers, and then only if Eva wanted it. That wasn't what he wanted, though. He wanted all of it. A whole life—with her.

But it was not in her best interest to complicate her new life with such a distraction as his love. Besides, whether he loved her or not made no difference. They could never live as one—he could never be her mate, and she his. It was time to accept the dictates of his situation with some adult grace of his own.

But she had no idea how vulnerable she was, and he ached to protect her, to give her what she needed to live safely and well.

In Garthius's hall she had cared more for that dog than for her own safety. Her look of horror that he would kill a dog to save her from death came back to him, along with his rage at how close someone had come to killing her tonight. If he hadn't been there to sense the spell, it would have been her convulsing on the floor... No. He firmly set aside the thought. How he had wanted to wrap her in his embrace, then to kiss away her fears and bring her here. To his bed. Forever.

Talak found himself in a room with several of Eva's paintings. She had no idea he had them. He slouched in a chair with legs stretched out in front of him, staring at them. He was just torturing himself sitting here, feeling the intelligent, strong, mystical, beautiful woman behind the paintings, feeling the voluptuous liveliness of her imagination... He wanted all of her, artist, woman, wife. And it could never happen.

Restless, he got up and walked toward the tower. Each piece of art along the way mocked him with its beauty, reminding him that in spite of all the care he had poured into gathering them, he would never be able to share them with the woman he loved.

Who had he acquired these things for, then? Just for himself? He'd always imagined that he'd created this setting of beauty to share with a wife when he'd been released from his sacred oath and was allowed to age again. He'd always intended this to be a setting of peace and harmony where two could live as one, raise a family, and grow old together.

Now his own heart had betrayed him, pulling him into love for a woman he could never have. Yesterday in the royal walled garden, he had—for the first time in four hundred years—contemplated asking his monarch for release from his oath of service.

But such a release would not accomplish anything except allow him to begin aging. Eva would still be of royal blood, and he would still be a magician—never her husband, never the father of their children. Then again, maybe finally growing old would be a release from this impossible love that consumed him.

He squeezed his eyes shut and slammed his fist against the stones framing the tower door, ashamed. He was behaving like a teenage boy.

He climbed the stairs of the tower to its roof. For a long time he stood staring at the night sky, drinking in the light of the full moon as it bathed trees, gardens, and lake in cool silver.

Slowly a resigned calm returned to him. He knew his place. He would help Eva safely gain hers, and take care of her as long as the queen allowed.

If everything went well, he would outlive Eva, and Eva's children, and their children's children, serving and protecting them all. That would be how he could love Eva. He sealed up the hollow ache in his chest with resolve, and let the peaceful night flow around him, cool and healing.

Chapter Thirteen

The next morning Eva and Talak sat on a broad semicircular stone patio nestled against his house, surrounded by a lush garden at once both formal and vigorously free. She'd been nervous coming downstairs, worried that last night's argument would still hang in the air. But it seemed they had both resolved to do better with each other, and she was relieved.

Eva sighed as she put down her fork. The frittata had been delicious—asparagus, tomatoes, roasted red peppers, and fresh basil, with parmesan, mozzarella and fontina cheeses, plus something delicate she couldn't identify. She looked at the platter of bruschetta with its bowls of sweetened ricotta and sliced strawberries but decided she'd had enough, and picked up her coffee cup instead.

"My compliments to your chef. He must be Italian."

"Thank you, Serenissima."

Had Talak blushed?

"Sometimes I think my heart is Italian. I...I have spent a great deal of time in Italy, and love its energy, its cuisine. I have cultivated a garden—"

"You cooked this?"

"Yes and took great pleasure in doing so."

"So on top of everything else, you cook—and have had four hundred years to practice." Eva squinted at Talak seated across the table. "Somehow that just seems unfair."

Talak laughed from deep in his body, and it took Eva's breath away. She realized it was the first time she'd seen him do it. There were few sights more magnificent than such a beautiful man laughing—mouth wide, head thrown back and throat exposed, his eyes half-closed to the morning sun, black hair tumbling around his ears.

"I apologize for the injustice, milady." He sat up, and his voice softened as he stared at her. "I would consider it a privilege to cook for you as often as you wish." He sipped his coffee, his face suddenly full of sorrow, and looked away.

Eva's gaze followed his, out past the old tower wall and across the lake, then returned to the garden surrounding the patio. "This place is beautiful. So peaceful. Everything is perfect."

"Yes, peaceful—by intention and care. I dislike hasty decisions, and as you now know I have had a long time to shape this setting." He smiled, boyish and proud. "Even so, it's still a work in progress."

"You said you had some new acquisitions. I'd love to see what you've found."

A ghost of concern flickered across Talak's face. "Of course. If you would follow me." They walked across the patio and through the large french doors back into the house, and Eva blinked to adjust to less light. Talak guided her down a wide hall. Each niche held a well-lit sculpture or some intriguing object that she wanted to examine, but Talak didn't slow his pace.

He led her to a heavy arched door. He opened it, and stood aside, head lowered. Eva stepped into a room that would have served any major gallery—twenty-foot ceiling, perfect light, the only furniture a cream leather chair facing the far end of the room, and a small table next to it. The long walls of the room's rectangle ended in a church-like apse. She gasped.

This was her work. Eva Milaras, artist. Her Forest Triptych hung at the far end, as if above an invisible altar. To her left, two large abstracts she'd painted last year were displayed, perfectly spaced, and to her right hung two five-by-three landscapes she'd only recently completed—the two the gallery had been slow in paying for, even though they'd sold as soon as they went on display. Eva took a deep breath and let it out, feeling proud. They looked absolutely spectacular hung this way. She was impressed, actually.

Then a chill of suspicion wormed up her spine. All of these had sold when she was desperately broke. Had Talak bought them just to keep her going? Was this just pity or patronage, more of his be-hind-the-scenes manipulation?

She glared at Talak. "So you rescued me from losing my apartment at least twice by buying these pieces. I suppose I should be grateful, but I'm actually feeling pretty cynical and insulted."

Talak nodded. "I thought you might, but I had to show you any-way." He gestured to the room. "I won't pretend that knowing my purchases helped you make ends meet didn't bring me pleasure. It did. But if that was all there was to it, I could have put your paintings in a warehouse. I didn't need to create this setting for them."

He moved toward Eva, then stopped, gazing at her with unnerving intensity. "The truth is," he said softly, "I fell in love with your work before I fell...before I felt I knew the artist. I bought your work because it is superb. It speaks to me, and it deserves this place of honor."

It seemed she could feel his sincerity vibrating in her body, but she refused to believe him. "So you say. But you're wealthy enough to afford any number of rooms to display anything you wanted to own, whatever the reason."

"It is now my turn to be insulted, milady," he said in gentle reproach. "You already know I take the greatest care with every aspect of the beauty of my home. If it took me twenty years to decide against keeping that fine sculpture you saw last night... Nothing—and no one—comes into my home so capriciously as you suggest."

He turned toward the door, and gestured for her to follow. "Please, let us leave this room. Your words insult your own art."

They walked down the hallway in silence. Now Eva felt intimidated by the artwork, rather than inspired by it. How could Talak believe her paintings belonged in this company? She certainly had never received such critical praise back home. Back home. What a laugh. Eva pushed away her bitter hopelessness at the thought of a place she would never see again.

As they came again to the atrium of the house, Talak pointed to a small box sitting on a table next to the door. "I see Page has gathered your jewelry in preparation for travel. It is time we returned to Riardan. Do you want anything before we go? Food? Drink?"

"No, thanks. I'm ready." She didn't really believe her own words. Ready for what?

The carriage sped across the meadow and again passed through the stand of old conifers before Eva spoke, feeling obligated to say something appreciative. "Thank you for all you've done for me, Talak. I expect I often sound ungrateful and spoiled to you. But I am grateful."

Talak returned a guarded smile. "It is my great pleasure to serve you, milady."

"I'm sorry I didn't see more of your home."

"Another time." He smiled again, with more enthusiasm. "While it's not inappropriate for you to have accepted my hospitality last night, your presence in my home without a formal relationship is unusual and possible grounds for speculation at court. It is best for both of us if we return quickly."

After traveling in silence for a while, he adjusted the course of the carriage and they began to climb toward the barren cone of Riardan. "Besides, I have heard messages that you have important clan business to address today."

"What do you mean, you heard a message?" Eva felt left out.

Talak turned to her with an inscrutable smile. "You need a skilled house magician to serve you, milady. One with ready access to such important information."

He lifted his shoulders, almost imperceptibly. "You should see who might be available—and willing. There might be someone quite close at hand who would love the job if you offered it."

Chapter Fourteen

B efore their carriage had come to rest in front of the house, Rachel, Eva's secretary, and Hulvis, her protocol advisor, emerged from a side door and hurried toward them. Talak opened Eva's door and stepped back enough to grant them access.

Rachel curtsied and presented Eva with an envelope. "Clan Athat meets today to select a new ambassador, milady." The agitation in her voice surprised Eva—usually she was such a calm and stabilizing presence. Hulvis, on the other hand, always seemed agitated, and this morning was no exception. "Soon. You haven't much time to prepare."

Eva glanced at Talak, who nodded slightly. "Would you mind taking me there? I'll be as quick as I can."

"Of course, milady." Talak bowed his head more deeply. "I am completely at your disposal."

After little more than an hour, bathed and dressed in fresh formal wear, Eva again sat in the carriage next to Talak, going somewhere new and probably dangerous. She'd never seen the Clan Forum, a hall used only for assemblies deciding matters of clan governance. All she knew was that it was situated at the outer edge of the city, just like the ones for the other clans—as far apart from each other as possible.

She rolled her family ring around her forefinger, feeling its weight, and squared it to her hand. She needed Talak's advice, and swallowed her pride. "Do you have any useful advice for me going into this event? What should I expect, or at least, what am I expected to do?"

"You will sit with those who wish you well and those who wish you dead, milady, and together choose a new ambassador to the throne." Talak's smile was grim. "The current ambassador will resign in complete disgrace, having allowed an illegal murder attempt in the embassy."

"He has to resign because of last night?"

"It was a profound abrogation of his duty and an insult to the queen. If he doesn't resign, he will be dead within days. He'll resign." Talak looked at her gravely. "It's an echo from the time when the clans had chiefs—first hereditary ones, then elected. The chief was murdered by his own people so often that eventually nobody wanted the position. Now major clan decisions are decided by direct and immediate vote, like today. The position of ambassador was created as a substitute for chief—more limited in power, but still empowered to be liaison with the queen and at court." He laughed. "And an office much less likely to speed one's final appearance upon a catafalque."

The carriage stopped in front of a squat two-story stone building ringed by a deep indentation that might have been an ancient moat. The windows were few and very small, and the entrance was guarded by soldiers in colorful dress—the same livery Eva had seen last night at the ambassador's residence. The building itself felt ancient, like an old church, or the ruined tower in Talak's house.

Talak escorted her toward the entrance. "Only clan members are allowed inside, so I cannot protect you as I would like. Be wary of everything. Your presence is what's important today. Promise nothing. Don't get involved in even a long conversation unless you can't avoid it."

His comments were hardly comforting, but Eva nodded as if they were and entered the hall, pausing inside to let her eyes adjust to its dim light.

The Clan Forum was a big single room, from what she could see, finished in rough simplicity—almost coarseness—that contrasted with the sophisticated and often highly ornamented architecture she had seen so far. Here massive squared beams, each rough-hewn from a single tree, spanned the ceiling from side to side. The small windows, mostly high up, had opposing sets of narrow steps rising to them. The windows also revealed just how thick the walls were. The place was built like a fort, for strength rather than looks. The air was thick and sweet with the smell of age and oiled wood, rich as an old library. It didn't feel like the forum was used very often.

Eva looked around. Several tiers of plain benches enclosed at each end ran like bleachers along the long walls facing each other. On the far short wall were several large chairs grouped around one that was raised on a small dais, which she assumed was for the ambassador. Its brilliant red and gold looked out of place next to the plain dark wood of the other chairs and the tiers of benches.

Clusters of people, probably no more than one-hundred and fifty in all, made shifting islands of color on the central floor between the bleachers and behind the chairs at the far end. Strange, this was the first building that Eva had immediately felt comfortable in since arriving.

Eva realized she knew almost no one, although it seemed everyone knew who she was—Madris's daughter from the Lower World, the assassination target and the catalyst for the ambassador's resignation. She walked to the head of the chamber and stopped a man who appeared busy organizing, like he knew what was going on.

"Where should I sit?" she asked, forcing herself to use her new name, a name she'd never spoken aloud. "I'm Eva bryl—"

"I know very well who you are," he snapped. Eva didn't know whether it was just his mannerism or anger directed at her. He pointed to the second-level bench. "This row, at this end. The heads of bloodlines sit at this end." His smile became a smirk, and it wasn't friendly. "As long as they can."

A gong sounded, making the air shiver from floor to ceiling. Silently, people took their places. When all were seated, the red and gold chair remained empty. The ambassador—or former ambassador, Eva supposed—was nowhere to be seen. She looked down the rows back toward the main entrance. The color and opulence of the costumes and adornments on the people gathered was breathtaking. She noted that her bench—her bloodline, she supposed—was nearly full. She sat back and turned again to the cluster of chairs. A man she didn't recognize stood in front of the empty chair and began to speak.

"Honored members of Clan Athat," he intoned. "Former Ambassador Garthius sends his regrets for not being present but has asked me to deliver his resignation, which has been recorded. His replacement must be chosen."

It didn't take long. Eva was relieved to see that her clan didn't put much value on long speeches. Women and men stood when they had something to say. The man officiating recognized each in turn, whereupon they spoke. The brusque but civil exchange proceeded with businesslike speed. Three men and two women were nominated.

A show of hands narrowed the field to one woman and one of the men. Another round of voting chose the man. There was no applause—in fact, the atmosphere was heavy and humorless. A mundane necessity, like the removal of a dead body from the room.

The gong sounded again, and everyone rose to leave. Some gathered around the new ambassador, but Eva remembered Talak's advice and headed for the door.

Chapter Fifteen

T he next morning, while Celine fussed with Eva's hair, Rachel
listed matters that called for her attention that day. Gardeners
needed to consult with Eva concerning the new water feature and its
gazebo. She also had another session with Hulvis to review various
invitations, and then another of his history lessons.

The workmen had finally finished her new studio, and it was ready
for her inspection. It seemed to Eva that it had taken a long time, but
to be fair she'd ordered larger windows cut, the removal of an interior
wall to create more space, and then a new floor of blond hardwood.
She was eager to get to work in it.

"Let's do the garden and the studio first," Eva said. "Then the
lesson, if there's time before lunch. I get sleepy in his lectures if it's
after lunch. Maybe we can do the invitations this afternoon."

There was a tap on the door, and before she could say "Enter,"
Efron, the house manager, swept in, carrying a salver bearing an envelope. Eva watched him ignore Rachel—deliberately, it seemed to
her—and present the tray to Eva. Behind him, Rachel dropped her
head, lips pursed.

"Thank you, Efron. Please give it to Rachel—as you must with
all my correspondence," Eva directed. Efron's eyes widened for an

instant, and then glittered with something hard before he lowered them.

He bowed with obsequious perfection. "Of course, milady," he said softly, and turned to Rachel, first taking the envelope off the salver and handing it to her with the ghost of a sneer. He bowed again to Eva, and withdrew.

Rachel's hands shook as she opened the envelope and read. Her hand flew to her throat. "The new ambassador, milady," she gasped. "He invites you to court in his entourage!" She extended the letter to Eva, her face radiant. "Such an honor... Shall I call for Hulvis?"

"Please." Eva smiled, surprised at the jolt of anticipation she felt. "It seems that his lesson today will be more interesting than I thought."

The ceremony in which Welryck bron Ryckmet, Clan Athat's new ambassador, presented himself to the queen and then introduced Eva and the other five who accompanied him in his office had been brief but impressive. They had entered to a brass and drum fanfare, and knelt before the throne until bidden by the queen to rise. The ambassador wore a ceremonial robe—reserved for state functions only, one of her fellows in the retinue had whispered to her. All in attendance had donned the full regalia of their clan or office, and it made a spectacular sight.

Now Eva surveyed the sumptuous apartment that would be her residence while at court. In fact it was easy enough to get home between sessions, but in case she chose to rest here instead, or wanted a private place to meet on neutral territory, this space was now hers.

There were even small rooms for accompanying staff. She'd bring a few furnishings from the house and make it an extension of her home.

Her duties, as she understood them from Hulvis, were simple but diverse: attend the ambassador, assist him in hosting officials from other clans, and perform other tasks on his behalf as necessary, often negotiating contact with other clans at his request.

Hulvis had also insisted that her appointment to court dictated that Eva marry as soon as possible, that it was inappropriate—even dangerous—to remain single at court for long. When she protested, Hulvis had been uncharacteristically blunt. This was not negotiable. Her position and pedigree both demanded a husband and offspring. For her own sake as well as the sake of her clan, she should quickly announce her readiness to receive suitors.

Eva had known that it was expected but hadn't realized this appointment would hasten the necessity. Something in her twisted in resentment. It would limit her freedom, she was sure, and only now was she familiar enough with her situation to begin doing what she wanted. She'd felt bullied and pushed around by events since her arrival. Now she would begin shaping her own destiny. She knew marriage was inevitable, but she would put it off as long as possible. Maybe Talak could help her navigate her path through the marriage market.

There was a knock on the door, and Eva opened it. A young servant in the queen's livery looked surprised to see Eva at her own door. He'd probably expected a servant to answer. With a bow he gave her an envelope with the royal seal on it and then knelt, apparently waiting for a reply. She opened the envelope to read that Her Royal Majesty

Queen Rhianna had granted Eva bryl Madris a private audience this afternoon. It was a summons.

"Please inform her majesty that I am honored to be received into her presence," Eva said, unsure of the proper protocol. The page stood. "But," she continued. The page dropped quickly again to one knee. "Please send someone at the right time to guide me, as I don't know where to go."

After the page had gone, she sent word to Talak. She didn't know exactly why she wanted him to know, but she did. And she'd ask him about how to delay her marriage.

Chapter Sixteen

Instead of being escorted to a stateroom in the castle as she'd expected, Eva was led through long passageways and down two narrow flights of stairs to an enormous walled garden. She looked back over her shoulder at the castle, but didn't recognize its façade—she guessed she had passed through it and come out on another side. Her armed escort ignored her pause, continuing at a steady march, and Eva had to lift her skirts and hurry to catch up.

They passed through a gate and turned, following a path around a large fountain. In a shaded grotto ahead, she could see a familiar slender figure dressed in white. Queen Rhianna was waiting for her.

Near the grotto's entrance, the escort detail parted in the middle, opening a direct line of sight between Eva and the queen, and stopped. She stepped forward until she was even with the lead guards and knelt, waiting.

"Eva bryl Madris, welcome." The queen's cool silver voice flowed over her. "Rise, dear child. Come sit here with me." She dismissed the guards and gestured to a marble chair in the grotto.

"Thank you, Majesty," Eva said, and sat with her hands folded in her lap. She was surrounded by the beauty of growing things. From behind her the smell of ripening grapes wrapped her in their rich sweetness.

"We are pleased that you are present in Our court," the queen began. "But even if your new ambassador had not brought you with him, We would have contrived your presence some other way."

Eva was certain her surprise registered on her face.

Rhianna smiled, beatific and maternal. "It's true. For several reasons. Which is why We wanted to speak with you—away from other ears."

She lowered her voice, as if sharing a secret. "Even though Our decree prevented you from returning to the Lower World, Our hope is that we can become steadfast friends."

The queen leaned forward with conspiratorial intimacy. "I want your help," she whispered, abandoning the formal plural. Eva was stunned. This was hardly the opening to their conversation that she'd expected.

"Majesty, whatever—"

The queen cut her off with a wave of her hand. "I expected your loyal willingness, child." She paused, as if Eva had interrupted her train of thought. She leaned against the back of her bench, arms outstretched. They could have been sitting on a porch swing talking about the weather, instead of in the walled garden of a royal castle.

"Your mother and I were close childhood friends," she said. "More like sisters, really." She was quiet for a moment. "I was devastated when she was killed and immediately assigned Talak to watch over you."

She stood and beckoned. "Come walk with me."

Side by side, they strolled toward a fountain that emptied into a pond with water lilies and large colorful fish. Dragonflies clattered all around.

"I had other problems, also precipitated by your mother's death. It was an indirect but effective attack on my reign. Your clan lost a powerful leader, and significant influence. Her death disrupted a delicate balance of power among several prominent clans, and two of them have since joined forces to force my hand in certain matters."

Rhianna turned to Eva and smiled, but sharpened steel glittered beneath her sweetness. "I very much dislike having my hand forced, and it is in this matter I would appreciate your help."

She pointed to a tall bush covered in white flowers the size of gardenias. "That is one of my favorites. I love the fragrance—go smell."

Eva walked toward it, and well before she was close enough to touch the petals, she was enveloped in the scent of its blossoms. Like lavender and lime combined, it was intoxicating.

"It's wonderful," Eva said, eyes wide. "I've never smelled anything like it."

"It's very rare." The queen took Eva's arm, as good friends might as they strolled through a pleasant garden. "About your help, which would be a great service to the realm," she continued. "You must marry soon, for your sake and for your clan. I would consider it a great favor if you allowed me to select the clans from which you received suitors."

"But why must it be soon?"

"So you can stay alive, child." The queen was businesslike, but seemed slightly amused. "Lower World royals are of great value as genetic enrichment, and you are the last of your generation of seeding. That makes you a prize, but also a prime target for assassination—as you have learned the hard way already. Until you are married, your major threat comes from your own clan, and the two attempts on your life so far are without doubt from ambitious members of your own extended family." She shook her head indulgently, as if she contemplated the pranks of mischievous children.

"When you marry, another clan becomes involved, and will offer protection to you from your own people. Likewise, your clan will help protect your husband from his clan. Each side, then, becomes more inclined to protect you from the other, and together you will learn to balance the dangers and protections from both sides."

The queen gazed at Eva, her face a thoughtful mask. "That is a lifelong task. May you have opportunity to practice your skills in it for many, many years."

"It doesn't sound like love has much to do with who I marry," Eva said, trying to keep reproach out of her voice.

"It doesn't. Not at all," the queen said without a trace of apology. "You will choose a husband who is a peer in genetic quality, and who can offer you suitable protection and privilege. Marriage is for offspring, and if you're lucky, some affection. Love is another matter altogether, and you are free to love whomever you will. Your husband will understand that and will hold exactly the same view for himself."

They walked in silence, the queen holding Eva's arm in her own as Eva labored to comprehend. Rhianna patted Eva's hand and said, "Let's sit here in the shade for a while."

She led Eva to a stone bench nestled in a small stand of bamboo. All around them, the slender long leaves whispered in the soft breeze.

"I understand you haven't yet chosen a house magician," the queen continued. "I suggest you consider Talak for that office."

"But he's bound to you by oath," Eva blurted, and instantly realized she was in perilous territory. "Not that that would ever create a conflict, of course."

The queen laughed, quiet and joyless. "Of course not." She looked at Eva. "I am being completely selfish in recommending him. He is more likely than any other magician I trust to keep you alive, and your health and safety are important to me. He is one of a handful of the most skilled magicians in the realm. And in addition to all that, he is desperately in love with you. He would do his job very well for that reason alone."

Eva's body stiffened, and her eyes lost focus. "He can't be in love with me—he treats me like a stupid child." She tried to think, but her brain was a block of ice. "I thought I felt a personal interest from him sometimes, but..." She couldn't finish the thought. But what? Why would she even care? Why couldn't she breathe?

When she could think again, all she could think of was a string of moments when Talak had said something about how he felt and she had completely missed what he'd been saying. He'd fallen in love with the art before he... Why hadn't he come out and said something? Why had he hidden it so well? Why hide it at all?

"You know how old he is, don't you?"

"Yes, he told me. About the oath and the spell."

"What you probably don't know is that when he was about a hundred and fifty, in service to one of my forebears, he fell in love. A beautiful woman, I'm told. A musician. Harpist, I think. I've forgotten her name." The queen shrugged.

"They loved each other so deeply that in spite of the requirements of Talak's...office, they married. They had three children, who all turned out to be musicians like their mother, with little magical talent. While Talak remained young, his wife grew old, and eventually died. His children did the same. Their bloodlines died out over a hundred years ago, and not a trace of his family is left. Talak, of course, remained faithful to his oath of service, though his heart was broken."

Eva gasped, tried to breathe out but couldn't. She hadn't thought of that. The agony of staying young as your mate aged and died was too awful to imagine. No wonder he kept this all to himself. She shivered, imagining the loss and loneliness that he'd endured. His oath to the throne had cost him all personal fulfillment, and still he referred to it as the sacred chains of his honor. Oh.

The queen watched Eva process the information, then looked out at the garden. "You are the first woman he has loved since then," she continued. A bird landed at her feet, and she smiled with childlike pleasure. "So you wouldn't need to marry for love. You could have Talak for as long as it pleased you."

Eva's head still spun. "He's terribly attractive, but I don't think I love him—and besides, we could never marry."

"Of course not, child! How could you think that?" The queen looked horrified. "He's a magician! He's not allowed to even touch you without your permission, except to save your life." She paused, then said with a chilling laugh, "He would be your adoring and loyal servant. But mine first."

The queen rose, and Eva followed. "Sharing him could be a wonderful link between us, don't you think? A bond of shared devotion. I'd like that very much."

Eva's legs felt like stone. Somehow she managed to keep up with the queen, who headed toward a massive wrought-iron gate. Beyond it, Eva could see a short path leading to a large door in the castle wall. It looked like the audience was over.

"So will you help me by allowing me to suggest the clans of your suitors? I would be...extremely grateful."

Eva felt like she was deep underwater, and something in her let go. She had to marry just to have a chance at staying alive, and she didn't know anything much about any of the clans or their eligible bachelors. What difference did it make if the queen chose the clans? At least she could choose the man. "And if none prove satisfactory from those, will you suggest others?"

"Of course, child." The queen patted Eva's arm again as guards appeared from somewhere and swung open the gate. "Remember, I have a vested interest in finding you a good husband, and in keeping you healthy and safe. You have a good friend in me."

She turned to the guard. "Escort Our loyal and beloved subject to her ambassador."

Eva dropped to one knee, but the queen had already turned away, strolling back into her garden.

Chapter Seventeen

As Talak drove her home, Eva studied him in silence, trying to process everything the queen had said. It was as if she were seeing him for the first time. She looked for the traces left by hundreds of years of loyal service and personal emptiness, but found none. No, around the eyes...and his lips, that gentle, guarded smile... Suddenly that smile looked incredibly sad.

Respect flooded through her, and right behind it, a pulse of hot desire. He was noble and beautiful. Disciplined, loyal, artistic, relentlessly passionate. He would be a spectacular lover. But was a lover what she wanted? It didn't feel like enough, but maybe it was all she'd be able to have.

Eva turned and looked out at the passing scenery. This was crazy. Yesterday she thought he was overbearing and condescending, and now she was thinking about what kind of lover he might be. She tried to banish the image of them in bed together, twisting, panting, their bodies hot and slick. But the vision wouldn't go away. Instead, she felt the sweet stir of arousal. Now that the idea had taken root, it wouldn't leave her alone.

If Talak noticed her scrutiny at all, he hid it well. He seemed perfectly relaxed and happy, even nonchalant. Occasionally he enthused about her appointment to the ambassador's retinue and what might be involved—including the necessity of accepting suitors.

When the carriage stopped in front of Eva's house, she waited for Talak to open the door. As if she had a choice—he was at her side before she could make a move. She stood, looking at the terraced gardens that flanked the wide marble walk, and remembered she'd postponed the meeting with the master gardener.

"I'd like to talk to you, Talak," she said, trying not to make it sound important with a capital I.

"Of course, milady," he bowed. "I am completely at your service."

She blushed at the thought of the queen's offer. Was that what he wanted? "Inside, though."

Talak followed her into the house and down the long hall to her study. Rachel rose at her arrival, then curtsied at Eva's request for privacy and disappeared through a side door.

Eva settled in a large wingback chair and gestured to its mate. "Please make yourself comfortable."

"Forgive me, milady, but I prefer to stand." He stood next to the chair, one hand on its back, as if using it as a shield between them. "But if you insist, I will sit."

She shrugged, and smiled cautiously at him. "My audience with the queen today was...surprisingly informative."

Talak's hand on the chair tightened, his fingers digging into the upholstery, but he remained silent.

"She told me about you...your wife and family." She searched his face for some response. There was none. "And she told me how you feel about me."

He stiffened, and his lips pressed into a thin line, but still he said nothing.

Eva realized she didn't know what to say next. "I don't know what to make of it all. I guess I just wanted you to know. That I know, I mean." She looked at him standing beside the chair, proud, haunted. She waited for him to speak. He didn't.

She felt trapped in the lengthening silence. "I wish you would say something."

"What is there to say?" His grip on the chair loosened. "I didn't expect or want to fall in love with you." His smile was sad. "I promise it will not interfere with my service to you."

"But what will you do about it?"

"Do?" he snorted. "Nothing. There is nothing to be done. You must live your life fully. If we are both fortunate, I will see your great grandchildren flourish."

In a flicker of movement, he knelt in front of her, his eyes fierce as thunderstorms. "You must invite suitors and choose one, Eva. Milady. Marry. Have fine children. Render service to the realm. Paint your soul onto canvases for the world to see. Your health, safety, and happiness are the greatest joys I can hope for."

"But you—"

"There is no 'but'!" He cut her off with a quick shake of his head, so sharp that his hair whipped over his face. He pushed it behind an ear and gazed at her passionately. Several times his lips moved as if to speak, but he made no sound, as if he were calling to her in a vacuum.

"Nothing else matters." His voice had thickened to a harsh rasp. "It will be my privilege to assist and protect you every step of the way. Never doubt it."

"But how can that be enough for you?"

His smile tore at her heart. "Because it must be," he said, his voice gentle and low. "I once scolded you to accept gracefully what is beyond your power to change. How—" His voice cracked and his eyes clouded. "How can I not heed my own advice?"

Eva watched his face as he spoke. This was too one-sided. It scared her, made her feel helpless. "I wish I didn't know this."

"And my hope was that you never would." Talak gazed at her a moment longer, then stood up and strode to the window. He leaned on the ledge, looking out. "But the queen saw fit to tell you."

Again he pushed his hair back behind one ear. "Perhaps it's for the best. As careful as I've been, I've almost let my feelings for you slip several times myself." He stared out the window. "I would probably have let something out by mistake at a much less opportune time."

He stood silent, pensive, focused on something Eva couldn't see. "Yes, better to have it out now, so we each can focus on what we must."

"What we must," Eva repeated, resenting just about every obligation she could think of. All she needed was another reminder of how profoundly not in control she was when it came to her life.

"That's not all." Eva forced herself to say the words. "She suggested I take you as House Magician. And as a lover." Talak's eyes widened, and Eva could feel her face flush.

He turned to her, a lean, graceful silhouette against the bright window. "You must marry well and safely and raise a royal family. I must serve you until the queen directs otherwise. If you took me as a lover, nothing could give me more happiness. It is the most I can hope for."

After a pause, he added with palpable tenderness and regret, "Perhaps I am more fortunate than you. At least I am allowed to serve the woman I love."

Eva rose and joined him at the window. "I want you to know I'm—" She took his hand and they both started at the physical contact. She realized she hadn't actually touched him since her crass attempt at escape via seduction weeks ago.

But this was so different—a surge of warmth blossomed up through her, lighting her core, flowing out to him, rippling and opening, spreading like a flower, petal after petal, so powerful that she had to widen her stance to keep her balance. "Oh..." she gasped.

His hand closed on hers, strong yet breathtakingly gentle. He took her hand in both of his and raised her palm to his lips in a kiss so physically delicate that only the warmth of his mouth signaled first contact. But the fire that raced between them was anything but delicate.

When he looked up from her hand, she could see the same heat blazing in him. It burned through all her peevish rationalizations. She wanted him—always had, from day one. Where a permanent relationship between them was forbidden, it seemed having him as a lover—even while she chose a husband—might be a possibility. But there was a bigger problem now. She knew that if he became her lover she couldn't keep their relationship separate from the rest of her life. She would fall in love with him completely, she knew this. She couldn't afford that luxury. She couldn't.

She took a deep breath and let it out slowly, drawing her hand out of his, wishing she could let it stay. "Thank you, Talak. I'm going to ask you to leave before I...before this gets more complicated."

Eyes ablaze, Talak dropped his hands and bowed. "You are wise, milady," he murmured, "as well as beautiful. But should you ever—" He bit off his words, and then was gone.

Eva stared out into the garden for a long time, until her heart slowed to normal. Queen Rhianna had offered Talak to her as casually as if she were loaning Eva a prize stallion to ride. Or had it only seemed so casual? Why else might she suggest that Eva get involved with him? The way she felt right now, she didn't need much more encouragement to saddle up. She grimaced at her callous metaphor. But there was such intoxicating power—proud and wild—in the man, in spite of the queen's bridle on him.

The afternoon shadows lengthened, stretching out into each other, before she could force herself to stop thinking with her heart and accept what she couldn't change.

Even Talak couldn't keep her alive while she remained un-married, apparently. If she needed the protecting balance of a husband's clan to save her from her own, she'd better let the ambassador know she was ready to receive suitors.

She took a deep breath, still resisting the inevitable. How could she separate love and marriage? It was so alien. But then she'd heard that arranged marriages sometimes grew into love. Was she even capable of having children by a man she might not love? Especially if she loved someone else, someone she could never marry?

A nameless procession of faces from centuries of her own world's history rose before her. She was hardly unique. Countless women had been caught in her predicament. Some of them had found a way—she would, too. After all, her survival depended on it. Everyone said so, even Talak, and she believed it now. With resigned calm she rang the bell to summon Rachel.

Chapter Eighteen

E va's messages, one to the queen and one to the ambassador, announcing her readiness to accept suitors were well received.

The ambassador's reply waxed enthusiastic. He would hasten to initiate the official proceedings and notify Eva of when the formal announcement could be made at court—probably in the next few days. She should ready her house for the coming parade of suitors.

The queen's response was cooler, but nonetheless clearly approving—and mentioned again unspecified rewards of royal favor for her cooperation. Her instruction to Eva was to welcome any clan's offer of a suitor to maintain appearances of impartiality, then make her formal choices from the queen's selection—choices she would provide once she had seen which clans came forward.

Hulvis, of course, quivered like an eager spaniel pup at the news, and insisted on providing his own historical assessment of all the clans he felt were of adequate standing to vie for her hand in marriage. Eva finally had to ask him to stop when she hit an emotional wall, unable to absorb even one more breathless anecdote.

Eva's declaration of availability for marriage would be made at court today. The hum of anticipation and activity in the house had gradually increased from happy applause from her staff at her announcement to intense teamwork of readying the house to receive clan messengers and their gifts.

For the past day and a half, Celine had bustled around, ensuring that the pale cream dress worn by Eva's mother on this occasion had been let out slightly to reveal a little more of her breasts, then aired, cleaned, and pressed. Yesterday she'd spread half a dozen trays of jewelry about the bedroom for Eva to choose from, and had applauded like a young girl when Eva selected a necklace and earrings made with large blood-red stones that looked like garnets, strung among hammered gold discs.

"Oh, yes, milady," she exclaimed. "Akzul—the red stones—are for blood and fertility. A perfect choice!" Now she nattered happily about what a wonderful occasion this was and how the suitors would vie with each other for Eva's hand, as she wove a series of webs into Eva's hair. It was the same design she had created for Eva's fateful banquet at the ambassador's residence, but this time instead of pearls in a silver weave, the web was gold, and from it dangled scores of slender stylized leaves of varied lengths, also in delicate hammered gold.

Eva smiled into the mirror, forced to acknowledge that the combination of gold, akzul, and her white dress was stunning. But even if he said nothing, Talak's eyes would be the real test.

In the traditional three-day period that followed, elaborate gifts accompanying formal offers of marriage arrived from a dozen clans. With help from Rachel, Eva recorded and acknowledged each gift, while Hulvis gleefully commented on their relative significance as an indication of how serious each clan was. There was a white mare from one, a small box of gemstones from another, a graceful sword with emeralds in its hilt from a third.

"And remember, milady," crowed Hulvis, "these are mere gifts of introduction. We will see more extravagant bidding soon, amongst the clans most earnest in seeking your alliance." He shivered in his nervous excitement. "In time past, one clan went so far—"

"Thanks, Hulvis, but I'm not really interested in those comparisons," Eva cut him off as gently as she could, "since I'm pretty much just a prize mare myself." In a flash of insight, she realized the image she'd used for herself was exactly the same as she'd applied to Talak. They were both horses in someone else's stable.

Hulvis gasped, looking mortified. Slowly his hand rose to his lips. She watched half a dozen arguments gallop across his face, but to his credit he remained silent—until the door opened to a messenger from Clan Occitanto. Their gift, he exclaimed, with his former enthusiasm instantly restored—a lute exquisitely inlaid with iridescent shell, colorful wood, and ivory—must be from their museum of art and a clear indication of the seriousness of their bid.

At the end of the third day of introductions, Eva was frantic. She was hemmed in, more a prisoner of her wealth and privilege than ever, desperate for the fresh air of independence.

The white mare had been transported to Albessind, the other gifts placed on display in the entry hall of her house. She finished all the related correspondence with Rachel, and told her to let the queen know who had initiated courtship. As if she didn't know already—Eva had come to suspect that the queen was watching her closely. And watching the clans that came with offers of marriage, too, no doubt.

She was already tired of the elaborate public ritual that had just begun—she needed to escape and do something more private, more creative. That was it! She had barely used her new studio, although it was fully furnished and supplied. She'd spend a day or two painting. Eva rang for Rachel and sent another message—to Talak, asking him to come and pose for her tomorrow. Finally she would be able to study him while she drew. They would be alone for hours, but she would be safe behind her easel.

Chapter Nineteen

"I hope you don't mind doing this," Eva said, suddenly feeling a little intimidated at the prospect of using Talak as a model.

The man melts your insides and saves your life—twice—and you use him as a model? Do you really think your concentration is good enough for that? On top of that he's an art connoisseur. He'll recognize bad work if you turn out a crappy rendition...

"I've wanted to do your portrait since...that day in the grocery store. It was the first thing I thought of when I saw you—you have such a strong face."

Talak dipped his head. "I'm delighted you think so, milady." He looked around. "Where do you want me to sit?" He tilted his head at an upholstered bench set on a low platform. "Or lie?"

"I'd like you on that bench, facing the window. You can put your clothes over there."

"You want me naked?"

Don't even make a little joke about it. Don't.

"Do you mind? If you get cold I'll get you to raise the temperature of the room."

Don't make a joke about that, either. Once you start...

Talak's smile was enigmatic. "Milady, finally you will see that I hide nothing from you, and that everything I have is yours to command however you desire."

The sudden burn in her neck told Eva she was blushing, but she pretended she wasn't. "Once I've got you posed, I'll do several quick sketches from different angles to find what works best. Then I'll adjust your pose and paint from that."

She looked up from adjusting the drawing paper and easel and stopped breathing.

Talak was staring at her—naked, sitting on the edge of the couch, legs splayed slightly apart, relaxed as if he were waiting for a bus.

Concentrate. Breathe. I said, breathe now. Good. Now concentrate.

Sunlight streamed through the arched floor-to-ceiling windows across Talak's shoulder, turning the rest of his body into a maze of planes, curves, and hollows.

Her throat became dangerously tight and she coughed, trying to relax. "Actually, I'd rather you sat facing the other direction, with your back to the window. Okay, turn your head toward me. Can you lean down on your left elbow? Yes. Now bring your right foot up toward your...butt, knee raised. Not quite that far. Good. And rotate your hips slightly toward me just a bit. Let your left leg relax, maybe bend at the knee a little. Good. Is that a pose you can hold for a couple of hours at a time?"

His stare burned into her. "However you desire my body, Serenissima, it is yours."

He was playing with her, dammit! Deliberately trying to fluster her. He had to be. All she had to do was say the word and he would take her, right there on that couch... His skin glowed in the sunlight.

Concentrate. Get to drawing!

Eva tore her attention away. "Um, I think I'm going to cover you with some fabric, for textural contrast." She got up and pulled a swath of sky-blue silk from a shelf and draped it between his legs, across his groin, and down over the edge of the bench, fighting the magnetic urge to caress him.

"And I'm just going to pull your hair back so it falls behind your head, and over this shoulder..." His hair swirled warm and thick into her hand, so heavy she suddenly couldn't move, couldn't let it go. She wanted to fall into it, fill her mouth with it, disappear inside it. It scorched her fingers and still they ached for more. The scent of sandalwood, his warm skin, his intoxicating maleness wrapped around her, pulling her down toward him.

She bolted back to her easel and shifted it slightly, as if it might shield her from the dangerous heat of his beauty. She studied his pose for a moment, absorbing the play of light and shadow, and started to draw. The lines of his limbs and the angle of his head emerged quickly, as if they'd been inside the paper, waiting to leap to the surface. She began drawing the draped cloth and frowned.

"Can you smooth out the cloth a bit? It's gotten bunched up somehow."

"It is not the fault of the cloth, milady. I was in control of my body until you touched my hair."

A hot coil of desire pulsed, turned, and began to wind open inside her, snaking along her thighs. She licked her lips, and knew if she went over to adjust that cloth, she would never make it back to her easel. "Well, smooth it out as best you can."

Talak adjusted himself, but the cloth seemed only to emphasize the outline of his erection. Eva stole one more glance. He resumed his pose and smiled, his eyes burning into her—a smile that had the attentive patience of a wolf stalking prey. Eva shivered and focused on the paper in front of her.

After a few minutes, she changed the placement of the easel and started another sketch. And then another. When she'd finished the sketch from a fourth angle she looked up.

"Okay, let's take a break. I need to look these over."

Talak sat up and stretched. "May I see?"

"No, these are too raw. I'll choose one of these and then do a second one from that angle. You can look at the one I pick to paint from."

She arranged the sketches in a row on the floor and studied them. They all had potential, but the one drawn from almost square to the bench was clearly the one. She put the others aside, placed her choice back on the easel, and then moved to the position she'd used to create it. Talak stood at the tall arched windows, looking out to the grounds below.

"Ready for another round?" *Damn. I didn't say that. At least I shouldn't have.*

"Always ready, milady," Talak said softly, turning away from the window. He sauntered back to the bench with the blue silk hanging over one shoulder. Eva fought down her desire. The way his body moved in the sunlight...

He leaned back on the couch and resumed the pose perfectly, arranging the silk to hang like a blue waterfall flowing over his thigh.

She studied him from the selected angle, blocked out the fact that he was staring back at her, and began. Again the lines of his body flowed up to the surface of the page in composition both strong and subtle. Hand and pencil became attuned to her eyes as she concentrated. She tumbled into the portrait, caught in the curves and planes of his body, in the way his hair brushed his shoulder, in the potency and pride that radiated from the seemingly languid pose. She lost herself in the arch of his foot, in the long curve of his thigh, the flow of his calf. The thin trail of dark hair that rode down his chest and disappeared under blue silk. His hands, the hollow of his throat...

Eva looked up to discover the light had changed too much to continue. She took a deep breath as she put down her pencil, letting it out slowly. She stepped back and looked at her work. It was really good.

"May I see?"

"It's not done, but yes." The words were out before Eva realized he'd be standing next to her—naked. Before she could tell him to put some clothes on first, he was too close behind her, looking over her shoulder at the easel. His body heat pressed against her back, gentle, insistent. "It is very good. You honor my body." Without taking his eyes off the easel he murmured, "You know, milady, when you are aroused your body smells of mint and fresh-ground coriander. Perhaps no man has told you that before. Your aroma is utterly intoxicating."

"Who says I'm aroused?" Eva tried to sound offended, but failed.

Talak smiled and shrugged, as if she had announced that the sun wasn't shining.

She gave up. It was pointless to pretend she wasn't. "Please," her voice weakened into pleading. "Please put some clothes on. We'll start on the painting tomorrow morning."

"If that's truly what you want. But remember, the queen's generous offer stands." Talak handed her the blue silk. It was still warm from his body. He bowed and walked to where he had placed his clothes.

Eva closed her eyes—she couldn't bear to watch him get dressed.

Chapter Twenty

E va propped the finished painting against the wall on a ledge at eye level and stepped back. With silent satisfaction she acknowledged that it was one of her best portraits ever. Maybe her best. It didn't matter if she'd never get it into her old gallery a world away, she wouldn't sell this one. This was hers to keep.

There was a tap at the door, and Efron whispered in, pausing inside the door to bow before approaching.

"Yes, Efron?"

"A matter of some delicacy, milady." He stopped, and seemed to be waiting.

Eva grew impatient. She wasn't finished studying the painting. "Yes?"

"Delicate, yes. The entire household is gossiping about your magician friend posing," he said with obvious distaste, "in the nude." He winced and put his pudgy hands on his belly, as if suffering gas pain. "Would it be possible for milady to at least keep him away from the windows? I am hard pressed to maintain proper decorum in your house, especially as a crowd of suitors is imminent."

She almost laughed out loud. Efron was trying to manage her as well as her house. "Say his name."

Efron stiffened. "I beg pardon, milady?"

"My 'magician friend,' as you insist on calling him, has a name. What is it?"

His face darkened. "His name is Talak, milady," he said with a curled lip.

"Yes. So you will use it when speaking of him." She folded her arms. "You don't like him, do you?"

Efron bowed deeply. "My feelings do not matter, milady."

"I note your evasion of the question," Eva said, not bothering to keep anger out of her voice, "but you're right. Your feelings don't matter and mine do. The queen would have him in my bed, and I doubt she consulted your feelings. Would that development render you unable to extend him due respect or to properly manage my household?"

"Absolutely not, milady." Efron's lips pressed into a nasty smile, a thin curve that reminded Eva of a shark's mouth closing.

"I'm glad to hear it. That will be all." She watched him depart, remembering Talak's remark that the clan member who'd recommended Efron might not be her friend. Who had that been? She couldn't remember.

Maybe she should take the queen's suggestion and make Talak her house magician. He was fulfilling most of the duties anyway, and would certainly keep an eye on Efron.

Eva sat beside the delicately carved writing desk, in her study, and scanned the message bearing the royal crest. "From the queen," she said to Rachel and Hulvis, although she knew they already knew that. They had arrived bearing the envelope and now hovered, waiting. She broke the seal.

"It's her list of approved suitors. Rachel, send for Talak. I need his advice on this matter as well."

Rachel curtsied and disappeared.

She handed the letter to Hulvis. "What do you make of this?" She grinned. "The short version, please."

"Yes, milady." Hulvis nodded, frowning, as if her order to keep his assessment brief was the most difficult task he'd ever faced. He studied the list, brow furrowed. "It's a bit puzzling," he said eventually. "She offers you the best of the current court as if you were her favorite, except for Clan Pandrakis, which hasn't been a significant force at court for decades. She either means to draw them in with this inclusion, or," he mused with worry in his voice, "to move you to the periphery of court influence. I don't know what to make of that, but I recommend great caution concerning Pandrakis. Perhaps she is offering you that choice—center stage or out of the political marketplace entirely."

Later, Eva and Talak sat in a shaded corner of the garden where a carved lion's head set in a low stone wall spouted a stream of water into a lily pond. The plashing of the water and the dance of insects above its surface filled the fading afternoon with a lively calm. Eva watched Talak watching the dragonflies, his eyelids partly closed, lips pursed. Brooding. Dangerous and beautiful.

"I share Hulvis's concern about Pandrakis," he said after a long pause, "but not for the same reasons. Something about it doesn't feel right."

"There are seven clans on her list. He said I don't need more than three, so I can just ignore them."

"At the very least you should choose four to give yourself a little more room to maneuver. But it's not that. I wonder why Pandrakis is on the list at all. Besides the fact that their inclusion will cause serious commotion at court."

Talak squinted into the sun, as if the answer was just behind it. "About sixty years ago Pandrakis attempted a coup against the throne, which was then occupied by Rhianna's uncle Arvon. One of the conspirators killed the king, but the coup was shattered by a rival Pandraki faction which claimed to be loyal. In spite of their great loyalty, they conveniently waited until the king was dead before acting. The rebels were slaughtered, their wealth divided among the so-called loyal, and the whole clan was banished from court for a generation. That meant they lost all their political currency, since only at court are the arrangements of power made. Even now, any political overture from Clan Pandrakis is generally viewed with disdain or suspicion, which makes their inclusion on this list...dangerous." He gazed at Eva, looking so uneasy that she felt a pang of fear.

The queen..." Talak took a deep breath, and shook his head. "The queen is using you, as she uses everyone. I'm not sure what she intends with this."

"That sounds vaguely disloyal of you."

Talak spun to face her, gazed at her for a moment, then smiled. "I have decided not to take offense from now on when you question my honor and integrity. But my loyalty is first to the dynastic throne, then to its occupant. In the course of my service, that throne has known both noble occupants and less than noble. My service, sometimes in spite of the occupant, is to that throne." He was silent for a moment, as if struggling toward a confession. "Such is the case at present, but it is not the first time."

He brightened a little, and shrugged. "But even so, the queen has commanded me to see you married well and safely. I am simply following her orders, even if it's in a way she might not want."

"So where were you when Pandrakis tried to seize power?"

Talak's smile was thin. "Here and there. Very busy. I was unable to save the king, even though I anticipated the attack. I had set effective wards and guardians against an attempt on his life from outside the castle, but had discounted an attack from within. One of his own attendants wielded the knife. But by then I had trapped a group of conspirators in an old horse barn, which I was about to burn to the ground—with them in it." His lip curled. "Facing immolation, they quickly rediscovered their loyalty to the throne, and denounced their relatives marching on Riardan. The rebellion was crushed."

"Couldn't you just have cast some spells or something?"

His laugh was grim. "That's the ongoing puzzle... Royal blood is impervious to magic. That is both its significance and its strength, but also its weakness when it comes to protection. No spell works directly on a royal, so both magical defense and attack must be indirect, like burning down a barn on those inside, or casting an accuracy charm on an arrow. That poses certain professional challenges to magicians. And that is why most royals prefer using physical techniques for security, magical techniques for gaining information and logistics."

"Well, I guess the safest way to deal with Pandrakis is to not choose them."

"On the contrary, milady," Talak said with a firm shake of his head. "The safest course of action is to include them on your list. There is a reason the queen has put Pandrakis there, so we must take the bait. We have to learn what that reason is if I am to keep you safe."

He looked away, as if he had come to the garden just to contemplate the late afternoon light slanting across the lily pond. When he spoke again, his voice was gentle, calm. "Even, if necessary, from the queen herself."

Eva started to make another joke about divided loyalty but bit it off, shocked. Talak's comment was treason. He had just surrendered his life into her keeping, and the knowledge made her tremble. She put her hand on his and forced herself to ignore the rush of heat flowing between them.

She stared into his eyes, acknowledging the significance of his words. She ached to tell him how grateful she was to him for his care and protection, for his love, dammit, how noble he was, how beautiful his ferocious sense of integrity. "Thank you," was all she could say.

He smiled, looking sad, and slowly drew his hand away.

Chapter Twenty-One

Talak leaned toward Eva, a sardonic curl on his lips. "Prepare for an entirely new level of involvement in court society," he whispered. "Now you will no longer be viewed as simply a scion of Athat, but as someone able to develop alliances involving your clan and the clan of any of your suitors."

The akzul necklace felt heavy around her throat as they strode into the castle. Blood and fertility, Celine had said the stones represented. That about summed it up. She took a deep breath, feeling like an awkward cross between a reluctant debutante and a prize brood mare. Today the four clans she'd chosen would send suitors after that prize.

Never mind, she told herself, she would learn how to navigate all this maneuvering to her advantage. She glanced sideways at Talak. Even though his posture was deferential, his eyes were alert as a raptor hunting.

Then the doors swung open and she strode in with Talak almost at her side.

The swirl of color and energy that made up the Royal Court still made Eva giddy, and she admitted to herself that she had begun to enjoy it. Yes, it was dangerous, but nothing was without risk. And at least here at court, protected by the pact, nobody could kill anyone except by order of the queen. Safe to seek alliances for something as small as a festival held under the queen's aegis or as dark as the removal of a shared political foe, representatives of the clans and their entourages swirled and eddied about the hall in an elegant waltz of power, moving slowly to the quiet music of ambition and intrigue.

It was in her blood, she told herself, and she would learn to dance as well as any.

Amidst the steady murmur of the court, the queen's herald mounted the lowest step of the dais below the empty throne, and struck his staff on the floor three times. Its heavy thud reverberated through the hall and all sound evaporated in a heartbeat, leaving behind an expectant silence. The herald puffed out his chest and began.

"By the grace of Her Serene Majesty Rhianna, Queen and Mother of the Realm," he declared in a voice that filled the hall and curled off the vaulted arches far above them. "Be it known to all here and throughout the realm that Eva bryl Madris of Clan Athat shall receive suitors in marriage from Clans Kotor-Brod, Morindiere, Occitanto, and Pandrakis."

At the pronouncement of the last name, surprise and speculation buzzed through the assembly, so persistent that it delayed the rest of the proclamation. The herald waited a moment, then repeatedly struck the floor with his staff until the noise subsided.

"The Lady Eva's choice of husband," he continued, "shall be declared to all before sunset, forty-two days hence."

As the herald withdrew, Talak whispered to Eva, "Hulvis has given you the formal response that is expected to any overture?"

"He said, 'I look forward to that possibility with you' is how I'm supposed to answer."

"Perfect," he murmured. "Nobody really believes it, but all will take offense if they don't hear it." He nodded toward an obese woman in gem-encrusted scarlet brocade approaching. She beamed at Eva as if she were about to sit down to her favorite meal.

"Here comes your first invitation." He stepped back, immediately the deferential servant as the woman closed in, over-large arms extended, their pendulous undersides wobbling as she moved.

The evening breeze was deliciously cool on Eva's skin as it flowed around her, a relief after the dense air of the court, thick with dazzling light and color as much as with people and perfume. The route between her house and Castle Riardan was familiar by now, but as they passed along the quiet canals, she still felt novel pleasure in the beauty of the homes and the delicate fragrances of their gardens drifting over the water.

Her first obligation had been to her suitor clans, agreeing to the traditional exchange of visits—she would host each man in her home for a single dinner, and each of them would host her in their homeland for a week. The disparity was to show off the homeland's attributes as well as the man's. In addition, she had spoken to dozens of clan representatives and individuals with their own agendas, doing her best to hold her own in their conversations, checking with a glance to Talak when she was unsure.

She had flushed warm with pleasure at discovering she could follow his slightest gesture or set of his face as he helped her navigate her entry into court politics. It was an intimate, even playful, kind of secret communication that she had never experienced with a man before.

She wanted to let herself love him for it, but two-sided love would just make them both more miserable. It was awkward enough with him being so open in how he felt about her. Better to be loving friends, even if she had to fight her desires. Yes, that was the better way.

They stopped in front of the house, and before she could gather the heavy folds of her skirt, Talak was holding her door open. She smiled at him, and decided she wanted to take a long bath. With him? Yes. No. She needed to get Rachel working on the overtures and events that would be coming now.

The door opened, and Efron bowed as they entered.

"Efron, Talak will be a guest here tonight, and we'll need something to eat soon. Will you please have Celine draw me a bath, and send Rachel in so we can start working on a calendar."

Efron bowed even lower. "Of course, milady." He made a discreet cough. "Except that I was forced to dismiss Rachel today for insubordination."

Eva wheeled to face him. "You did what?"

"I had no choice," his voice grew oily, placating. "I'm terribly sorry for the inconvenience. Allow me to help you find a suitable replacement."

"How dare you? That is not your decision to make!"

Efron bowed again, so low his voice bounced to her off the marble of the foyer tiles. "Milady, if I am to run your household—"

"I run this household, Efron. Never forget it!" This was her house, not his. She might be subject to the queen's decisions, but in her own home, she would never be subject to Efron's. If she couldn't choose where her home was, she could certainly choose how to run the one she had. She looked at Talak, who seemed to have difficulty keeping a straight face. His eyes blazed in support.

She forced her voice into a flat calm. "Summon the staff, please, Efron. My staff. Now. All of them, right here."

He bowed and melted away.

When all eighteen of her staff had gathered, Eva stopped pacing. "Today Efron dismissed Rachel," she announced, hands planted on hips. "The reason doesn't matter. He overstepped himself. I want each of you to know that he does not have authority to take on or dismiss staff. Only I do. If there's a problem with one of you, I want to know what it is. I will probably speak with you about it, and I will make the decision as to whether you stay or not. Is that clear?"

There were tiny nods and murmurs of assent, some of surprise—and maybe relief. Efron looked as though a thunderstorm were building behind his face.

"What's more," Eva continued, "I have not asked him yet, but I request that Talak serve as my house magician." She looked over at Talak, and he bowed. "Good. He accepts."

She turned back to Efron. "Have the house magician's quarters prepared in the suite next to my chambers and furnished appropriately. It is your top priority. Spare no comfort. Is that understood?"

Efron, his face now purple, nodded, as if the slightest motion was agony. "Very good, milady," came out more as a gurgle than a response.

"Good. Talak, will you please locate Rachel and explain to her that there's been a terrible mistake. Bring her back here as quickly as you can, and make sure her reinstatement is complete. I also want to compensate her family for their distress."

As the door closed behind Talak, Eva turned back to her staff. "Thank you all. You may return to your duties now." She turned toward the stairs and her chambers, and Celine bustled toward the service stairs in the pantry. That bath was going to be even more welcome now.

Dinner was served in the lantern-lit solarium, with all the doors open to the warm and fragrant evening. Eva sat at the head of the table, and Efron had set Talak's place two places down, on her left. She'd suggested he move up, but he declined, saying Efron had followed the correct protocol.

"Is making you house magician going to change the way we relate?" she asked after a particularly long silence. At least it seemed to her to be unnecessarily long.

"It will, milady." Talak looked up from his plate and gave her an encouraging smile. "In many ways it makes our relationship easier. It formalizes my ongoing role as your bodyguard, and as a member of your household." He paused. "It gives me reason to be near you night and day. You need but call to me." His eyes said more.

Eva broke their linked gazes and studied her plate.

"It also allows me to advise you more directly on a wide range of matters," he continued in a businesslike tone. "And my first such advice is to discharge Efron. He does not have your welfare at heart, and poses a potential danger to you from inside your own house."

Feeling defensive, Eva shook her head. "I want to give him one more chance." She'd just chastised Efron for interfering with her staff choices, and now Talak was doing the same. It seemed like authority she mustn't surrender—even to him. "I think he's learned his lesson, but if he hasn't, I certainly will."

Talak's face hardened. "As you wish, milady," was his only reply. She hated it when he retreated into formality, and even more when he said nothing.

"Thank you for dinner. Your chef is talented," Talak said when he'd finished eating, "but lacks the finished skill you deserve in your food. With your permission I will enhance her palate, and show her some techniques I acquired some time ago in the Grand Duchy of Tuscany. It was after the Medicis, during the rule of the French on behalf of the Holy Roman Empire. It was an interesting time." He pushed the plate away a quarter of an inch.

Eva bit her tongue. How could she possibly hold her own against this sexy man who probably had dined with the Medicis, might have watched Tiepolo paint frescoes in Venice, and on top of that studied cooking in pre-Napoleonic Tuscany? It wasn't fair.

But as experienced and skilled as he was, this was her house, and she would run it her way. She wasn't even sure herself why she refused to dismiss Efron. Was it just pride and stubbornness? Maybe. But she had a right to be stubborn. She'd been pushed around too much already. Or maybe she was right about Efron, and Talak was wrong. That would be something of a relief. Either way, she'd keep Efron on a much tighter leash. That would suffice for now.

Chapter Twenty-Two

"I'm honored that you have chosen Occitanto to be your first visit, Lady Eva," Salar said, waving off a shouted jibe from friends in the carriage nearest them.

The late morning light sparkled on the water below them and glinted off the gilt and silver and jewels of the passengers, and from their eight ornate carriages as they followed a canal away from Riardan and toward the lip of its volcanic cone.

Eva shivered, caught up in the color and excitement of being the fêted guest of honor, carried so exuberantly into the unknown. Riding at the center of this flotilla was like sitting on some noble Elizabethan barge on the Thames, or in a celebrity's open limo wrapped in a motorcycle escort—without the engine noise. She wanted to feel apologetic, that this carriage was too big, too opulent, that it shouldn't be hers, but she couldn't get her heart into feeling it. She liked this. It was fabulous and fun, even the extravagant attention. Maybe especially the attention. If she had to be a prize brood mare, she'd damn well enjoy the perks that came with the role.

Still, it was strange to be in the back seat of the same carriage that had belonged to her mother, sitting next to Salar, dashing blond scion of Clan Occitanto, while Talak sat alone in front like a chauffeur. She couldn't see his face, and she missed that. With a pang she realized he, too, was playing his role, which meant ignoring and being ignored by the revelers while he drove. Their celebration did not include him. The group had been boisterously envious that she had scored such a celebrity magician for her house staff, but their attention quickly moved on to other topics. For all his celebrity, he was just her servant and each carriage had a magician driver. In fact, most cars had other staff, presently busy spreading an elaborate airborne picnic.

It was easy for those in the other cars to call out to Eva and Salar in the center of the flotilla, making jokes, bantering about what marriage to Salar would bring her, even passing picnic food in silver chafing dishes and bottles of wine back and forth as they headed toward Occitanto and the fabled glamour of its capital.

They soon passed over the craggy lip of Riardan's cone. Eva laughed to see that as the mountain dropped sharply away below them, most riders raised their arms and shouted, as if they were passing the crest of a massive roller coaster ride. She always felt the same way.

Salar leaned toward Eva, gesturing at the horizon with his goblet. "Beyond those hills lies Occitanto. We have the best climate—enhanced, of course—but I think you will fall in love with my homeland."

"Attack!" Talak bellowed, "from below, to the south!" He pointed toward a tiny cloudlike smudge hugging the boulders of the mountain slope. It didn't look particularly dangerous to Eva.

Talak made a series of gestures, ending with a slap against the front of the carriage, then dropped the carriage away from the others and sped forward, making a tight arc to face into the oncoming threat. The rest of the cars scattered like a small school of bright fish. Before Eva could see where they went, they were enveloped in freezing darkness.

"Get down on the floor, and hang on to something!" Talak shouted back to them as a blast of freezing air knocked the carriage sideways. She and Salar slid onto the floor in a crouch just as a dagger of ice sliced open the seat where they'd been sitting.

Salar put a gallant arm around Eva, looking far more angry than frightened. "It seems someone does not want you to enjoy my family's hospitality, and I apologize for their intrusion," he growled. A rock the size of a man's head smashed against the side of the carriage, firing splinters in every direction.

He pulled her underneath him as the biting cold chewed at them. "We may not survive, but I promise the culprit will be uncovered," he shouted above the roar, "and dealt with." The carriage bucked and plunged as Talak fought to keep them aloft and upright.

As quickly as it had struck, the storm evaporated. Their battered carriage floated in the suddenly calm air. Eva looked up from the floor. A thin crust of ice that had formed on the edge of the red plush seat above them was already melting in the sun's warmth, darkening the fabric.

"Are you uninjured, Lady Eva? Lord Salar?" Talak twisted around to look at them, face tight with concern. Eva met his eyes and nodded from under Salar's arm. She could see him relax immediately, and once again she was filled with gratitude for his protection. What if he hadn't seen the oncoming threat?

"We're fine." Salar climbed onto the seat and offered Eva his hand. "Thanks to your keen eye and quick action." He brushed splinters from the heavy brocade of his sleeve. "Is everyone else all right?"

Talak scanned the air and shook his head. "I count only six cars, including ours. It may be the other two found a safe place to land." He peered down over the side, flying parallel to the mountain. A moment later he pointed down. "No. I see the wreckage of one below, perhaps both." He swung the carriage down to the grotesque litter of color and broken luxury strewn across the rocky mountainside.

Eva stared, forcing herself to accept what had happened. Debris from their carefree picnic, pieces of the cars, and twisted bodies lay strewn across the dark volcanic boulders of the mountain. It was all...wrong. Out of place. The sight was horrible, but its lifeless stillness was worse.

"Oh, gods." Salar groaned, his voice thick with emotion. "Brem and Galia. Occar. I am so sorry, my friends." His aristocratic face hardened into a cold mask. "You will be avenged." A tear trickled slowly down one cheek. He pulled his long blond hair back with both hands and began twisting it into a knot.

Eva watched him, confused but strangely moved. He had seemed almost effete to begin with, full of playfulness, even frivolity, as they had embarked on this trip. But in the face of danger, he had been more offended than afraid. Without the slightest hesitation, he'd protected her with his body during the attack. But now, as he spoke to his dead friends, tying his shoulder-length hair into a bun seemed odd.

"What are you doing?" Eva asked.

"It is our custom," Salar said gravely, "for a man to tie his hair in a battle-knot before entering combat. While it may be many months before I learn who is responsible for this outrage, I tie my hair now before the broken bodies of my friends in promise that they will have justice."

He pulled his gaze away from the wreckage below him and turned to Eva. "You will discover that while we Occitanti are famous for entertainment and revelry of all kinds, we also have a keen sense of honor and understand how to protect it."

He smiled at her sadly. "I apologize that this tragedy has put a blemish on your introduction to my family. And while we will mourn the death of my companions"—his voice cracked, but he swallowed and continued—"my friends—and burn them with honor, I ask you to learn of us, both how we embrace happiness and how we embrace grief. We are not afraid of either."

This man was no mere fop, Eva realized, pawned off on her by his clan as a potential husband. She was impressed. He carried his dignity and his sadness with the same grace and elegance for which Occitanto was so famous.

She touched his elbow. "Thank you," she said, "for showing me your feelings as well as your strength."

Salar shrugged. "My people believe that all feelings can be a source of great strength." He smiled again. "As you visit the homelands of your other suitors, you will find that our view on this matter is not universally shared. Part of your choice of husband should be based on the culture you want to live in." He placed a hand over his heart. "I am proud to show you ours."

Eva could feel Talak listening to Salar's words, and it hurt her to talk about marriage in front of him. She knew it was inevitable, and that she would have to get used to it, but still she hurt for him. Salar couldn't possibly know what Talak had been through with his own loved ones. If all emotion was a source of strength, then Talak was a massively powerful man.

The survivors landed their cars where they could and began the slow work of retrieving the bodies from the mountainside.

Talak leaned forward and whispered to Eva, "Stay close to this carriage. It is your best protection should any new threat arise. Tell Salar I have gone briefly to inspect the source point of our attack." With that he lifted into the air, vanishing like an arrow shot from a bow.

Of course! Eva realized with a shock. Carriages were for royals. Magicians wouldn't need such cumbersome things. She turned back to the wreckage and began gathering dishes and personal items in the improvised pouch she'd made in her voluminous skirt. She looked up to see that Salar was watching her with appreciation. "How much of this do you want picked up?" she asked, nodding toward the debris.

"Everything we can," he said emphatically. "We'll consolidate our group, then use one carriage to carry the dead and their belongings. We will send others to pick up the debris and anything we might not be able to take now." He strode to her side. "Thank you for your help," he said softly. "I admire your practicality in the face of tragedy. It speaks well of you."

By the time they had finished loading the carriage with the wrapped bodies and as many of their belongings as they could manage, Talak had returned and was standing next to Salar, speaking quietly. Eva assumed he was reporting what he had found, because Salar listened intently, giving a nod of comprehension or agreement now and then.

Four survivors joined Eva and Salar in her badly damaged carriage, and they took off again for Occitanto. A stunned quiet smothered all but the most necessary conversation. Three of their group wept openly as the hills marking the entry to their destination slowly approached.

When the spires and domes of the city became visible, the mood fell more somber still, heavy with the awareness of the news they brought.

"What did Talak find?" she whispered to Salar. "Anything useful?"

He nodded, grim and resolved. "Not much, but enough to begin my hunt for who might be behind this."

Chapter
Twenty-Three

As the funeral barge floated slowly toward them along the paved roadway, Eva stood, as did all the rest on the reviewing stand. A brass and drum ensemble followed behind the barge on a separate airborne platform draped in black bunting, playing a mournful processional. The barge stopped, and the music stopped.

After a long silence, the drums began a steady tattoo, gradually increasing in tempo and volume until they sounded like rolling thunder. Litters bearing the bodies of the dead rose into the air, trailing their long black pennons, and slowly floated up to settle on top of the pyre.

On the ground at the base of the pyre, a single flame burned in a black brazier. Obsidian, Salar had said, representing the eternal fires below the world. Next to it was an ornate vessel holding unlit torches. The head of each victim's family descended to the brazier, took an unlit torch from the container, and lit it from the flame. In unison they touched their torches to the base of the pyre, then threw the torches onto the pile. As the flames licked upward, the horns rejoined the drums in a soaring melody that pulled an involuntary sob from Eva's throat.

She grabbed Salar's arm. Without taking his eyes away from the funeral pyre, he put his other hand on hers, pressing her hand into the rough black ceremonial leather armor he wore.

She looked up at him in admiration. There was no effete luxury or extravagance about him now—he was a capable man prepared for battle. He stood focused and still, hair tied into that severe knot, his shoulders squared and body poised, his face empty of all but his promise to his companions. He exuded almost as much disciplined strength as Talak.

What would it be like, Eva wondered, to be married to such a man? What would it be like to live among his friends? There was a depth in him that had at first surprised her days ago, when their carefree picnic had suddenly turned to tragedy.

Since then she had accompanied him as he met and dined with the families of his murdered friends, had accompanied him in the official rituals of mourning that had occupied most of their waking moments. He bore his open-hearted grief with discipline and dignity, yet carried the same elegance she had seen at first—but now that elegance meant much more. Salar's depth no longer surprised her but inspired respect. He didn't have Talak's intensity, but she could do far worse in husbands, she was certain.

The flames licked along the top of the pyre. Raging heat stung her cheeks and forehead as the litters were engulfed in flame, barely visible through the shimmering fury.

The brass and drums stopped abruptly, except for a single trumpet which slowly ascended the scale until it reached an impossibly high note, wavering like the flames themselves. The other trumpets began the same climb together while the lower horns began a descent, mirroring the trumpets note for note. For a long moment, they all held their last notes in a heart-rending dissonance before falling silent, one by one, until again only the single trumpet cried its note. When it stopped, there was only the roar of the fire and the muffled sounds of mourning.

Much later, when the pyre had crumbled in on itself, swallowing the last remains of the dead, the torch-bearers turned to face the empty funeral barge, and their families filled in behind them. One old woman was carefully settled into a floating chair someone had brought forward.

The platform carrying the silent musicians began to glide back in the direction from which they'd come, followed by the empty barge and the mourning families on foot. Those in the reviewing stand waited until a respectful distance behind the families had opened, then one by one descended the steps to follow in the slow cortege.

Chapter
Twenty-Four

"I would be good to you," Salar said with quiet earnestness as he slowly walked Eva toward her carriage. "Our clan is strong, and although the hands of our families are not spotless, we prefer noble and open action over villainy. Your life would be good here and your allies at court would be many." He placed his hand over hers where it rested on his forearm. "And our children would be...fortunate, as well as beautiful. Like their mother."

Eva stopped and turned to look at him. Sincerity radiated from his eyes and earnestness had softened his voice into an intimate caress. She touched his cheek with a finger and smiled. "I've been deeply impressed by you and your people. I suppose it's a tragic gift born out of the senseless death of your friends that I have seen you handle adversity. I respect what I saw."

Slowly, they began to walk again toward the carriage where Talak waited, as if they had agreed to delay their separation for as long as possible, where Talak waited. "Please know," she continued, "that I hold you, your family, and your clan in highest esteem."

Eva laughed, covering her mouth. "God, that sounds so damn pretentious. I'm sorry. I didn't mean to be." She shook her head. "But it's still true. I must be learning courtly manners by osmosis."

Salar dipped his head and smiled, diplomatic but warm. "I cannot ask for more than that. I realize that you have obligations to the clans of all four suitors, and I respect the fact that those obligations must be met before you can make your choice of husband. I can only hope," he said with a small laugh, "that we have set the bar impossibly high."

He opened the car's front door and then turned to her, gently holding both of her hands. "Come back, please. Come back soon. Let us show you how we celebrate happy times, too."

Eva leaned into him and kissed him lightly on the cheek. "Thank you," she whispered. "I'd like that."

She turned away, climbed in, and Talak closed the door, the perfect chauffeur. Eva suddenly regretted kissing Salar in front of him. She turned and waved as the carriage lifted from the courtyard and swung toward Riardan.

Above the city, she sat back and let out a deep sigh. She looked around at the empty back seats, noticing for the first time that everything had been completely repaired and refurbished.

"Did you make all these repairs?" she asked Talak.

"I helped," he said with a smile. "I assisted Salar's craftsmen by making it possible for them to work day and night without fatigue. At present I expect they are enjoying a deep, well earned rest."

As the towers and rooftops of Occitanto grew smaller behind them, Eva pondered the events of the seven days she had spent there. It was a poignant mix of grief and beauty, but she'd felt very much at home in Salar's hospitality.

"So what do you think of Salar and his people?" she asked, turning to Talak. "I'd be very interested to know. Please be blunt."

Talak's jaw twitched. "He's a decent man," he said. "That in itself is fairly rare. His family has a good reputation, and in general his clan stays out of the dirtiest of court intrigue if at all possible."

He was silent for a moment but his jaw muscles kept clenching. "You could do much, much worse." For several heartbeats he stayed silent. "I believe he would be kind to you."

Eva felt embarrassed by Talak's discipline, his strength of character. He made no secret that he loved her, but when she asked him to evaluate a suitor, he didn't hesitate to offer honest and insightful praise. His words and behavior constantly reminded her that he could be her lover, but anything more was forbidden.

What would it be like to have Talak as a suitor? She likely would have made her choice already, she realized, dismissing the thought immediately. That cut across every law in Riardan. Besides, he was already married—to his four-hundred-year-old oath of service. She could never compete with that vow. He would stay young, while she aged and eventually died. She didn't want that—for either of them.

She forced herself to think back to what he'd said about Salar and his clan's reputation. "I'm sure that when they do enter the fray," she said with a small laugh, "they do it with their customary panache."

Talak gazed at her thoughtfully for a moment before turning his attention back to the terrain in front of them. "It is hard for you, I think, to understand how completely unavoidable conspiracy is in this realm. And murder, too."

He gestured, and the car's course changed slightly. "The way you were raised and taught, murder is a horrible crime—perhaps warranting the death of the one who commits the murder." He shook his head. "But here it has long been a commonplace diplomatic tool among those of royal blood—little more. Granted, it's a capital crime for any non-royal, even highly developed magicians. But among those of your caste, it's viewed as being mildly regrettable but often necessary, maybe on par with someone in your birth country regretting that they have to pay taxes. It is just part of the power royal blood holds over the rest of us."

Eva hadn't thought it through. She hugged herself, shielding herself from the reality. "You mean I have the right to kill anyone I want to—with impunity?"

"Anyone. Servant, magician, other royals. There might be political repercussions, but never prosecution.

"This is the third attempt on your life," Talak continued. "You saw firsthand how several people were killed in an attempt to kill you, and perhaps take out Salar, too. I'm sure the perpetrators of those murders didn't care in the least how many other people died in order to achieve their goal. Acceptable collateral damage, I think Lower World generals would say."

His face hardened. "And I have no doubt that the same people will attempt your death again."

Eva sat silent for a while, connecting the accepted norms of this violent culture to the sight of the bodies of Salar's friends lying lifeless and broken on the mountainside. Death as a way of life. Murder, the cost of doing business. She fought the blunt swell of nausea.

"Have you ever killed anyone?" she asked, not looking at him.

"In four hundred years of service to the throne?" His laugh was a joyless bark. "Of course," he said. "Both in defense of the throne as well as assassinations on order of the crown."

His face was grim and he looked suddenly tired. "Think of all the stories in your home country of special forces or special ops teams loyal to their government. They're sent on covert missions which they have no right to measure against their personal morals. That's me. I am part assassin, part soldier, part advisor, part healer, part creator of beauty. Every high-level magician is."

She pushed away her disgust, as well as a shadow of fear. She looked at his hands, relaxed and graceful. Strong. And no doubt deadly efficient. She needed to know about this side of him. "How many people have you killed?"

He looked at her, some kind of inarticulate pain burning in his eyes. "Too many," he said softly, gazing out at Riardan's peak. "I didn't really start counting until recently, sometime early in Rhianna's rule. She orders far more death than most of her predecessors did."

Talak took a deep breath and let it out. "Her taste for it," he said slowly, "has often made me wish I had a choice." He stopped, as if waiting for Eva to say something.

The silence grew long and awkward, but Eva had nothing to say. She could barely think. She watched the farms pass by below her, so peaceful, at least from this altitude.

She needed to get back to Albessind, connect with something wholesome, be nourished by the land, the mill, and the slow, manure-littered rambling of livestock. She stared ahead at the gaunt cone growing on the horizon. Instead of Albessind, she was headed toward a nest of rattlesnakes, where she was expected to become a rattlesnake, too.

"I'm sorry." Talak's apology pulled her back into the present.

He was sorry? For what? A terrible thought seized Eva. She felt her blood drain away from her heart, from her face, and pool in some hidden, protected cistern. She struggled to form the words. "Did you kill my mother?"

Talak's eyes burned into her, his face tight with pain. "No, I did not," he said quietly, and looked away. "I will be forever grateful the queen used someone else for that mission."

Slow horror filled her, as if her chest had been packed with crushed ice. She couldn't breathe. She let his words land in her, settle around her heart like vultures waiting for something to die.

The queen had murdered her mother, but had sweetly told Eva as they'd strolled together in her garden that they'd been dear friends. Eva didn't want to ask, but the words crawled their way out in spite of her dread.

"If she ordered you to kill me," she asked softly, "would you?"

"No!" Talak's reply was an explosion. "If the queen knew what I..." His voice thickened into a plea for understanding, or maybe a defiant declaration. "I have already committed high treason to protect you. I will never..." He stopped, breathing hard. "Never."

Eva watched him struggle for control of his emotions. He did love her, but his love was chained in a dungeon of class, custom, and law.

Then she realized that her feelings for him were also prisoners. She had to marry, but she could never choose Talak. She wasn't supposed to even think of marrying him. Worse, she was a real prisoner here in this deadly world. She could never confront the queen about her mother's death. She couldn't return to her former life, but she might not survive this one for very long. She was hemmed in on every side by death and the promise of death.

Apparently no one's life was exempt from this boiling witch's cauldron of murder and revenge, of plots and counterplots. Every royal had their knife at the ready and would use it without qualm whenever it seemed to their advantage.

She shuddered, grateful to feel something certain, even if it was revulsion. It didn't seem like her odds of survival were very good. Would Talak protect her, even against the queen's order? Yes, she knew he would—if he could. And taking a husband would bring more safety. At least it was supposed to work that way. Even Talak insisted it would.

"I believe you, for whatever that's worth."

His shoulders relaxed, but his smile was as sad as it was relieved. "It is worth far more to me than you can imagine. Thank you."

Chapter
Twenty–Five

T his was the first formal dinner held in her house, and Eva looked down the long dining table with satisfaction. She'd been focused on this project the entire week since her return from Occitanto, and it had come together well. Seated at her right was Tekkirouda bron Hannar of Clan Pandrakis, or Tekko, as he had insisted with a bow that made him look more like a friendly bear than a serious suitor.

Although not at all fat, he was huge, easily a head taller than Talak, with a broad, powerful frame that made the chair he now sat on seem dangerously fragile. His sandy-red beard formed a heavy bush along his jaw, which made his physicality even more overpowering, and he wore a vest and leggings of brown leather over his dark green clothes. His fist engulfed the silver goblet he held, and his voice rumbled along the table in an enthusiastic conversation about hunting.

Efron hovered discreetly beside the giant sideboard, overseeing the staff as they came and went. Everything from the setting through the second course now being cleared away was perfect.

Long before the guests were due, Talak had disappeared into the kitchen to assist Eva's chef, who hung on every word he spoke, her eyes bright with awe. Even though Talak and Efron were open in their dislike of each other, they had worked seamlessly to make her house glow with festive hospitality. Eva fingered the thick softness of her napkin and refocused her attention on Tekko. His face glowed as he wound up his story.

"...By then the stag was too weak to climb further up the slope, and we took him there. What a noble warrior he was! A real fighter." He took a pull from his goblet. "Sixteen points, a true monarch of the forest. Head's mounted in our hall now. I swear it was the finest hunt of the season."

He beamed at Eva. "We'll take you on a night hunt when you come to visit Pandrakis," he said. "You will love it, I promise. Family tradition. Nothing like it."

A night hunt? It didn't sound very appealing at all. She smiled politely. "I'm told you come from a long line of fine hunters."

"That I do," he said with obvious pride. "That I do. My family knows the forests of Pandrakis as well as any, and better than most. Our hounds are prized by hunters of many clans, as are the longbows we make." He leaned forward as if to whisper a secret, and Eva thought his chair creaked as his weight shifted. "You would marry into a fine house through me. I know our clan is not the most favored at court, but there's more to life than all that. Unless your heart is already set on politics, your life in Pandrakis would be full of rewards." He wiggled his eyebrows up and down, and Eva bit her tongue to keep from laughing. "And a fine passel of children, I guarantee."

Eva could feel herself blush. Brood mare, indeed. "I'll bear that in mind, Tekko," she said, looking up to see staff bringing more dishes from the kitchen. "Ah. Here comes our main course. At first I suggested we serve you venison, but I was advised that doing so might insult you rather than honor you. So we have lamb tonight."

"Ah. Terribly thoughtful of you, milady. You will eat the finest venison there is when you come to Pandrakis. I have no idea why, but cooks in other places want to fix it with too many herbs. Ruins the natural flavor completely." He leaned back so one of the serving staff could mound his plate with meat. "Two more, if you don't mind," he muttered to the server, with a broad wink at Eva. "I need to keep my strength up."

As the dinner progressed, Eva conversed with the others in Tekko's modest entourage—his uncle and aunt, as Tekko's parents were dead. She'd been careful not to enquire how they had died. Next sat his two sisters and their husbands on opposite sides of the table, and finally two young men from another Pandraki family who were somehow apprenticed to Tekko. "Learning to hunt like men," had been his gruff, good-natured comment while introducing them. They sat farthest down, talking animatedly to each other.

When Eva tried to engage them in conversation, they were responsive and polite, but able to discuss little beyond the subtleties of training hounds, which seemed to be their current area of study. As far as she could gather, their lessons in weeks previous had included proper knife techniques to use when dressing a boar, as opposed to other kills. Eva gave up with what she hoped came across as encouragement and retreated to conversations closer to her.

After walking with Tekko to his carriage, where they made their goodbyes until her visit to Pandrakis, Eva had Efron assemble the staff in the dining room. Talak, she noted, stood on the opposite side of the room from her house manager.

"I want to thank you all for a marvelous dinner," she began. "I'm sure you all put in great effort to make the evening such a success, and

I appreciate it." She surveyed the line of faces, two deep, all bright with careful pride.

"Entertaining my suitors well reflects directly on me and my clan, and you performed beautifully for me. Thank you. There will be three more, as you no doubt have already heard, and if you do as well for them as you have tonight, you will have done me a tremendous service in helping me get properly established. So thank you all."

She turned to Efron. "And a special thanks to you, Efron, for coordinating the preparations." He puffed and bowed with the slow and ostentatious humility of an opera diva accepting a third curtain call. "And to you, Talak, for your assistance to my chef in the kitchen."

Talak nodded slightly, and Eva thought he winked.

"Talak, would you and Rachel meet with me upstairs in my study? I'd like to schedule the other dinners and confirm my visits to the remaining suitor homelands." She turned toward the stairs, and Talak joined her.

"Rachel is already waiting for you in your study, milady," he said quietly.

"How did you alert her so quickly?"

He smiled. "Since her reinstatement I've given her more ability to communicate with me telepathically. She had the latent ability, it just needed activation. While it is a great convenience at moments like this, it may also be important to your well-being one day to have such a link between us."

Eva stood on the bank of the river Achthon, looking across to Albessind Manor. It had been more difficult than she'd expected to get permission from the ambassador to take leave from court for a few days of rest. He had not been pleased to say yes.

Already it was time to go back. She didn't want to leave.

Maybe she would never understand why she felt so at peace here, a place she had visited only a few times, yet felt so like home. Maybe it was because this had belonged to her mother, and now served as the only anchor to her genetic roots in this world. Maybe it was because she could feel the slower cycles of life here, or merely that the air wasn't cluttered with the constant traffic of artifice and intrigue of Riardan. And maybe it didn't matter why.

She filled her lungs with rich farm air, watching a heron in the river's marshy edge take a small fish. Whatever the reason she had for loving this place, it felt good to walk in these fields, smelling the earth and the animals, listening to the quiet voices of the river, feeling the morning sun melting into her shoulders. This place was her refuge, and with Talak beside her she could recharge and relax.

Together they had visited the schoolhouse, where the villagers were repairing and cleaning, preparing it for the arrival of their new teacher. She'd accompanied Talak to work on the ferryman's arthritis again. The old man had wept with gratitude as he opened and closed his hands in amazement at their restored motion.

She turned away from the river, toward the tenant farmer's cottage where Talak waited beside the carriage. She promised herself she'd return as soon as she could, and stay longer.

"So," Eva said, rubbing her eyes. She was grumpy and tired of talking about the dangers and benefits of getting married, but Hulvis could barely contain his enthusiasm for the intricacies of all the protocols leading up to the Ceremony of Selection, when she would announce the successful suitor and his clan. "What happens if I don't choose any of them? What if I decide on someone else?"

Hulvis' eyes jerked up from his papers, wide with horror. "Milady, you can't..." he gagged. "The suitors' clans would be..." His voice faded before the prospect of what was clearly unthinkable.

"I can't? I've now had advice from people at court as to why each of my suitors would be a bad, even dangerous choice." She heard the irritation in her voice, but she didn't care. "You said this was the time-honored way it was done. You didn't say it was the only way." She glowered at him, at the same time feeling pity that the poor man had to take the heat of her rebelliousness. "Is this absolute law?"

Hulvis looked down at his books and notes, stroking them with nervous fingers as if to draw comfort and strength from them. "No, milady. But the consequences of..." his voice faltered, "contravening the tradition would be catastrophic."

With obvious effort he pulled himself together to go on. "Your marriage is your best and most powerful opportunity to secure your place in the realm. You protect yourself from members of your own clan by forming an alliance with another through marriage. Then you and your progeny will draw benefit of association from both sides."

"Marriage as a political weapon. Yes, I'm well aware."

"I know you don't like to think of marriage in these terms, milady," Hulvis said, flushing with apology, "but be assured that everyone around you does. Everyone, without exception. Forgive me for being so forthright, but it would be folly to ignore the facts."

"Because..." She let it hang in the air.

"Because the status and protections are attached to the protocol." He paused. "If you chose a husband other than a declared suitor, you would forfeit any standing brought by an alliance. Your husband's own clan would remove him from any office he held, so it's unlikely he'd say yes to you anyway, because he'd be throwing his own status out the window. Even if he were foolish enough to say yes, you would rely exclusively upon your own resources and those directly under the control of your spouse."

"That doesn't seem so catastrophic to me."

"Milady..." Hulvis shook his head and wiped away beads of sweat forming on his forehead with a trembling hand. "Within the protocol, all your alliances will carry the power of the two clans behind them. The combined strength of those clans stands behind you and lends its authority to your actions. Outside the protocol there is no clan support—from either side. Whatever alliances you might be able to forge would be personal to you and your husband. Your influence—and your protection—would be nonexistent. You would be completely and perilously isolated. Even your own clan would turn its back on you, and your husband's clan would do the same to him."

He looked at her with pleading eyes. "You would also make bitter enemies of each of the suitor clans for the humiliation they would suffer by such a choice. They would be among the first to come after you. I doubt that you and your husband would live long enough to see your children become adults, and they would be pariahs as well. Even if they did survive by some miracle, they would be utterly without standing. They, too, would be horribly vulnerable. No, following the protocol is for your own safety and security, and for your children's."

"Such as that safety and security might be."

"Yes, milady. Such as it might be." Hulvis nodded gravely as he gathered his papers. "But even that much safety would evaporate if you were to spit upon this tradition."

Chapter
Twenty–Six

E va waited for Rachel to finish addressing and sealing the correspondence they'd been working on since lunch. Her schedule for visiting the remaining three suitor clans of Kotor-Brod, Morindiere, and Pandrakis was all set, and the same for hosting Salar, Kevs of Clan Kotor-Brod, and Alaric from Morindiere at dinner. She smiled wryly at how disproportionate the formalities of courtship were. Each man hosted her for a week, with feasting and their finest entertainment, and all she had to do was entertain them in her home over a formal meal.

Now all that remained was to inform the ambassador of her travel plans, as he'd insisted. Her gaze drifted to the arched windows and to the gardens below. The dozen fruit trees were laden with growing fruit, promising a generous harvest.

A sharp gasp behind her broke her reverie. Had Rachel spoiled one of the letters with an ink spill? She turned to see her secretary frozen at the desk, eyes blank and wide, mouth open, her face drained of color.

She rushed to put a hand on her shoulder. "What is it, Rachel, are you ill?"

"It's Talak, Lady Eva," Rachel whispered. "He's...someone is dead, killed. Morindiere. Alaric." She shuddered, but her face remained blank. "He was returning from a...a silver mine in the mountains. They were ambushed."

Fear chewed on Eva's shoulders. "Is Talak okay?"

"Yes, milady. He wasn't there. He...just received the news himself."

"This is ridiculous!" Eva snapped. It was downright exasperating. Did these people have nothing else to do but figure out how to kill each other? It was getting old in a hurry. Yes, she knew Talak was right when he spoke of the danger she was in, but really. How could she pick a husband if suitors were murdered before she could even visit them?

She calmed herself, feeling a little embarrassed that her first response to Alaric's death was irritation. But then she'd met him only once, when introduced at court. He seemed a nice guy, but she couldn't honestly say she cared about him, at least not yet. With a chill she wondered if this was how people knew they were becoming inured to all the killing, when emotional response was more anger about interrupted plans than it was about violent death.

I'm becoming like them, she thought. This damn place is changing me, and not for the better.

But what could she do? She was trapped here against her will, forced to marry just to survive. Those were the hard facts of her life. But she wasn't going to play victim. She never would. If these were the facts of her life, she'd make sure the whole world knew what she thought of them.

She turned back to Rachel, whose eyes had refilled with her own light, although her face was still pale. "Send a courier to each of the suitors' ambassadors at court. I want all four suitors, including Alaric's replacement, to meet me in my court chambers tomorrow afternoon."

Rachel looked up with surprise in her eyes, but said nothing.

"I'm tired of being bullied by all these deadly schemes around me. I'm going to lay down some courting rules of my own."

"Thank you all for agreeing to meet with me at such short notice. I'm sure it was an inconvenience, and I appreciate your effort." Eva looked in turn at each of the four men seated in her drawing room. Tekko looked a little uncomfortable, but that was probably his experience whenever he was at court. Graf, Morindiere's overnight replacement for Alaric, looked more nervous than anything else. He was lean and freckled, with sandy hair so light that his eyebrows were hard to spot at first glance. His green eyes were full of a quick intelligence that lit up a face that otherwise would seem too angular.

Salar was poised as ever, and alert. His warm smile of greeting had sent pleasant shivers through her. Now he sat watching the actions of his competitors, assessing each of the other men present, much as Eva was doing. Kevs, of Clan Kotor-Brod, seemed aloof and unconcerned, but Eva suspected that was more façade than reality.

She spread her hands apologetically and settled in an armchair set at the focus of the arc made by her suitors. "I'm sorry for the loss of your relative yesterday, Graf," she said, nodding to him. "And my regrets to you, Salar, for the loss of your friends at the beginning of my visit to your homeland."

Eva took a deep breath and let it out slowly, refocusing her resolve. "It is because of those terrible events that I've asked for this meeting." She shrugged. "I know this is unusual."

She checked their reactions. Now they all seemed on guard. "I know this kind of death is nothing new to you, but it's still new to me, and I refuse to let the death of one or more of you influence my choice of husband. Therefore I'm putting you each in charge of the well-being of your competitors. If one of you dies, I will assume that another in this group is responsible, and I will send all four of you away in rejection."

Salar's eyebrows arched, and he gazed at her thoughtfully. The other men were more visibly disturbed.

Graf leaped to his feet, his face flushed. "Am I supposed to set aside my clan's honor, ignoring that Alaric has already died while seeking your hand, so you can marry without further trouble? His body has not yet passed through the fire to the gods and you stay my avenging hand. That is too much to ask of us, Lady Eva!" He looked around as if seeking some sign of agreement from the others. Apparently not finding enough, he huffed and sat down glowering, arms crossed.

"Why would you think I'm asking you to set aside your clan's honor, Graf?"

"It's obvious. Suppose I find proof that one of these other men or his family is behind Alaric's death. Am I to sit idle—no, actually protect him from danger so you might choose him as your husband?"

"There are a lot of assumptions in your argument," Eva replied. "Most glaring is the assumption that Alaric's death didn't come at the hand of someone in your own clan. We know that's a possibility we can't rule out. Indeed, it might be the strongest possibility."

Graf colored, but fumed in silence, arms crossed. It was not a good look on him. Out of the corner of her eye, she saw Salar give a tiny nod. Approval? She hoped so.

"Besides," Eva continued, "right to revenge is the easiest defense. Raw ambition is probably more likely the motive for targeting one of you for death right now. But bring me the proof that you've found Alaric's killer, and I'll take steps of my own. Or see that the right steps are taken by others. But the proof had better be irrefutable."

She regarded each of the four men in turn. "Think about this, all of you. What I'm saying could also be seen as enlightened self-interest. I'm giving you all a better chance to survive my courtship." She laughed, trying to make it a joke, but nobody else joined her in it.

Tekko spoke, his voice a quiet, serious rumble. "Lady Eva, I have no doubt that your intentions are good. But for us to be asked to protect each other is, um, awkward. Contrary to tradition." He nodded vigorously, agreeing with himself. "Risky stuff. I expect there will be heated objections to what could be seen as your interference in my clan's affairs."

"You are probably right, Tekko." She realized there were more political smarts in the big man than he'd let on previously. "I expect this will be an unpopular act. But several from Clan Occitano were killed in an attack on me and Salar recently. Wouldn't you say that constitutes interference in their affairs? Alaric lies dead, another serious interference in Clan Morindiere's affairs—just a familiar, more traditional form of interference, I guess."

She scanned the group again. "You can accuse me of being nontraditional, perhaps even disrespectful of tradition. I'll accept that. But I assure you that I've never plotted against any of you, or your clans. It would be hard to mount a claim of meddling against me, which really is what your people do to each other all the time. All I want is to choose a husband from among you four without more bloodshed. That doesn't seem to me like such a big imposition."

Eva squared her shoulders. "In fact, if each of your clans is equally offended, wouldn't that indicate I'm not playing politics with you? I think it would mean that I'm being completely non-partisan."

"Making all four of our clans angry with you at the same time," Kevs grumbled, "would not be a good idea."

"But you're anticipating your own failure, Kevs. That's only true if one of you is killed in the next three or four weeks." She looked each man in the eye. "All I'm really doing is asking for your help. If all four of you really pitch in, then the worst never occurs and my horrible insult never leaves this room." She paused. "But that assumes all four of you are willing."

"I don't think I trust the others enough to do that," Kevs sulked.

"Then I suppose you could just withdraw your candidacy," Eva said, sick of his whining. "I'm sure there's some way you could do that without violating tradition. Is that what you'd like to do?" Out of the corner of her eye, she saw Salar's eyebrows lift, and a smile flicker across his face before it was suppressed.

"That's silly. Of course not."

"I'm glad." She fought to keep a straight face as another argument came to her. "Or I could just exempt you from this agreement. That would make it acceptable for any one of my other suitors to kill you, but only you."

Kevs flushed scarlet, but stayed silent.

She turned to Salar. "You haven't said anything yet. I hope you can find a way to agree to this."

"You are extremely persuasive, Lady Eva," Salar said, giving her a wry smile and lifting his shoulders in an elegant gesture of acceptance. "I suggest we swear to each other on our clan honor, invoked earlier, to abide by your request."

His face hardened. "I fear, though, that by making us safer, you may have increased your own exposure as a target for political murder. I hope you know what you're doing." He smiled warmly. "Each of us has a vested interest in your survival, too, you know."

Ambassador bron Ryckmet did not rise from his desk to greet Eva but instead took extravagant care not to notice her arrival in his study, even though she'd been ushered in and announced by his secretary. Apparently he was completely absorbed by the letter in his hand. In fact, he rose and went to a window, turning his back to her as if seeking better light for reading, although the whole room was bright with sunshine streaming through the tall vaulted windows. Eventually he turned toward her, still fixed on the letter in his hand.

Eva regarded him with an artist's objectivity. He had gained a fair amount of weight, making his effete features puffy. His heavy face spoke to her of ambition, cruelty, and love of power. Though she was certain they'd been tailored perfectly for him, his robes of office hung on him like a garish theatrical costume. They made him look pathetic, in a way. Mean, petty, and angry. She was glad she didn't have to paint him. She'd get caught in the red spider veins spreading across his cheeks and nose, and make too much of his ugliness. She sat down on one of the luxurious chairs close to the desk to wait out his transparent pettiness.

"I don't recall giving you permission to sit," he said without looking up.

This was just plain childish. Eva's frustration boiled over. "Then just send me home in disgrace for the infraction, ambassador. I wasn't aware I needed your permission to sit, but then I always seem to be bumping up against protocol and time-honored tradition here—everyday things like murder and the really awful crimes like sitting too soon."

He wheeled on her, his face purple, the letter crumpled and trembling in his fist. "Very cute. Everything's so simple for you, isn't it, Eva bryl Madris?" he snarled. "You think you're entitled to do whatever you want without ever weighing the consequences! How do you think this fiasco with your suitors reflects on your clan? The whole court is buzzing with news of your behavior. You are in my entourage representing Athat to the throne, but you are nothing more than a willful, spoiled brat."

"As far as I can see, I've done only what every royal does—use whatever influence they have to get what they want, regardless of who suffers. As long as they follow most of the rules, of course."

Eva stood and took a step toward him. She watched surprise, maybe even fear, scuttle across the ambassador's face as he backed away.

"But if I could actually do what I wanted, I would already be long gone—back to my real home. So why don't you just banish me and cancel my troublesome marriage-dance? Tell the suitors to go home now, as opposed to me sending the survivors home if another of them should be killed."

"How dare you!" He clamped his lips together, as if holding himself back from saying more. Eva shivered at his intensity, and in a blink of intuition realized that Welryck bron Ryckmet had not asked her to join his entourage at court because he liked her. He was trying to use her, too—and her marriage.

He had his own agenda, and somehow she was disturbing it. Did he have a hand in the murders? She knew it was plausible. Any scheme was plausible. She really was beginning to think like these people. It was not healthy.

The ambassador retreated behind his desk and leaned on it, again the aggressor. "We make far too much of you Lower World seedings," he said between jowl-shaking breaths. "You arrive here and think our whole world is yours, just waiting for you to play in it. Well, let me tell you, the rest of us are not here just so you can have a sandbox of carefree privilege and wealth to play in." He slapped the desk so hard that the inkwell lid plopped shut.

So this was more than just personal. On top of whatever beef he had with her, he didn't like Lower World offspring. Eva smiled at him sweetly. "Why, Ambassador, I had no idea you despised people like me. Have you ever murdered—or perhaps just tried to murder—a Lower-World royal before she could get here and find the sandbox you don't think she deserved?"

Bron Ryckmet's eyes bulged wider. His mouth fell open, then closed. Then it opened again, like a fish on the riverbank trying to breathe. His face darkened to a dangerous-looking plum.

"You little bitch..." the words came out of his mouth with a hiss like escaping steam under pressure.

"That's right, isn't it, Ambassador?" Eva stepped up to the desk, but this time he didn't back away. "That's what I am, a breeding bitch. I'm not supposed to care that I had a life in the other world, one that I actually liked. I'm just supposed to throw all that away, be grateful to be free of it even, come to Riardan, choose a husband with political clout, escape an early death, and breed for as long as I can, so people like you can have a refreshed stock of murder victims for your nasty little games."

She turned away and sat down. "I figure you want to take advantage of my marriage to score something you want. Maybe that's why you've been so interested in knowing where I was and who I was seeing."

"You may leave now. This meeting is over." Bron Ryckmet sat and began to shuffle through papers on his desk, but his hands shook and his voice was tight with rage.

Eva stood, brushing folds of her gown's sleeves into place. "Please remember, Ambassador, that if your schemes might benefit from my cooperation you're far better off approaching me as an adult than by treating me like the spoiled brat you think I am."

He leapt to his feet and pounded on the desk again. "Get out!" he screeched. "Go!"

"And who is acting the spoiled brat now, Ambassador?" Eva sank into an elaborate curtsy before walking out.

Talak's mouth still curled in a smile as the carriage settled in front of Eva's house. "Just remember you need more friends than enemies, Lady Eva. While I doubt the ambassador is a real threat, he has powerful friends in your clan. Still, I am gratified to see you establishing your influence with such...creativity."

He opened the door and walked with her into the cool house. "Salar is right, so please be careful. You may have made yourself more of a target with this move. I expect there are some around who would rather see that you not live to marry at all than marry an enemy, and you've taken away their opportunity to eliminate the man they don't want you to choose."

He lowered his voice to a whisper. "But still, it was a daring and unusual move, and I admire you greatly for it."

Chapter
Twenty–Seven

B elow them, dense forest stretched over hills and valleys as far as her eye could see, unbroken except for occasional meadows or lakes. The subtle variety in the shades of green captivated Eva, and she sensed the verdant, undulating carpet below her as a living thing, full of stories and forces, all hidden below the woodland canopy. They passed over a river churned milky with rapids, invisible from the air until they were almost directly over it, carving its way through a deep gorge in its run to the sea. It would be a real challenge to paint this from an airborne perspective yet retain the sensual fecundity of the land.

"This is incredible," she said to Talak. "No wonder Tekko loves to hunt. Is there any land dedicated to agriculture, or is it all wild like this?" She turned and smiled at Rachel, sitting in the back seat with a book in her lap.

"There are farms and fields closer to the villages and cities," Talak answered, "but nothing like the open farmlands around Albessind. The wealth of Clan Pandrakis comes from the forest—mostly from rare hardwoods, exotic leather from the hides of animals, and wooden weapons, especially longbows prized by archers everywhere. The great musical instruments of the realm are made in Occitanto, but the wood used to build them more than likely comes from Pandrakis."

Talak directed the carriage downward. "In addition, the bloodlines of their horses are superb, and they seem to have a way of training horses that makes them prized everywhere."

Eva watched the forest roll by below them. "What about their mutiny against the throne, what, sixty years ago? Have you figured out why the queen included them on the list of approved clans?"

"If you married into Pandrakis," Talak said carefully, "your political influence would be greatly reduced. There is no doubt of that." He scanned the horizon, twisting one way and then the other to make yet another 360-degree sweep. "As for the queen's motives, I think there are two possibilities. She may be giving you the option for a quiet, nonpolitical life." He shrugged. "That's possible, but I think unlikely. She is not in the habit of giving people choices like that."

Eva could easily believe that. "And the other motive?"

Talak was silent for a while. "I ask you to be patient with me. It's still a struggle for me to overcome four hundred years of conditioning and speak treason against the throne." His lips pressed into a grim, flat line. "The second possibility is that she means for you to come to harm here, then blame it on Pandrakis. It would be the perfect excuse to crush Pandrakis completely, and divide the territory among those she wishes to reward." He sighed. "I consider that the more likely."

"Lovely." Eva's skin prickled. This was how the queen really viewed her—and her mother before her, apparently. A pawn, and quite expendable. All the shallow hubbub about her unorthodox pact with her suitors meant nothing if she herself was destined to be a sacrifice to the queen's scheming.

Then she thought about the rest of what he'd said. "She would do that? Destroy an entire clan?"

Talak shrugged. "It's happened before. And worse."

They remained silent until Talak pointed to the horizon. "There is Pandrakis, the capital city."

He turned to Eva and extended his hand, which held a small box. "Before we get closer, I want to give you this. In light of what I've just said, I'm more concerned than ever for your safety, and there will be occasions when I'm unable to be physically next to you to protect you. Should you ever need to summon me, use this."

She opened the box. Inside rested a small silver pendant on a chain. It was as beautifully crafted as any jewelry she'd seen, but she knew it wasn't just a necklace. Eva ran her thumb over the surface, feeling the delicate craftsmanship that had created this elegant oval cylinder engraved with twisting vines of ivy.

"What is it?"

Self-effacing humor filled Talak's smile. "Think of it as a kind of dog whistle, milady. Since you cannot contact me directly using magic, I have charged this whistle with the capacity to make...overtones, if you will, that only I will hear. I'll come immediately to you wherever you are." He scanned the horizon again. "If you can blow it more than once, so much the better, but that may not be possible. Once will be enough, I promise."

Eva turned it over. There, at the bottom of the pendant, was a tiny hole. "Is that where I blow?" she asked.

"Yes. And the outlet is in the groove on the flat side that will rest against your skin, so should you have to use it, put that side up."

183

She unfastened the clasp and hung it around her neck. "Thank you," she said. She felt herself blush. "I say that a lot to you, don't I?"

He bowed his head. "And every time you do, it is the greatest reward I can hope for."

Talak cleared his throat. "Your festivities in Pandrakis will likely cover more physical territory than they did in Occitanto. Please be assured that I will never be far away, even when I cannot be immediately present.

"Ah." Talak pointed ahead. "Our escort approaches." Several black dots close to the towers of Pandrakis began to grow larger. "They will expect us to land somewhere convenient where you can board Tekko's carriage. You'll ride in with him."

Rachel leaned forward from the rear seat and asked, "What should I do—remain here, or accompany Lady Eva?"

"Only Lady Eva will change carriagess. You will stay in this one with me." He turned to Eva, his eyes full of a deeper meaning. "Neither of us will be far away."

The Pandraki contingent bore down on them swiftly, sounding a horn—a hunting horn, Talak remarked, laughing and shaking his head. The Pandraki group flowed around Eva's carriage with boisterous greetings as they arrived.

Eva was surprised to see that instead of the focus on luxurious appointments familiar elsewhere in Riardan, these boat-like craft were in themselves works of art. Beautifully carved wood decorated them everywhere, and each had a unique animal head on its prow like the figurehead of a ship. Tekko's was shaped like a wide canoe, made from some golden wood. It bore a horse's head on its prow, and an elaborate mane flowed out in wooden streams from its arched neck. There was a stag's head on one, a fish on another; a hawk, a wolf, and a sea monster adorned others. They all were magnificently carved.

Tekko pointed down to a meadow almost directly below them, and they all swirled down to land.

Eva noticed that, also like boats, these carriages were door-less—one would have to step in. Maybe they landed these on water as well as ground.

His face alight with good-natured enthusiasm, Tekko leaped from his and pulled steps from inside, bowing deeply in welcome to Eva.

"Milady, I am honored to welcome you to Pandrakis." He paused, proudly making a sweeping gesture at the forest all around them. "May you find our people as beautiful and bountiful as our land, and the welcome of our hearths one that you will not wish to leave."

"Thank you, Tekko," she said, stepping into the beautifully carved air boat. "I'm honored." She turned back to smile briefly at Talak.

Tekko got her settled, then waved his arm and shouted. With another blast of the hunting horn, the carriages lifted into the air, gained altitude, and in a high-spirited pack headed for Pandrakis City.

Eva looked at herself in the mirror, startled. It seemed like ages since she'd seen herself wearing pants. *I look like an extra from some Robin Hood movie.* The full-sleeved green tunic and tan leather jerkin looked good, and the leather pants accentuated her figure. All she needed now was one of those pointy hats with a long pheasant feather stuck on the side.

Although it was only late afternoon, she'd soon be summoned to the traditional light pre-hunt meal. Eva wasn't sure the meal would be all that light. She'd been in Pandrakis for four days, and she had yet to encounter anything remotely resembling a light meal. Even so, there were few overweight people in the clan, at least under a certain age—then there were plenty. Apparently, when they grew older and ceased the constant outdoor activity that characterized their culture, few reduced their food intake to match that change.

She looked around the large suite of rooms that she had been given. Like the rest of this huge house, they had the feel of an Austrian nobleman's hunting lodge, built around a core of massive timbers, paneled with gleaming burled wood, and furnished with large, squarish furniture upholstered in leather. To her surprise, she'd found it all extremely comfortable.

She was a little less comfortable with some of the decor, which consisted mostly of animal heads mounted on the walls—trophies from other hunts, no doubt. Many of the floor coverings were animal pelts, and there was even a heavy fur cover on her giant four-poster bed.

Tekko had proven a solicitous and enthusiastic host, personally carrying her luggage up the wide timber stairs, and ensuring that a welcoming fire blazed in the massive stone fireplace which occupied the majority of one wall.

"Our comforts may not be as polished as those of other clans, milady," he said, "but I believe you will find them to be more than adequate. Please ask for whatever you desire, and we will make sure you have it. After all," he said with a sly grin and a suggestive wink, "my goal is to entice you to stay much, much longer than a few days."

The dinner gong sounded downstairs, and Eva took one more look in the mirror. She looked alarmingly boyish.

I guess I've become used to seeing myself in ornate gowns, she thought. Such a far cry from the shapeless sweats she used to wear. Now she looked like she was about to meet up with friends for a Halloween party. Friends she'd never see again. She took a deep breath and pressed her palms to her eyes to banish the wave of homesickness. There was no point in dwelling on what she couldn't change. She'd already accepted that her old life was gone—at least in her head, if not yet in her heart. She had to make the best of this one. Eva looked around the room again. It was comfortable in a homey sort of way. In fact, it was a relief from the ostentation and artifice that characterized most of the other houses she'd seen.

It was hard to make these courtship formalities a matter of the heart, though. She was expected to choose someone who could help keep her alive, who could provide the kind of alliance she wanted, without the slightest concern for whether she loved the man or not. Or he her.

All her suitors had been genuinely affectionate and respectful, but not one of them had even mentioned love. Only children and lifestyle benefits of marriage. Talak had used the word, though, and she knew it was real. In this swirl of courtship and danger, it was his love that gave her a point of reference, and her heart filled with its warmth.

She opened the door to the hall. Her "light meal" waited for her downstairs, and after that, the famous Pandrakis night hunt—the subject of so many rhapsodic accounts from Tekko. Tonight, he'd said, shining with boyish excitement, they would hunt boar.

Chapter Twenty-Eight

E va was way, way too far off the ground. It was one thing to be in an airborne carriage operated by a skilled magician like Talak, but it was another thing altogether to be sitting on top of a massive animal that shifted its weight and tossed its head whenever one of the hounds bayed or someone shouted.

Even though it was restrained by a martingale and a livery boy who held the bridle, Eva felt like the horse might take off at any moment, carrying her with it into the darkening forest.

She fingered the sheath of the long dagger Tekko had insisted she carry on her belt.

"It is the first lesson for a youth of Pandrakis, milady," he'd said firmly. "Never enter the forest without a blade. Never. The forest is like her sister the ocean, bountiful and beautiful and wild. Completely impartial about what—or who—lives or dies in her."

He had taken great care to ensure that her saddle was adjusted perfectly. Her legs rested at the right angle on either side of her mount, her booted feet set in the stirrups. But the saddle was not the problem. The problem was the enormous and very powerful animal that the saddle was cinched around. Eva tried not to look down.

Instead, she concentrated on watching Tekko as he cantered back and forth along the line of beaters, spear carriers, handlers, torchbearers, and the other mounted participants. It was obvious he was in his element. He moved in unconscious union with his mount, as if he were a centaur instead of a man on horseback. She had never seen him look so comfortable, so animated, so clearly in command.

He called out orders with authority and the gruff good humor that she had come to know as his natural manner. His every movement was a declaration of his strength and competence, and Eva found herself admiring him. What he lacked in formal polish, he more than made up for with focus and energy. Here in his home environment those qualities radiated from him. When he had finished joking with the Master of the Hunt, Tekko wheeled his horse around and trotted to her side.

He beamed at her, then looked back over his shoulder at the restless assembly. "It's a fine night for the hunt, Lady Eva," he enthused. "Everything is perfect. A spotter has been tracking a large boar for over a day. The ground is neither too dry nor too wet, so we'll find and hold the trail quickly. The hounds are eager for the chase." He bowed his head with touching deference. "With your permission, milady, I will sound the horn to commence."

She smiled, hoping she looked more relaxed and excited than she actually was. "Then let's begin. But Tekko—please remember that I've never ridden a horse like this before. I rode a pony at the county fair back home when I was ten." She could feel herself blush in the twilight. "Please stay close and help me keep my seat." She squirmed in the saddle. "I promise to do my best." She was relieved to see tender concern in his face.

"Your mount is trained to stay with mine, and I will follow the gentlest terrain I can. But the very instant you tire of riding, milady," he said gently, "you can ride with me until we find a vantage point from which to watch the conclusion of our hunt. I promise I will not leave your side." He waggled his eyebrows. "For far more important reasons than your riding skills."

He grew serious and earnestness filled his face. "Our whole intention is that you enjoy yourself tonight, as well as see us at our best." He drew in his mount sharply as it tossed its head, huffing and nickering in its eagerness. "If all goes as planned, you will witness our unmatched skills in hunting on foot and on horseback. You will feel the great courage it takes for a single man to face a blooded wild animal that weighs four times as much as he does, armed with nothing but a spear to protect himself and to take the quarry. You will watch a pack of hounds follow their master's commands, all the while forced to resist their natural instincts to attack their prey."

Tekko stopped and shook his head, his smile warm and full of kindness. "But most important of all to me is that you share this wonderful event with me in safety, and in as much comfort as possible."

"Thanks, Tekko. I'll see how long I can last. I'm afraid my legs are already a little tender."

"Then let the hunt begin." He winked at her and gave his signal to the Master of the Hunt, who lifted his bugle. At its first note the hounds broke into a clamor, and they were off.

Eva clung tightly to Tekko as they galloped through the forest. Riding with him had banished all her uncertainties, and most of her discomfort. Now she was enjoying herself immensely. She had no idea how long she'd ridden on her own, but it had seemed like hours. She looked back over her shoulder, and as he'd promised, her mare followed behind faithfully, reins tied securely to the pommel of her empty saddle.

As the moon had yet to rise, their only light came from the torches that wove in and out of the trees in mysterious patterns, following the horns and the baying hounds. It really did have its own kind of beauty. At least this part did.

If he had seemed beefy and a little soft to her before, wrapping her arms around Tekko's muscular torso had banished that misperception. A bit of fat may have smoothed the lines of his body, but underneath that very thin layer were muscles of steel.

"Hang on, milady," he shouted back over his shoulder.

Eva clasped her hands in front of him just as his horse launched itself across a gully and landed without breaking stride.

With her cheek pressed against the back of his leather vest, she watched the circle of light cast by their torch flow over the undergrowth, rocking to the horse's powerful gait.

The moon broke over the forest horizon, bathing their trail in its pale light. At the edge of a clearing, Tekko sounded his bugle in what must have been a signal of their location. In answer another horn sounded from the woods ahead. He blew a reply and let the horn fall on its lanyard to his side.

"We are not far now, milady," he said. They changed course slightly and struck out across the clearing toward the clamor of the hounds.

He turned his head and called out to her, "I think I know a good place where we can watch the kill. I expect you're ready to get down?"

"Yes!" she shouted into his shoulder gratefully. "It'll be a relief to sit still for a while."

"Then it will be only a moment, Lady Eva." He spurred his mount toward the dark line of trees on the far side of the meadow. They slowed to pick their way along a stream until they came to a trail, which they began to follow uphill. The sounds of the hunt became more distant.

The trail leveled off just as they emerged from the trees, and Eva could see that they were on a steep bluff, looking down on a meadow bordered by the rock face below them and on the left by a stream. Straight across and to the right the forest formed a dark wall.

Tekko extinguished their torch. "So you can see the kill more clearly, milady," he explained. "Your eyes will adjust quickly, especially now that we have the moon."

He dismounted and lifted Eva down from the horse as if she weighed nothing. It felt sublime to stand still with her feet close together. "You did very well indeed," he beamed at her. "You're a natural. You'll make a fine horsewoman. If you wish," he added hastily, and waggled his eyebrows.

Eva couldn't help but grin back.

He busied himself, removing the blanket rolls and spreading them on the ground at the edge of the bluff to give them a clear view of the moonlit meadow below. Closer to the forest, the horses began grazing, quietly champing the thick grass.

Tekko placed his bow and quiver beside him, then looked across the clearing. "Hah!" he exclaimed. "The quarry!"

With heavy grunts an enormous boar crashed out of the brush into the meadow, an arrow sticking from one shoulder, another from his flank. Behind him the baying and yelping of the pack grew louder. The boar stumbled, then made his way to the base of their bluff to take shelter in a thicket. The ensuing silence was terrible. Tekko unsheathed his sword, placing it next to the bow and arrow.

"Would it really try to climb up here?" Eva wasn't so sure this was still the perfect spot to be.

"No telling what a wounded boar will do," he whispered. "He could try anything. We must always be prepared."

The dogs burst out of the forest, baying, sniffing, clustering to follow the scent. Behind them came two men on foot and several on horseback. They extinguished their torches.

"By the Forest Mother!" whispered Tekko. "They've given the spear to young Aldris—he must have distinguished himself in the chase. What an honor!" Tekko looked at Eva. "He came to your table with me. The dark-haired boy." Tekko took a deep breath. "This will be his rite of passage into manhood." He returned his gaze to the scene below and added, "Assuming he succeeds."

At a shouted command, the hounds formed a kind of semicircle, open toward the thicket. The lone figure with the spear stepped through, walked another twenty yards, maybe, halfway to the thicket, and stopped. Again, the scene became painfully still, the silent tension like thunder all around Eva. Maybe it was the blood pounding in her own ears. Everything seemed frozen in time.

With a bellow the boar burst from the thicket and charged the spear carrier, covering the distance with breathtaking speed. Aldris stood motionless for a heartbeat, then planted the butt of the spear in the ground and knelt, just as the boar lunged for him. The beast made a horrible sound, a cross between a roar and a squeal, as it impaled itself on the spear, sinking along its shaft, its shaggy body pinning Aldris to the ground.

There was a triumphant shout from everyone behind him, and several men rushed forward to free him from the massive carcass of his trophy.

"Is he okay?" asked Eva.

"I'm certain of it," replied Tekko, without taking his eyes off the scene below. "Usually it's when the man's body goes flying through the air that you know a tusk has caught him. Then his chances are not so good."

They watched the hunters gather around, congratulating Aldris. Leaving a few behind to dress the kill, the rest headed home, already celebrating. Tekko turned to Eva, his face shining with pride and excitement. "This is the best possible, Lady Eva. You experience our night hunt and witness my young colt's passage into manhood." He lifted her hand to kiss it. "A memorable night in every way."

Eva was about to reply, but the sound of dogs still on the hunt drifted out of the forest behind them.

Tekko stiffened. "Those are not ours," he said in a hard, flat voice. "Please crouch down, milady. Right now."

Eva's mare whinnied and dropped. Two arrows stuck out from her flank. Then Tekko's stallion fell. "Crawl to the horses, use their bodies for a shield. Stay low!" He reached back to collect his weapons and slithered toward the fallen horses.

From the shelter of her dying horse, Eva heard a soft whizzing sound, ending in a thud. She looked up to see Tekko staring down with what looked like irritation at an arrow sticking out of his shoulder.

"Crossbow. Who..." he muttered, reaching for his bugle. He fumbled it to his lips, then dropped it. "Can't blow the damn thing...this little stick in me."

"I can make a signal," Eva said grimly. She drew Talak's whistle from her tunic and blew. No sound came out. She hoped it had worked. She blew again.

At the edge of the forest a pack of snarling, long-haired hounds appeared, their tongues lolling, jaws froth-lined and dripping. Eva looked around. She and Tekko were pinned between the dogs and the cliff.

As if they were one animal, the dogs lowered their heads and advanced slowly. An arrow shooshed from beside her, and one of the dogs fell with a yelp. She saw Tekko had already nocked another shaft in spite of his injury. She said a silent prayer and blew on her whistle again.

Tekko let fly, and another dog dropped. That left three. He would never get them all. Eva pulled her blade—she wasn't going to go down without a fight.

Just as the closest dog leapt for her, there was a flash of pale blue light and the dog fell to the ground. Then the other two yelped and fell as the same light struck them. I know that light, she thought. I've seen it before...

Then Talak was kneeling beside her as another man was bending over Tekko. "Are you unharmed, Eva?" he murmured, his voice rough with emotion.

With wordless relief she sagged into the strength of his arms. She looked up, realizing that his face was so close she could easily brush his chin with her lips...

"Kernan is Tekko's House Magician," Talak's voice was steely, cutting through her fog of relief. "He'll take you and Tekko to safety and have him cared for. This needs finishing. Tonight."

Chapter Twenty-Nine

T alak watched as Eva and Tekko sped away in the carriage Kernan had summoned. That had been much too close. She could have... He drove away the image of Eva lying against the dead horse with an arrow in her heart, or worse yet, torn apart by the hounds. Tonight he would find out what was really going on, and who was behind this string of violence.

In suggesting Eva take a suitor from Pandrakis, the queen had used her as bait in a cynical ploy—that was certain. But who had tried to take the bait?

He turned his attention to the mess in front of him. Two dead horses, two dead hounds, three more unconscious from his spell of defense. They were purebred giant wolfhounds, the signature hunting dog of Morindiere. Was that a real clue, or subterfuge? The crossbow bolts carried the markings of Morindiere. That was just a little too tidy.

He crouched down, searching the three hounds that were still alive, finding a diaphanous glimmer of magic. They'd been ensorcelled. Whoever had loosed these dogs on Eva and Tekko tonight had bound and guided them with magic.

Talak stood with grim satisfaction. If a spell had guided the dogs to their quarry, then another spell could hunt down the one directing them. With a muttered command, he bound the sleeping hounds in pale blue ropes, levitated them, and called to the spell that had controlled them to lead him back to its source.

A delicate pulse answered—more than enough to follow. The caster had not bothered to hide himself. Either he had been too confident to care, or he wanted to be found. Talak would find out which. He wrapped himself and the animals in the folds of an obscuring spell-cloak and sped into the darkness.

They flew along the trail, the creek, over the forest to a hammock at the edge of a marsh. Ahead, mage-light flickered in the undergrowth. He set the dogs down gently and dissolved the rope, adjusting the original spell so that when they awoke they would be bound to his command and not another's. He made certain his cloak of hiding was intact, then floated slowly toward the light, as if borne on a passing breeze.

A man in soldier's gear lay on his back, unmoving. Dead. Another, clad in simple dark garb, knelt over him. The man straightened and the light caught his face. Talak froze, and a wave of bitter resignation filled him.

This made ugly sense of the puzzle, exactly the answer he hadn't wanted to find. It was the magician Balrestin, his cohort, sworn to service before the queen. Talak wakened the dogs, keeping them immobile and silent, but ready in case he needed them.

"My dear Balrestin, greetings," Talak said as he dissolved his obscuring cloak. "It seems you've been busy this night."

Balrestin jerked upright, a flash of shock and fear on his face before it became a mask of polished neutrality. "My dear, Talak," he reciprocated, his voice hard with sarcasm. "It seems you've been busier this night than I expected."

"Would you care to explain your intrusion into my mission from the queen, and thus your invitation to her displeasure?"

A nasty bark of a laugh, humorless and cold, burst from Balrestin's lips. They curled into a sneer. "Invite her displeasure? Do you really think I am here against her instructions?" He lifted his right hand, palm to his face.

Even in the soft light, Talak recognized the ring on the other magician's index finger. The queen's own seal, a sign of her overriding authority, as if she stood beside him. Talak had worn it himself on over a dozen occasions, but had never encountered another bearing it.

The queen had intended Eva dead. This was the fell moment of choice between love and loyalty, from which there was no turning back. But he'd known this was coming, and he'd already chosen. Weeks ago.

"Stay out of my way, Talak," Balrestin warned. "It is treason to interfere."

"And what of the Lady Eva?"

"She dies." The magician laughed, and Talak fought the urge to silence him where he stood. "If not tonight then tomorrow. She has already served most of the queen's purpose, setting the stage for the coming conflict. Her death starts the war."

Now he's showing off how much he knows, Talak thought. Good. He is overconfident. My advantage.

"Pandrakis will retaliate against Morindiere," Balrestin gloated. "Both clans in the ensuing fight will be depleted. Oh so reluctantly, her majesty will be forced at last to intervene, and form a new balance of power here in the eastern reaches. Her old grudge with Pandrakis will be settled as their territory is divided amongst more loyal clans, and Morindiere's influence, which has grown too great for the queen's liking, will be broken. Very efficient."

"And you expect me to allow you to murder the Lady Eva without objection."

"You have no choice. It is your required proof of loyalty. You no longer enjoy the queen's unquestioned favor, Talak," Balrestin sneered. "I imagine your very survival depends on your cooperation."

"Senznach attaburneen," Talak muttered, mobilizing the dogs.

"What did you say?" the other magician's head jerked up.

"I said I serve the queen."

"A wise choice, my friend. Now I have work to do. Go. Enjoy one more tryst with your doomed Lady Eva." Balrestin knelt again beside the body in Morindiere armor, but spun around at the first growl. The three giant hounds advanced from the brush and crouched within striking distance, their teeth bared.

Taking advantage of the other magician's alarm, Talak cast a web of immobility around Balrestin, binding his limbs before he could act. "I think I have a choice or two that you may not have accounted for, my friend."

"You fool! The moment you kill me the queen will know. I'm wearing her signet! Don't you know she can follow the wearer through another magician?"

"Ah, but that's why I will take it from you while you live. It will seem to her that you are still alive."

"Her magician will recognize your imprint the moment you touch the ring!"

"And that's why I will not touch it."

Balrestin laughed hysterically. "You expect me to remove it for you? Just hand it over? You are an idiot!"

"No," replied Talak as he bent over the body of the dead soldier, drawing the sword from the corpse's scabbard. "That is why I am going to take your hand as well as the ring. While you live. Raise your right arm, I command it." He gestured, calling on the spell he had cast.

Balrestin's eyes bulged as his arm slowly lifted against his will. He began to scream before the arcing blade sliced through his wrist.

The severed hand dropped to the ground and Talak wound it in an obscuring spell. With a stick he pushed it into a leather bag while Balrestin screamed and bled.

He tied the bag to his belt. "You were careless, Balrestin. Far too confident. Your last lesson is a hard one. Even the queen's ring will not save you if you get careless." He floated into the air. "You placed a ravening spell on these hounds to kill Eva," he said.

"I think you deserve a dose of your own medicine—a nasty death, even for someone like you." He looked around. "You picked a good spot to die, though. The swamp animals will make your body disappear in very short order. No one will ever find your remains."

Talak gestured at the hounds. In unison they leaped upon the bleeding man, their jaws seizing, tearing. He heard bones crack. The snarls and snuffling wet growls overtook the last of Balrestin's screams.

Talak strode into the upstairs sitting room where Tekko, bare-chested and bandaged, sat propped against the cushions of a makeshift bed next to a crackling fire.

"Huh!" Tekko grunted. "I see you spilled blood tonight. Hope most of it belongs to the bastards who tried to kill us."

Talak weighed how to frame his response. "None of it is mine," he said with a bow, "but I couldn't collect enough. The villain is still at large."

Eva sat in a large leather chair holding a goblet, her lap covered in furs. She looked shaken—pale, even in the firelight—delicate, brave, beautiful. In a different and better world he would gather her up in his arms this instant, carry her to safety, and drive away her fears with kisses along her neck, never again to leave her so exposed to danger. He'd come so close to losing her tonight, in spite of all his effort. If he hadn't given her that whistle, the dogs... He couldn't finish the thought, it was unbearable.

He bowed more formally to the Clan Pandrakis leaders standing at the foot of Tekko's couch, noting Haran bron Sarkscun among them. Good to notice his old enemy before he said too much. He would take extra care with his words.

"Thank you for assembling, my lords. And Kernan, for getting my urgent request out. It was essential that you hear my news immediately. I've learned that this incident was intended to spark armed hostilities between Clans Pandrakis and Morindiere. I can assure you that Morindiere is not behind this."

"But the wolfhounds. The crossbow bolts. All the evidence we have so far seems undeniable," bron Sarkscun protested.

"Exactly as it was intended to look, my lord," replied Talak. "In fact, there is more. I tracked down one of the conspirators in this deception. He was preparing a man's body dressed in full Morindiere uniform and armor—soon to be planted somewhere you could easily find it, I have no doubt."

Haran held old grudges against him, and Eva was still in too much danger for him to give much of anything away. "That man escaped, but I examined the corpse he left behind. I cannot disclose more at the moment, but your enemy in this intrigue is not Morindiere."

Gratefully, he took the warm tankard proffered by a servant and turned again to the assembled group. "But the danger of open conflict is not over. I think it's unlikely, but there may be a mirror to this incident, even now being perpetrated against Morindiere, using arrows with Pandrakis fletching and a corpse clad in brown leathers and green. I urge you to send a message immediately to their leaders, warning them of that possibility and assuring them that it is not your doing.

"Whatever you do,"—Talak took a draft of the warm spiced ale—"it is of absolutely highest importance that you do not retaliate for this attack. That would play into the real enemy's hand, whoever that is, and I'm certain you don't want that."

After an intense whispered consultation, one of the Pandraki leaders nodded and left the room with Kernan.

"Further," Talak continued, "I judge that a grave threat to Lady Eva's life still exists. I apologize for the social awkwardness, but I must remove her to safety for tonight. She will return to you tomorrow, but leaving her here tonight entails more risk than I am willing to accept." He shook his head. "Believe me, I intend no insult. But given the events of the evening, I must insist."

"Have a care not to interfere with clan activities, Talak," growled bron Sarkscun. "You are not in charge here."

"True, my lord—I am not in charge, nor do I seek to be." Talak made a small but conciliatory bow. Out of the corner of his eye, he saw Tekko scowl at Haran. "I am in charge only of the Lady Eva's safety, as commanded by the queen herself. Because I'm convinced she is still in mortal danger tonight, I remove her from your hospitality, but only briefly—and with sincere regret."

He locked eyes with bron Sarkscun. "Beyond that, do what you will with the information I've provided in good faith. Attack Morindiere if you choose—that is a decision for your clan. And with a single order you can stop me from offering any further information or counsel."

Haran looked away.

"But why would anyone wish to instigate a fight between Morindiere and our clan?" Tekko asked. "True, we are not on the best of terms, but we're nowhere near engaging in armed conflict."

"The reasons are not clear to me yet," Talak replied, "but it appears that this plot was set in motion to profit from a war of attrition between your two clans."

"And you think they would use Lady Eva's visit as their opportunity?" Tekko's face flushed scarlet. "That is purest cowardice."

"I agree," Talak said. Good. Tekko's reaction rang true. He wasn't involved. "Whoever wishes to see Pandrakis falter surely knows how difficult it would be to mount a frontal strike against you. No doubt subterfuge seemed to offer a more effective attack."

"Indeed," grumbled Tekko. "Our geography has always been our best defense. For generations our enemies have crept into our forests, only to leave their bones in the undergrowth."

"I ask you to protect Rachel in our absence, Tekko," Talak said with another bow. "Again, I mean no insult. I have more to take care of tonight, requiring more attention than I could give it without knowing that Lady Eva is completely safe."

"Understood." Tekko lifted his good arm in salute. "Until tomorrow."

Talak turned to Eva. "Milady, the sooner I can get you to safety, the better."

Eva rose from her chair and knelt to take Tekko's hand. "Thank you for your quick action tonight," she said. "Without that, we wouldn't have had time to defend ourselves at all, and this plot would have succeeded."

"All part of my hosting duties, milady," Tekko rumbled gruffly. "Besides, you are far too pretty to let some assassin shoot you full of crossbow bolts."

Even in the firelight, his blush of embarrassment was obvious to Talak. Tekko was a good man, but he wasn't enough for Eva.

Eva stood and turned to Talak. "Where are we going?"

Talak shook his head, unwilling to say more in front of bron Sarkscun and whatever other enemy might be present. "Where I can protect you against further threat."

Chapter Thirty

E va hadn't realized she was hungry until she opened the basket of food that Tekko's steward had insisted on sending with them. She wiped her fingers with a napkin. "You're sure you don't want something to eat?" she asked, ready to put everything away.

Talak shook his head. "Thank you, milady, no."

She couldn't look away from his face, tense and pale in the moonlight as the carriage skimmed over the trees. She ached to reach out and touch his cheek, to kiss him. Why couldn't she? There was nothing to stop her, even as she was choosing a husband. Ironically, she'd begun measuring her suitors against him as her standard. But why not have the real thing, then, as a lover? He was intelligent, kind, gorgeous, artistic. Not to mention loyal to a fault. Her body stirred whenever he touched her. No one would bat an eye, not even her suitors. Was she afraid of what would happen next? Yes.

But what was she so afraid of? The answer came as cool and clear as the moonlight. Because once she'd kissed him, she wouldn't be able to stop. She loved him. She was in love with him already. She tingled when he stood close to her; she warmed when he smiled. It was too damn late, and it already hurt. They could never actually belong to each other.

The queen owned him and could take him away from her with a single command. What kind of relationship could they have? Lovers, until the queen put a stop to it? They could never marry, never have children. It was hopeless. To start something now would only hurt too much when it ended.

"Milady, are you crying?" Talak's voice cut through her thoughts.

"No, not at all," she said, laughing in bitter embarrassment as she wiped her eyes.

"I suffer when you are unhappy."

"Then this trip should be a festive evening for the record books. Sorry."

"I wish I could—" He clenched his jaw shut.

They sped through the night in silence.

Eva decided to distract herself from her misery. "Where are we going?"

"To my home. I know you will be safe there, and it's the best place for me to finish the work I must complete tonight. It won't take long, but it's essential." He paused. "And I have information for you that is too dangerous to share anywhere else."

"Earlier you wouldn't say where we were going."

"Because I don't trust everyone who was in that room. In fact, I'm certain someone in Clan Pandrakis helped facilitate this attack." He gave her a reassuring smile. "I'm quite certain Tekko's not involved, but I can't say the same about the others."

Eva said nothing. She looked out at the dark landscape passing below them, but often found herself turning to watch Talak. His skin was like ivory in the moonlight. He could feel her gaze, she knew, because several times he turned to smile at her. Maybe he meant those smiles as encouragement, but they were breaking her heart.

Eventually he pointed ahead. "Welcome again to my home, Lady Eva." She looked in the direction of his gesture and saw the lights wink on in greeting.

Page was standing at the open door when they landed, twisting a corner of her apron in her hands. She beamed and bobbed her head as Eva approached, and curtsied low to Talak. "Everything is ready and baths are drawn, Master Talak."

"Thank you, Page."

He turned to Eva. "Page will give you fresh clothes when you've had a chance to bathe. By then I should have finished what I have to do." His face softened, wistful and tender. "May you soak away all your sadness, milady."

Eva smiled but said nothing, afraid that her voice would crack if she tried.

Page held a towel as Eva stepped out of the bath, then retreated to the bedroom. As she dried, Eva could hear her busy in the other room. When she entered, she found a stunning light blue dress laid out on the bed, with a midnight blue cloak and shoes. On each item, delicate patterns of silver filigree shimmered in the soft light.

Eva had grown used to the most sophisticated clothing, but the sheer simplicity of this ensemble took her breath away. "Wow. Who did these belong to?"

Page blushed slightly, as if confessing a secret. "They are new, milady," she murmured. "Master Talak had them made for you, not a month ago."

"They're beautiful. But why?"

She held up the dress as Eva stepped into it. "That's not for me to say, milady. I'm sure Master Talak can tell you."

It fit perfectly, and the thick, soft fabric caressed her skin, flowing sensuously with every movement.

"He's asked that you join him in his study upstairs, milady," Page said as she fastened the cloak with a silver brooch. "I can take you there now."

They climbed the spiral stairs in the old stone tower and at a landing went through a heavy wooden door into a modest hallway. Page passed a door on the right and stopped to knock gently at the first on the left. She opened the door and curtsied.

Eva entered and heard Page close the door behind her. The softly lit room was long and relatively narrow, spartan in its furnishings. There was little of Talak the art lover here.

All along the wall facing the doorway she'd entered were shoulder-high shelves of books, topped with vaulted windows looking out onto the lake. The moon cast a brilliant silver path along the water's surface and shone directly into the room.

In the middle of the near wall, facing the windows, stood a massive desk coupled to a much larger worktable covered with books, papers, and a strange array of objects that Eva didn't recognize.

Talak looked up. A plain black box, lid closed, rested between his hands. He pushed the box to the middle of the desk and rose, smiling. "Milady, you are exquisite." He dipped his head slightly and gestured toward two large chairs. "Welcome to my study. Forgive me if I seem abrupt, but I have news you must hear, now that I can tell you in safety."

She passed him and walked to the windows, looking out at the moonlit lake. "Then let's stand over here and talk. I have a feeling I don't want to hear this sitting down."

Talak joined her and began without preamble. "My worst fears were confirmed tonight. The queen herself ordered this attempt on your life. This poses great difficulty for us."

"Us?" Eva cupped her heart around a spark of hope. Talak would find a way for them through this, she was sure.

"Yes. I killed her agent tonight, another magician of very high rank. Equal to mine. My treason may never be discovered, or it may come to light next week. Until then, I will protect you with my life. I have made...certain provisions that may save you even if I am executed."

Eva's skin contracted, as if she had been wrapped in a shroud of ice. There was no hope after all. How could she survive against the queen's plans without Talak? "But you told the Pandrakis that the perpetrator got away."

"Again, I couldn't trust all present. All it would take is one report, and I would be in prison tomorrow—awaiting execution."

Part of her wanted to sink into one of those chairs now, but instead she leaned forward on the bookcase and stared out at the lake. A deeper discovery surfaced and overtook her.

The thought of Talak dead was unbearable. It made her earlier angst-ridden reluctance to show him how she really felt about him seem downright childish. Petty. She would make her moments with him count, without insisting on some imagined marriage, impossible to attain.

She took a deep breath and turned to him, reaching up to take his face in both hands. Her body began to tremble with the heat that rose from his skin and tingled through her hands.

"Then there's no time to waste, is there?"

Talak tensed. "What do you mean, milady?"

"I mean that I love you. I want you. Never address me by title again, please. Only as Eva. And while the queen will no doubt tear us apart sooner or later, I want what time we have together to be full. Full of what we've felt for each other for a long time. I've been so stupid to avoid...this. You. Us." Her right hand slid down to his chest, her fingers resting on the bare skin above the open neck of his shirt. "I've..."

His breath caught. "My la—Eva—have I permission to touch you?" His voice was thick and rough.

"Yes. And you need never again ask permission to touch me." She gazed up into his face, parting her lips in a prayer for his. "In fact, I insist that you touch me. Now. Often..."

His kiss was slow in coming, and indescribably tender, as if he still couldn't believe it was permitted.

The certainty of what was going to happen made her shiver. She could feel her body warming, ready to flower open. "I want to see your bedroom. Your bed."

With a groan of wonder, or liberation, or of relief as if a dam built against his longing had crumbled, he crushed his mouth to hers and lifted her into his arms.

Eva began to laugh softly against his lips.

"What's so funny?"

"Last time you carried me like this I was trying to kill you with a coconut." She giggled. That had been a world and a lifetime ago.

"I will make sure...there are none...to...hand... tonight—Eva. Eva, my love..." His words tumbled and fell as they escaped his mouth between kisses pressed against her forehead, her hair, her mouth, her eyes.

He carried her through a double door, and they were in his bedroom. It had the dense atmosphere of a lair to it, heavy with his presence, which somehow made her feel vulnerable. And incredibly hot.

He set her down next to the bed and unfastened the brooch holding her cloak. It whispered to the floor. For a heartbeat they stood gazing at each other, motionless.

"Oh, yes!" she exclaimed in a whisper, and they lunged to embrace, pulling at each other's clothing until it was strewn across the floor and they lay wrapped in each other on the bed, laughing and kissing.

Talak propped himself up on one elbow to trace slow, wandering lines along her shoulder, throat, between and under her breasts, down to her navel. His hand stopped there, palm resting gently on her skin. Eva put both her hands on his, pressing him to her more firmly.

Their silence was full. She sighed, deeply peaceful, satisfied, like when she knew a painting was finished and she put down her brushes. She pulled him closer, shivering at the heat of his skin, and the delicious rough weight of his thigh as it slid over hers.

For a long moment, he gazed down into her eyes before lowering his head to brush her lips with his. His hair fell forward, hiding their faces from the world, making a secret chamber that only they could share.

"I have dreamed of loving again for hundreds of years," he whispered, so close she could feel the breath of his words on her lips. "The moment I first saw you at the gallery and realized you were the artist who had created those incredible paintings, I knew you were the one."

She lifted her head to kiss him. "That's a long time to dream. I hope we haven't made a terrible mistake."

"Never!" His eyes blazed, the hot certainty in his voice melting her fear. "No matter what happens."

He gently peeled her hands away from her navel and he slid down to kiss it. "Never." His mouth continued its slide farther down. "Never."

Eva woke as the skies began to turn pale, pulled from her sleep by the unfamiliar heat of Talak's body spooning against hers. She lay motionless, listening to the deep, slow rhythm of his breath, feeling it flow against her neck as he exhaled. She nestled back into him as the memories and sensations of their loving came back to her. She'd had her share of lovers before, but this had been a completely new experience. It felt as if she were an explorer discovering a new world.

For the first time it seemed enough to know and be known without words, sharing a language of breath, sharp and short or long and soft, and eyes, closed or open wide, and touch, gentle or fierce—the supple voices of their bodies telling each other deep and marvelous secrets, giving each other their mysterious and precious gifts.

Talak's breathing shortened, and she could tell he was awake. His arm drew her back into him, and she could feel him hardening. She rolled to him, pushing him onto his back. "Good morning," she said, kissing his chest, kneeling to straddle his hips. She watched fire blossom behind his eyes and laughed softly as he drew her down into a tight embrace.

Chapter
Thirty-One

The carriage lifted and sped north toward Pandrakis. Eva relaxed back into the seat, her hand resting comfortably on Talak's thigh. Their morning had been idyllic, bathing together, quietly sharing a hearty breakfast prepared by Page, who fussed around them like a mother hen, obviously delighted that Eva had not slept in her own bed.

Now, as she watched the trees and farms roll by below her, she began to think about the impact that her relationship with Talak would have on the process of selecting a husband. It was unfair that she should be in such a grotesque position, having to take a husband when she'd already found love. An all too familiar voice inside reminded her that she would need Talak's help to find a way to avoid marriage. But she already knew he'd insist on her marriage to one of her suitors.

She shifted to look squarely at Talak and squeezed his thigh. He turned to give her a tiny, knowing smile. Happiness, like a fountain, bubbled up through her to meet him.

Then his face grew serious. "Before we get to Pandrakis I need to tell you about these things," he gestured to the black box and a thick bundle underneath it on the floor between them. "You will have to take these back to your house in Riardan, and place them somewhere absolutely secure. If you don't have such a place already I'll build one for you."

He took her hand in both of his. "No one but you must be able to find them, let alone look at them. They may save your life should the queen find me out and have me executed, but in the wrong hands they would spell your death, too."

Heavy dread crushed Eva's happiness. Would all this intrigue still destroy them, now that they had finally allowed themselves to share the love they felt for each other? It was so unfair. The deadly politics of Riardan would destroy them both.

"But you said the queen wants me dead anyway, so what's the point?"

"I suspect the queen will change her plans concerning your fate, now that you've survived this plot. I've witnessed her habits of strategy many times. If one plan fails, she rarely tries to repeat it but rather takes advantage of the effect of the failed plan."

"And in my case?"

"She'll pretend that she's delighted you survived and use you in some other way. Probably through your marriage, still."

Eva swallowed her disgust and let her gaze fall to the two packages next to her feet. They looked so plain. She wasn't sure she really wanted to know more about them, as if knowing would somehow hasten disaster. But this was no time for denial. She knew that much.

"What's in them?"

"The magician I killed," Talak began carefully, "was wearing the queen's own signet ring. The box contains his hand—with the ring still on his finger. It is incontestable proof of her involvement in this incident in Pandrakis. Both Morindiere and Pandrakis would consider that an act of war on her part—against them both."

Talak gazed at her. "The box is magically sealed to hide the ring from those who might try to track it down. Once you open the box, that obscuring spell will dissolve and it will be a matter of only a few hours before the queen's people know where it is. So don't open it unless you are ready to use it."

A severed hand in a magic box. It couldn't get more ghoulish than that. Eva nodded in resignation. Yes, it probably could.

She was only mildly ashamed that she felt no revulsion whatever at possessing a box with a dead man's hand in it—proof of a monarch's conspiracy against her life that she might have to use in a time of crisis as evidence. In fact, it seemed perfectly understandable. How she had changed.

"If I'm dead, then this would be a way of gaining the protection of Morindiere and Pandrakis against the queen." Talak looked away, then continued. "But it would be a desperate measure. The very men you show it to might have been part of the conspiracy, too. Disclosing it in public might give you your best chance." Talak shrugged. "As I say, it would be a desperate move, worth the risk only if you had nothing left to lose but your life."

"And the other?"

"You may remember I said I started counting the killings that the queen ordered me to perform for her." His eyes flashed. "Well, at the same time I began to document them, too."

He pointed at the bundle. "That is the detailed record of my assassination assignments over the past twenty years. Together, they are proof of how the queen has used covert murder to instigate discord among the clans in order to keep them fighting amongst themselves."

His lip curled in disdain. "Her philosophy has been that if the clans are busy fighting each other they are less likely to plot against her." He shook his head. "It's been a remarkably effective strategy. Divide and conquer has always been effective, especially for those who don't mind sowing the seeds of discord and watering them with someone else's blood."

"Well. Those are pretty dangerous little treasures," Eva said, pleased at the steel she heard in her voice. Would she have the guts to use these? If her back was to the wall, absolutely. "I'll have Rachel secure them in my luggage as soon as we land."

Again the city of Pandrakis rose out of the trees as they approached, as if the cedar and stone towers reached up to welcome them back into their forest world. Tekko was waiting for them as they landed, looking much improved from the night before. Eva waved to him warmly and beckoned Rachel to come forward.

She curtsied. "Where are the...items, milady?" her voice was no more than a whisper.

Eva couldn't suppress her smile. Of course. Through their telepathic link, Talak would have already let Rachel know about them. She was going to have to start taking that as a given. She tilted her head toward the carriage. "On the floor." Rachel scurried over, scooped them up, and hurried away.

Eva greeted Tekko, letting him dwarf her hands in his. He held them gently, although his face clouded with anger. "I'm delighted you've returned, Lady Eva," he said. "I hope you will not let this unpleasantness reflect badly on us. Heartfelt apologies on behalf of all Pandrakis."

"I'm certain it had nothing to do with you or your clan," she said emphatically. "Thank you for allowing me to disappear last night. It seems that the most immediate danger has passed, so again I gladly offer myself to your hospitality." She was careful to use the formal phrasing for her visit. Maybe that would help get things back on track.

But he shook his head vehemently, clearly not ready to let it go. "An attempt on your life during courtship on Pandraki soil is an attack on me and on our entire clan, Lady Eva. We'll get to the bottom of it, don't you doubt it. Put things right." Tekko's voice was cold as a river stone in winter, and hard—a tone she'd never heard from him before. She could sharpen a knife on its edge.

He offered his good arm to her, and she took it as they strolled back to his lodge. Eva glanced around to see where Talak was, but he had disappeared.

Tekko placed his hand over hers. "Is he your lover?" His voice was gentle, nonchalant.

Eva stiffened and had to make an effort to keep walking. She knew he deserved a real answer. "Yes. Only recently."

"Ah. I thought maybe for a long time. From the first time I met you, he's watched you like one." He stroked the back of her hand to comfort her. "It doesn't matter. I would not want to interfere with your happiness. But I would expect children."

"I understand. Of course." The thought of having children with anyone but Talak seemed incomprehensible, a chilling impossibility remote as an unwelcome dream. She tried to sound bright and unconcerned. "That's what this is all about, after all."

She looked up at him with new respect, and he met her gaze. "You are more observant than I first gave you credit for, Tekko. I apologize for not seeing you better at first."

He chuckled, affable and forgiving. "Think nothing of it, Lady Eva. Most people would prefer to think that a big man is not as bright as they are. It seems to make them more comfortable with his size." Again, he chuckled. "And that's often an advantage for me, so I do little to change their minds. Unless I need to."

"Still, that's very observant of you." They mounted the broad stone steps to the main entrance, and guards pulled the doors open for them.

Tekko shrugged and winced slightly at the movement of his injured shoulder. "When you survey a pack of hounds in a run, you have to be able to learn their personalities and relationships through their interaction. Which is the lead, which the smartest, the most loyal, the loner, the bravest and most adventurous? You'd be amazed how most rooms full of people are exactly like a pack of hounds. And much easier to read."

Eva laughed aloud. "Even at court?"

It was Tekko's turn to laugh. "Especially at court. I'm dismissed immediately as a country bumpkin and not worth anyone's serious attention. That leaves me free to evaluate the hounds at my leisure."

She imagined Tekko standing in a quiet corner, ignored by the colorful throng of courtiers in constant search of the important and the interesting. "You'd be a great ally to have there."

"Never doubt it, Lady Eva." His voice was firm, eyes clear with deeper meaning. "Never doubt it."

His demeanor shifted smoothly back into the gruff and amiable hunter as host. "And now, if it pleases you, milady, you should change for an outdoor excursion. A feature of Pandrakis that you may not be familiar with is our medicinal gardens, which are supervised by expert nature witches. We benefit from a good relationship with them, which I doubt any other clan can say. In fact, most clans are prejudiced against them because their magic isn't politically useful, but we Pandrakis respect their link to nature's wisdom. I thought to show you some of those gardens before your farewell feast tonight. As far as I know, they're unique in all Riardan."

As the forests of Pandrakis disappeared behind them, Talak reached for Eva's hand and drew it to his lips. He returned it to her lap, but Eva pushed it to rest on his thigh.

He turned to Rachel in the back seat. "I apologize for leaving some of my recent thoughts unguarded," he said gently. Surprised, Eva turned, too. Rachel's face was scarlet, even though she continued to study the book open in her lap.

She turned back to Talak with a soft laugh. "You've embarrassed her. But at least she knows how we feel."

"Oh, she knows all right." He chuckled. "In fervent detail. This is not the first time I've found my connection with her unintentionally open while I thought of you."

He drew his fingers gently along her forearm. "I still feel the newness and danger of touching you unbidden. I have hundreds of years of conditioning to overcome before I can sit with you like this and touch you as I want, without concern that I'm putting my life in jeopardy."

His face lit up, and he threw back his head in hearty laughter. "It is far too late to worry about putting my life in jeopardy, I suppose, as we have plunged together into greater peril than there are words to describe."

"We'll be careful," Eva said, knowing that she was speaking to herself more than to him. A fierce rush of love, maybe defiance, too, rose in her. "And we'll fill our time together with the very best we have to give each other. However long that is." Her fingers traced small circles along his thigh. "I, for one, would like to do some of that as soon as possible after we land."

His hand stopped hers with a tender squeeze. "That is probably not the most diplomatic way to conclude this courtship journey." His voice thickened. "Although I would like that, too. More than anything."

"Speaking of courtship," Eva said. "Tekko knows about us. He asked." She struggled to keep a new fear at bay. "He said he wouldn't want to interfere with my happiness, but that he would still expect children. I said of course, that's what all this marriage drama is about." She paused, looking at Talak for guidance. "But I don't think I can do it."

"Do what?"

"I can't go to bed with another man. Not now." She felt tears building and blinked them back. "Let alone have his children."

Talak tilted his head back, closing his eyes. "You must. It's our only hope for happiness. Or even survival."

He turned to Eva, his whole face radiating pain. "I have had over four hundred years in this society to help me cope, and I still burn when I think of another man touching you as I would." He looked away. "Having you...having his children with you, while our love stays in the shadows. But you have to marry another royal and have his children to stay alive."

"But—" Eva began, but he swung back to her, shaking his head.

"No, let me say just a little more, my love." He lifted her hand to his lips and set it back down on his knee. "My love. This is not about what we want, it's about survival. As horrific as this may seem to you right now, it's the only way. The queen will never let you return to your world, I'm sure of it now. You're here for the rest of your life." His lips curled in a tiny smile. "May that be long and happy." He gazed at her with heartbreaking tenderness. "Happy as possible," he added.

"What if I marry but refuse to have children?" Eva asked.

"There is no one so expendable as a royal caste woman of childbearing age who cannot or will not bear children," Talak said with surprising coldness. "They last no more than a few years. Your children will let you live much longer."

"Then there is no hope," Eva said quietly. "I live only if I marry and produce royal-blood babies."

"But that is not the whole picture, my love—you said so yourself!" Talak's ferocity startled Eva out of her trance of despair. "You said we would fill our time together with the very best we have to give each other. However long we have." His voice softened. "We can still do that. We must do that. For both our sakes." His eyes burned into hers. "The rest is just...necessity."

He blew out a deep breath and looked out over the landscape, which had changed from heavy forest to open farmland and canals. They traveled in unhappy silence for a long time.

When Talak spoke again, the fire in his voice had cooled. "After we returned to Pandrakis yesterday, I was confronted by a senior member of their ambassador's retinue. He was furious that I had spirited you away and invoked the clan's honor, saying I had violated it." He turned to meet Eva's eyes. "On its own, it probably would have meant little, but this man's family and I go back a long way, and it's not a happy relationship. I could feel his personal rage inside his official objection, and it occurred to me that he actually might have been part of this conspiracy against your life."

"But what could he have possibly gained by having me killed?" Eva asked.

Talak again lifted Eva's hand and kissed her fingertips. "It's possible that both of us were targeted in this plot. The queen commissioned me to protect you. If you had died under my care while in a courtship visit to Pandrakis, it is conceivable that in response to my failure the queen could have thrown me to Pandraki officials clamoring for someone's blood."

His smile was grim. "It wouldn't be the first time that a magician's life was sacrificed to satisfy some clan's honor." The way he emphasized the last word made it clear what he thought of that.

"That possibility casts a very different light on recent events, making me realize I may have made a serious mistake a while ago, one that might cost both of us our lives." Talak gazed a long time at Eva, his face full of love and regret, before he continued. "Out of duty, my centuries of loyalty, I told the queen I loved you. Really loved you." He looked away. "I see now that in that moment, I may have signed both our death warrants. The queen might have decided—quite rightly, as it turns out—that at some critical moment I might choose my love for you over my loyalty to her. She would never tolerate that and might have decided then that we were both expendable."

"That could explain the attack on the way to Occitanto," Eva thought aloud. "Pandrakis could just have been plan B."

She took Talak's hand in both of hers, feeling his strength and warmth flow into her. "So she might have decided to get rid of me at the same time because if you were executed I might harbor resentment against her?" Eva shivered, appalled at her vision of the queen sitting like a merchant at a long table in some bloodthirsty marketplace, trading human lives like bushels of wheat to gain some advantage.

"Exactly." Talak shrugged. "Or she just decided on a new plan. She does that sometimes. It's part of why she's so hard to predict. And why she's still in power."

Eva watched the farms drift by below them. What Talak said made so much sense. They were both targets. It wasn't just about her. It was the two of them against the rest of the world. "So what do we do? Anything?"

"First, this means beware of Haran bron Sarkscun. And second, I think this means that you can't afford to choose Tekko as your husband. He's a decent man, but bron Sarkscun may not be the only member of his clan plotting against us. Living among them may be more danger than you need."

"Well, I've already got far more danger than I need!" She hoped Talak would laugh. He didn't. "That was supposed to be a joke. It wasn't very good, I admit." He smiled, but there was no humor in it.

"Tekko is very sensitive to his clan's honor," she continued. "But from what he said to me, it seems he's assumed that the attack came from outside and has sworn to catch the conspirators." Eva shivered, remembering the tone of Tekko's voice as he made his promise. "I don't give any odds on their survival if he does."

Talak nodded in agreement. "I think that would be true even if he found the conspirators among the ranks of his own clan." His lips pressed together into a grim smile. "I know I wouldn't want to be a guilty relative of his hiding in the forest, knowing that he was coming after me."

They fell silent for a long time, and Eva mulled over everything they'd shared. By the time they touched down in front of her house, she felt calm. As long as they could face these dangers together, she knew that somehow they'd survive.

Chapter Thirty-Two

"D on't bother taking off your cloak," the queen said impatiently. "You won't be staying long."

The figure in front of her bowed low and adjusted the cloak obscuring the face. "My queen is gracious to summon me. I had not hoped for another audience so soon."

"Your queen. Your queen is most certainly gracious but sorely displeased with you." The figure in front of her bowed again, much more deeply.

"We regret lending Our magician and Our Royal Seal to your little scheme. You bungled your opportunity to serve Our throne in this."

"We nearly had them both, Majesty," the muffled voice pleaded. "But for Talak, we—"

"You failed!" The queen's icy tone cut off the rest of the explanation. "Nearly had them? No, Haran! You never had them. You have thrown away your chance to gain the ambassador's chair and that coveted piece of your neighbor's territory."

"Majesty—"

"Leave Us now. You have earned Our displeasure and failed Our trust. Nevertheless, We may yet give you an opportunity to regain

Our favor, so be ready to serve. In the meantime, you will continue to provide Us with information concerning your clan's leaders."

"Your Majesty is merciful as well as gracious," the oily voice said. "I remain your loyal servant and beg for an opportunity to redeem myself in service."

"Go!" she shouted. "Get out before I have you executed where you stand!"

The bundled figure snatched up his cloak more closely around him, bowed, and scurried into the darkness.

For a long time the queen drummed her fingers against the armrest of her chair, pondering this turn of events. She wished Balrestin would return. If the Seal fell into the wrong hands, it could be used as proof of...no, that did not bear contemplating. Other magicians were searching for it even now and would find it soon. Balrestin was probably dead, but if anyone else had the ring, its signal would lead her people to it. No, there was no danger in that. At least not yet.

Maybe the failure in Pandrakis was for the best after all. Eva was alive, and Talak could still be useful. Perhaps if she forced Eva's hand, pushing her to choose a husband before her formal courtship was complete. That could be used to set the aggrieved clans against the others. Yes, that had possibilities. Perhaps when only one clan had not had opportunity to entertain her...

And Talak, what of him? He was still hers, at least for now. She would bide her time and seize the first opportunity to eliminate him. Perhaps bron Ryckmet's source inside Eva's house would provide an adequate pretext.

Whatever happened, she could not be discovered as the author of Talak's demise. She would make sure of that. And without Talak, Eva could be manipulated in any number of ways. Yes, much better that Eva remain alive. She could be a very useful pawn for a long time.

She hummed a little tune, full of pleasant anticipation. The best course of action was simply to apply pressure to Eva and then wait for someone to make a mistake. Maybe even Talak. That would be the best of all.

The queen rose and summoned her guard, feeling much better about things. She couldn't help but smile as several new possibilities began to take shape in her mind. This surely would work out for the best in spite of—maybe even because of—the collapse of her earlier plan. This was very good.

Chapter Thirty-Three

E va put her sketch pad down beside her on the stone bench. The light in the garden was perfect, but she just couldn't concentrate. She missed Talak. Still, it was good to be home, and good to have sunlight.

In spite of the fact that her visit to Morindiere last week had been free of any violent incident, or even the slightest hint of danger, it had been by far the least enjoyable to date, at least in terms of the formal courtship. Graf had been polite and formal but remote, even distracted, and Eva got the impression that he had little personal interest in courtship. He was just doing his duty. Maybe it was because he was a replacement for the fallen Alaric, hastily picked by his clan's leaders. Whatever the reason, he spoke and interacted with her through a faint atmosphere of sacrifice, as if fulfilling a formal obligation even though he would really rather be doing something else.

On top of that, what conversation he did make made it clear that he believed his family's wealth and prestige offered more than sufficient reason for selecting him as her husband, and seemed shocked—suspicious, even—whenever Eva tried to engage him in any discussion of his personal life or even his interests. But she soon discovered that he came by that view honestly. His whole family approached the courtship as a business proposition, nothing more.

The gloomy weather of Morindiere had certainly not helped to create any atmosphere of celebration or festivity. A persistent cold fog hung against the craggy mountains and over the capital city, cloaking everything in a dull silver light. It rained every day, and periods of sunlight were rare.

Graf took Eva on tours of silver and gem mines, the university with its massive library, and innumerable ateliers showing jewelry of astonishing beauty and imagination. But he himself didn't show the slightest personal interest in any of it except the library. Then his passion for books and knowledge lit up his face, and he would have gladly stayed there all day, sharing its wonders with her. In all the other venues, his conversation was formulaic, no more friendly than that of a bored guide leading a group of tourists through a museum.

The food had been wholesome enough and well prepared, but showed no sign of the creativity that she had seen in the jewelry. Worst of all, the entire city had seemed drugged by a dull self-satisfaction, with little laughter or playfulness.

So it was no surprise that they had parted easily, both pretending not to be relieved when her stay had come to an end.

Still, the trip had been a wonderful one for her—the very best so far. Without doubt, the most glorious part of her sojourn in Morindiere had been a direct result of Graf's lack of personal interest in her. She and Talak had been free to spend long and uninterrupted hours together, as well as every night in her ornate apartment. They had talked and cuddled and made love like a couple on a honeymoon.

No one in Graf's family, and certainly none of the servants, showed the slightest concern that she spent as much time with Talak as she did with Graf—or that Talak's bed remained unused, or that she was so obviously happier in the company of her House Magician. In fact, they seemed to take it for granted. It was then that Eva realized that a magician lover was far less a threat to an arranged marriage than if she had taken another royal to her bed. At least there would be no competing children, no confusion of status.

In an act of will, Eva pulled herself back from her memories. Glancing appreciatively around the garden, she picked up her sketch book, headed into the house, and climbed the stairs to her study.

Seated at her desk, she focused on the week's calendar Rachel had drawn up. Talak wouldn't be back until tomorrow—ages from now. She ached for his touch, to feel his quiet, powerful presence. She toyed with the idea of asking Rachel to contact him telepathically, but she'd already done that twice this morning, and both times Rachel had alternately blushed, giggled, or gasped as he conveyed his messages through her.

After the last one, Rachel said in a shaky voice, "Milady, forgive me for saying so, as it's not my place, but you are very lucky to have someone love you like he does. Even though I'm only the messenger, I feel his...intensity. Like a river at spring flood. It's quite...unsettling, if you know what I mean. He's a very passionate man." She'd busied herself then with the letters in front of her, but her hands trembled.

No, it was really unfair to Rachel to have her call to Talak again just because she wanted him. He'd be back tomorrow. In the meantime, she had Kevs of Clan Kotor-Brod to entertain at dinner tonight.

Dinner had been an ordeal. "I don't know, Celine," Eva said, rubbing her eyes. "This all seems so bizarre. I'm expected to choose a husband from these four suitors, and in spite of myself I compare each of them to Talak. And of course they all come up short."

She watched Celine fuss with her hair, unwinding the intricate web of jewels she'd worn to dinner. It had been a complete waste of time and effort. "Especially Kevs. If he's typical of what Clan Kotor-Brod has to offer, they're in real trouble, socially speaking."

"I know, milady," Celine cooed, "but duty is duty, and you'll be able to lead a good life with one of them, I'm sure. And Talak will always be your love. Everyone understands that."

Eva scrunched her face in frustration because she couldn't shake her head while Celine was working. "That's the part that's hard for me, though. I'm having an awful time separating my concepts of love and marriage. It just seems so unreal."

"Yes, milady, but that's been our way for longer than anyone cares to remember." Celine patted Eva's shoulder, motherly and comforting. "It will all work out just fine, you'll see."

At the moment Eva couldn't see it at all. Kevs was a whiner. He'd complained about being left until so late in the process to be entertained, then spent a good part of their dinner chastising Eva for extracting that oath of mutual protection among the suitors. After all, Tekko had nearly been killed only a week later.

Kevs was certain that the attack was Morindiere's doing, even though Eva wouldn't hear of it. He'd actually called her naïve for believing it wasn't. Definitely not husband material.

Then there was Graf, who just didn't seem interested in marriage at all. The prospect of living out her life in fog-shrouded Morindiere, married to an aloof husband, was truly depressing, even if she would be clad in the realm's finest jewelry. She already had more money and jewelry than she knew what to do with.

Tekko was kind, brave, and sensible, as well as astute in his observations of people, but they both had tacitly acknowledged that most of their deeper interests lay in different spheres. She would never take to horseback riding, and although he tried hard, he couldn't understand why anyone would want to paint abstracts. Still, if someone put a gun to her head—or a knife to her throat, given the prejudices of this world's technology—she could probably lead a decent life with Tekko.

Salar was far and away the best choice. He was intelligent, strong, disciplined, courageous, graceful, and good-hearted. He lived in a vibrantly artistic culture that Eva knew would suit her well. Her painting and artistic sensibilities would be welcome. But as handsome and gifted and goodhearted as Salar was, he still wasn't Talak.

All her thoughts led back to Talak. She closed her eyes and sighed. "Yes, I suppose it will work out, but working out isn't the romantic ideal where I come from. When Talak told me—ouch! Careful, Celine! When Talak told me how he had dreamed of loving deeply and devotedly again after hundreds of years—ouch! Anyway, we've already acknowledged how deeply devoted we are to each other, exchanged promises of devotion, really... Ouch, that really hurts, Celine! What are you—"

Eva opened her eyes to scold Celine's reflection in the mirror and saw her face beaded with perspiration, bright pink, and agitated. Then over her shoulder she saw why. Efron stood quietly behind her, looking indescribably humble, in his officious way. He hadn't knocked.

She slammed a fist on her dressing table, making Celine jump. Efron's eyes widened for a heartbeat, then lowered again. "Efron!" she shouted, "I will not tell you again. You will knock on my door and wait to be invited in. You are not to enter unannounced and sneak up behind me."

"I apologize, milady," Efron murmured in his most obsequious voice. "I had thought simply to leave this note which Lord Kevs just had delivered. I didn't even think you were here..."

"I repeat, you are to knock and wait to be invited in!" Eva was surprised at her own anger. This was unacceptable and had to stop. "Will this unannounced intrusion happen again?"

"No, milady." Efron bowed low before advancing to place the message on the edge of her dressing table, and scuttled away.

Once the door closed with a soft click, Celine began to sob. "Oh, I am so sorry, milady, for hurting you, but I was trying to warn you that he'd come in. He just stood there smiling that ugly smile and listening to what you were saying. I know he means you no good. I was only trying to get your attention. I am so, so, sorry." She turned away, wiping her eyes with her apron.

Eva stood and put her hands on Celine's shoulders. "Don't give it another thought, Celine, it's my fault for not paying attention. How much do you think he heard?"

"He heard all you said about how much you and Talak love each other, milady,"—Celine sniffled, "—and how devoted you are to each other. I tell you, his face changed when he heard that. His eyes lit up something horrible, and his smile…" She shuddered. "I just know he means to do something evil with that information."

A cold chill swept through Eva. How could anyone use a simple declaration of mutual love and devotion against them? Oh. Of course. Loyalty. The queen. The sacred chains of his honor, as Talak had once called his obligation to the throne. Gods, how their lives had changed since then…

Eva fought a thick wave of nausea and tasted salt rising along her tongue. "Forget about my hair for now. And thank you for your attempt to help me tonight. Please go get Rachel right away. Hurry!"

She had to let Talak know what had happened. In the pit of her stomach, she knew something terrible had occurred, but she couldn't see exactly what.

What was clear was Efron had information that could conceivably hurt Talak. He wouldn't dare pass that information on to Talak's enemies—would he? He might. He hated Talak. And Talak's enemies must be everywhere. Who were they? Yet the queen herself had suggested Eva take Talak for a lover—she couldn't possibly object!

Eva knew she was trying to rationalize something that didn't need any rational justification. She had just put a long, sharp knife in Efron's hand, and he would use it to strike at the man she loved.

Chapter
Thirty-Four

T he next morning Eva and Talak stood side by side in her study, gazing out the windows at the garden bathed in bright sunlight. It was far too cheerful a scene. "I could have Efron killed before he has a chance to use the information against us," Eva said grimly.

"Too late, my love." Talak's voice was calm, resigned. "That information is long gone from this house. It was on its way no more than a matter of moments after he left your chamber last night."

He drew her close. "No, unfortunately, you can't get rid of Efron right away," he said.

She ached, seeing him so calm in the face of this betrayal, as if his life wasn't in danger.

"When I'm arrested—and I will be, probably within the next two or three days—his murder, or even his immediate dismissal could be interpreted as proof of your deeper connection to me."

Talak turned to grasp both her shoulders, his stare burning into her. "It must appear to the whole realm that I was your plaything, nothing more. Anything we can do to create an impression that you are the unwitting victim of my treason will help keep you safe."

Eva closed her eyes and leaned into him. "I wish I could remember who recommended Efron to me," she said. "That might give us a clue as to who the viper informed."

He lifted her face, his brows arched in surprise. "I thought you already knew. Welryck bron Ryckmet, before he became your ambassador. Efron has given him the information."

"Oh, gods. He won't help us—he hates me." Then the cold realization landed. "He planted Efron here—right at the beginning—as a spy! And I can't do anything to him because now he's ambassador."

"But by the same token, he can't do anything to you. He's both protected and defanged by the neutrality of his office." Talak stroked her cheek. "Besides, he's not that important, except that he'll convey Efron's information to the queen, who will in turn have him lodge the formal complaint against me so that she can appear impartial. There will be a tribunal, and a guilty verdict for treason is already certain."

"Based on just a private remark about devotion?" Eva burst out. "That's ridiculous!"

"All the queen needs is a pretext," he said, stroking her hair. "Believe me, as flimsy as this one is, it's more than enough."

Talak kissed her forehead and stepped back. "We've no time to waste, love, and we have so much to take care of before the inevitable happens. So we should get started. You might be more comfortable sitting." Eva sank into a chair, hugging her arms, hating the distance between them. She wanted to be anywhere else with him, doing anything else than this.

Talak gestured to a trunk that he'd brought with him that morning. It rose into the air a few inches and floated to settle in front of Eva. Slowly its many heavy clasps opened and the lid tilted back.

"Since we returned from Pandrakis, I've been busy preparing against this eventuality, now certain." He reached into the trunk and drew out a small sheaf of papers bound in a scarlet ribbon. "Everything is in place. I've transferred title to my house and all my other property to you. These are the deeds and other documents that record the legal transfer. All I own in this realm is my house and its surrounding land, but in the Lower World I have extensive holdings in Italy. Those also are yours now."

"But I'm stuck here!" Eva exclaimed, fighting a wave of hysteria. "I can't escape."

"If things become desperate, yes, you can." Talak smiled reassuringly. "I've created an escape route for you. In my house is a portal to the Lower World that no one else knows about. I've had it for centuries. It's at the base of the stone tower."

He drew a ring from his pocket and gave it to her. "If you can get to my house, this ring will guide you to the locked door behind which the portal lies, and let you in. There is a small carriage set right in front of it, already spelled to take you through the threshold and to Italy. I've also set wards and spells so that only you can use the portal. After you've gone through, the house will catch fire and burn to the ground. Anyone who might have tracked you there will assume you were incinerated in the fire."

Reaching into the trunk again, he drew out a matchbox-size carriage. "Carry this with you everywhere now. While wearing the guide ring I just gave you, place this on the ground and tap it twice with the ring. The carriage will expand, large enough to accommodate you and at least one other. It's already spellbound to take you directly to my house and to your escape."

Hope burned in Eva like a sudden fever. She jumped out of her chair and ran to Talak. "Then let's go right now!" she exclaimed. "You and I can be long gone before they know what happened."

"No, love." Talak shook his head and pulled her into an embrace. "It wouldn't work."

"Why not? You just said it was an escape for me if things get desperate." She gazed up at him. "This is desperate. An escape for me and one other." She brushed a finger along his lips. "You."

"I wish it was that simple," he said, holding her fingers to his lips. "But it's an escape for you, not for us. First, no one would believe that I died in a fire in my own house. The queen would declare a huge bounty on our heads and the hunters would search both worlds. Relentlessly. It would take no more than a few weeks before someone found and killed us. You would never be safe if we both disappeared. Your only chance of survival is if I am arrested."

Talak began speaking faster, and his voice rose in a fever to convey all the information he had to give her. "But that is just your escape as a last resort. I am hoping that with my demise the queen will leave you alone to marry and live out your life here in relative peace. Please marry Salar. He is the best man for you"—his voice caught and he forced a grin as if making a joke—"That is, the best man for you once I'm gone."

"Please don't talk like that!" Eva hugged him tightly, feeling her tears soaking into his shirt, and his heart pounding below her ear. "Let's talk about something else, at least for a little while."

Talak grasped her shoulders, pushing her gently away so he could look into her eyes. "I would love to, but we can't afford denial. Or delay." He tilted his head toward the open trunk. "This is what my love for you looks like now."

"It's not fair!" Eva sobbed, raging into his chest. "We deserve more!"

"Eva. Love." Talak's voice was gentle and soothing as a lullaby. "You have no idea what it's like to dream"—his voice cracked and he cleared his throat—"to dream for hundreds of years about being able to love again. You've made that possible. You've given me the greatest gift I could ever hope for. For centuries my heart was in prison, and you set me free." His eyes shone with an ecstatic light that made her heart groan.

He drew her in a tight embrace, kissing the top of her head. "Yes, of course I wanted more. I wanted a lifetime with you. But this...this brief miracle has to be enough, because it's all we're going to get. Please understand that it's not what I wanted, but I'm a dead man. There is no way you can save me. The queen will have my head, or worse. And the best I can give to you now is a chance to live a full life with Salar, and, if all else fails, a chance to escape to the Lower World."

Talak settled Eva back in her chair and placed the deeds on her lap. "There's so much more I have to tell you," he said, his voice a rough and urgent whisper—as if the queen's guards would knock on the door any moment.

"I've made a list of everything in here already, so you don't have to try to remember it all. But I want to go through the main items so that you know what you have."

He put his hand on the deeds. "In with the deeds are two Swiss bank account numbers. There's probably about twenty-five million euros in them. You'll be well provided for, between that and the properties—an apartment in Rome, another in Florence, and the villa. It's on the Adriatic, near San Vito Chietino. There's a map in there along with the deed. It's not particularly easy to get to, which is one of the reasons I chose it."

If she didn't say something, or hold him, she would break into pieces. "But—" Eva began.

He held up a hand. "No, my love, let me get through this without interruption. We can talk later. I have to get through this." He drew a piece of paper from his pocket and unfolded it. "Even though you can't get rid of Efron yet, you should be safe to fire him in a month or two. In the meantime, you need to surround yourself with people I know you can trust."

He handed her the paper, his eyes searching hers for agreement. "You'll need a new House Magician." He raised a hand as if to forestall her objection. "And although I know you're very sensitive about other people making decisions for you, I've already chosen him. He can be trusted completely. He'll be able to help vet a new house manager once you've fired Efron." He pointed to a line on the paper. "You'll also need at least two able bodyguards, and I've retained three for you. They're coming this afternoon so that I can introduce them to you. And I've also added three others to your staff. They'll watch out for you in ways you can't. For example, they can be your eyes and ears among the staff. Ernesta is quite elderly but don't be fooled by her appearance. For reasons of her own, she'll keep a watchful eye on Efron until you can get rid of him."

Talak knelt in front of her chair, gazing up at her, wiping her cheek dry, and Eva leaned into his touch with a soft moan.

"There are other things in there," he said, tilting his head toward the trunk. "Most are self-explanatory. An assessment of people in your clan and at court that will be useful in choosing long-term allies. Background information concerning some current political issues that most people don't know."

He looked over at the trunk and then back at Eva. "Depending on how much time we have left, I can go over more of them, or all of the rest. But I think we've covered the critical items now."

As if he had just set down a heavy load, Talak's shoulders dropped, and he breathed out a deep sigh. "And finally, I have a personal request, love—that you take in my housekeeper, Page. She'll be content with any position. Her family has served in my household for hundreds of years, and I'll feel much better knowing that she is in good hands. She likes you, and you'll love having her around. She's got a good heart and is very capable."

Eva knew that she couldn't speak without sobbing. All she could do was stroke his cheek, nod, and blink hard against the tears she refused to let spill.

Chapter Thirty-Five

The thought of having dinner served in her dining room with staff bustling about was more than Eva could handle, even if she knew Efron wouldn't be anywhere nearby. He'd remained in his quarters all day, pleading an illness. She was sure he wasn't anywhere near as ill as she would like him to be.

Still, to make sure he understood her grasp of the situation and to ensure he didn't do any more damage, she informed him that she expected him to stay in his quarters until further notice, and she had posted one of her new guards at his door to make sure he remained there.

Wanting nothing more than quiet time alone with Talak, she'd had their dinner brought up to her suite. Although Talak ate with some enthusiasm, Eva could only poke listlessly at her plate. She was sure the food tasted fine, but her taste buds weren't functioning. On top of that, it took real effort just to chew and swallow.

They'd been busy all day, briefing the bodyguards and getting the new staff added. Talak's choices had been flawless. Eva was fascinated by Ernesta, the old woman whom Talak had hired to keep an eye on Efron. She walked with a cane and her shoulders were stooped, but the light in her eyes spoke of an internal fire and intelligence that was startling.

Best of all, the new house magician, Yurud, was Talak's young protégé. The silent but unmistakable accord that existed between them was a real source of comfort for her. It was clear that Talak had briefed him about the situation in great detail, because Eva could feel the compassion—even tenderness—from him as they spoke briefly about the household, the staff, and about Efron's betrayal.

Eva felt empty. It was as if she had already lost that part of herself which made sense of everything else. She'd have to get used to it eventually, she thought. This is what her life would be like without him—secluded meals with tasteless food, and emptiness. The ache of his absence was like missing a part of her body—a hollow pain that prevented her from being alive, allowing her only to exist.

No, she would not fall into self-pity. Not yet, anyway. She looked up from her plate to see Talak gazing at her, his eyes radiant.

"What?" She asked, feeling her eyes fill.

"I am memorizing you," he whispered. "No matter what happens, I will have you with me."

She couldn't bear looking at him but turned away and rang for a servant, unable to speak. When the dishes had been cleared away, she stood and took his hand. "Let's go to bed."

Their lovemaking was alternately careful and delicate, as if too firm a grasp or too hard a touch might damage the other, and then so ferocious that it seemed each was attempting to devour the other, so that there would be nothing of either of them left for the queen's soldiers when they finally came.

Through the night they lay cradled in each other's arms, barely sleeping, dozing and murmuring in the sweet comfort of their embrace. Eva started at the slightest noise, burrowing into Talak when it became clear that the unspeakable moment had not yet arrived.

Toward dawn she heard him sigh as he turned away from her to sit on the edge of the bed. Before he had a chance to stand, she knelt behind him, throwing her arms around him and burying her face in his neck. "I can't do this. I can't let you go," she sobbed. "I feel like I'll break into pieces without you."

"You must," he said, his voice calm, heavy. "It is selfish of me to ask, but you must." He stroked her arms. "All I have left is the hope that you will be happy. I can endure anything if I can believe that you are safe and well."

He dropped his head back against her. "Promise me that you will marry Salar, raise a family, and live well."

That was the last thing Eva felt like doing and the words tried to stay in her throat, but she whispered, "For you, I promise. But only for you."

"Thank you. That is all I can ask." He drew her arms apart gently but firmly, and stood. "I'd like to bathe," he said. "Would you join me, my love?"

After the sun had risen, they ate again in Eva's sitting room, speaking rarely, voices muted. It felt as if the world was about to stop, so there was little left to say except to comment on inconsequential things—did the other want more coffee? How the fruit had come into peak season, so delicious.

Afterward, they went down into the garden and strolled, arms around each other, leaning on each other. The morning sun streamed down on them, and the bright beauty of the garden was a painful contrast to Eva's dread.

"Maybe we've just imagined all this," she said turning to Talak. "Maybe we've created this horrible scenario, but it's not going to happen."

Talak took her in his arms and kissed her with overwhelming tenderness. "They're already on their way," he said quietly. "I received a message while we were eating. They will be here soon."

He took her face in both hands and kissed her again. "Remember. You have an escape. You have weapons of information. You have a powerful and kind future husband." He drew her into an embrace, kissing her hair, her lips again and again. "I want to say goodbye to you here," he murmured. "There must be no display of affection once they are here. You can't afford it."

"I can't say goodbye," she wept into his chest. "All I can say is I love you. I love you and I always will." She looked up at him, her vision blurred by welling tears. "Whatever I do, whatever I do for the rest of my life, I do for us."

They stood a long time, locked together, silent and fierce. Finally, Talak said, "It's time. They're arriving, and we should meet them at the front door. I don't want any of those jackals inside your house."

No sooner had they stepped outside the front door than three carriages settled in front of them. In the largest and most ornate sat Welryck bron Ryckmet, Clan Athat's Ambassador to Queen Rhianna, and two other men dressed in official robes. Eva didn't recognize either of them. In the second carriage rode five magicians, all wearing the livery of the royal court.

The third vehicle was little more than a black barge with three bench seats, the middle one smaller than the other two. In it stood four soldiers clad in armor of brass and leather, armed with crossbows and swords, two at the front and two in the rear. The empty middle seat, Eva knew, was for Talak. A soft groan of despair escaped her, and she clamped her lips shut. She would not dishonor her pain by showing it to these animals.

The ambassador approached, followed by the magicians, who spread out in a wide arc behind him. The soldiers disembarked but stood at attention along the sides of the prisoner's barge.

Welryck drew a document from his sleeve with a slow flourish. It was clear that he was having trouble refraining from openly gloating.

"Talak dun Rashbon dun Brekst," he intoned, reading from the document. "You are hereby charged with the crime of high treason against her Sovereign Majesty Queen Rhianna, and by her order you are taken this day into custody for trial. You are hereby relieved of all offices, honors, protections, and authority previously vested in you by her majesty and her forbears, expressly dissolving the bond of extended life-service to her most serene throne, pending the verdict in these charges against you."

Talak stepped forward slowly, arms at his side. "I surrender peacefully, proudly declaring my innocence, but yielding to her majesty's will—as all good subjects must."

"Bind him!" Welryck commanded the magicians.

From one magician's hands, long silver lines no thicker than a thread floated forward. They stitched shut Talak's lips and eyelids. From the second magician emerged a heavier black cord that encircled his throat and wound down like a black vine about his shoulders, binding his arms to his body in coils down to his knees. From the remaining three magicians came a conjoined snake of light that struck the center of Talak's chest. Eva heard him grunt behind his sealed lips. He staggered and slowly sank to his knees.

Eva wanted to scream, to vomit, to kill. She stood motionless, letting each detail of this atrocity be seared onto her heart.

The soldiers stepped forward and in an obscene redundancy tied his hands and shackled his feet with rope. They jerked him to his feet and forced him in a grotesque shuffle to the black barge. They shoved him into the middle seat and then roped his helpless body to the bench.

One magician sat on either side of Talak in the middle seat, and they lifted into the air. The remaining magicians boarded their carriage and hovered, waiting.

But Welryck apparently wasn't finished. He stepped closer to Eva, so close she could smell his fetid breath as he spoke. "Let this be a lesson to you, my dear," he said, smug and venomous, all official solemnity discarded. "This could happen to anyone who throws their weight around just a little too much, or disrespects those who rightfully have authority over him. Or her."

It was all Eva could do to stop herself from spitting on him. "I will remember your lesson, Ambassador bron Ryckmet," she said in words of ice. "I will remember your lesson for the rest of my life."

He arched an eyebrow and sneered. "I'm sure that wasn't intended as the threat it sounded like, Lady Eva. For your sake." He turned on his heel and marched back to the official carriage without looking back. It, too, lifted. They turned in formation and sped away.

Eva stood rigid, forcing herself to remain standing until they were out of sight. Then she turned to go back inside, boiling with helpless rage.

Chapter
Thirty–Six

T he house seemed hollow now, gutted of something essential to its function, let alone its well-being. Eva wandered from room to room with no sense of belonging or purpose, as if maybe in some unexpected corner she'd find what was missing.

But everything about the house was in order, horrifyingly normal. Except that Talak was gone, leaving an unbearable void, and Eva was lost in the labyrinth of her own home. Housekeepers performed their tasks, the gardens were tended. Messages came and went via courier. Unbelievably, the aromas of cooking food still drifted out of the kitchen. Nothing had changed, except he was gone.

Finally Eva wandered into her study, where Rachel was organizing the day's messages, events and appointments. Rachel jumped up when she came in, her face drawn and eyes red. Eva sagged into a chair. "I don't suppose you can still contact him, can you?"

Rachel shook her head, eyes brimming. "No, milady. Since they took him. It's like he was never..." She sat heavily, and wiped her cheeks with her palms. "I am so sorry."

"I know, Rachel. Anyone who has a heart is devastated. But I need your help to keep going. I can't afford to be paralyzed by this horror."

She settled in her chair and took a deep breath. "I want to send a message to the queen, asking for an audience."

Chapter Thirty-Seven

I must be careful, Eva thought as she walked the corridor guided by the queen's page. She would have to act like a desperate subject begging for the release of her lover—completely unaware that the one to whom she made supplication was the heartless bitch that had thrown him to the wolves.

For Talak, she could carry this off.

The page opened the heavy door, revealing a spacious sitting room, dazzling in its white and gold brilliance. "Please wait here, milady," he said with a bob of his head, "for Her Majesty's arrival."

Eva settled carefully on a brocade and gilt-covered chair. Maybe by some change of heart—or opportunistic change of plan, more likely—the queen would intervene and liberate Talak, at least until the trial. That would give them more time to look for some way out, an escape that wouldn't bring a stream of bounty hunters after them.

The door opened and a bailiff carrying his staff of office stepped into the room. "Her most Serene and Glorious Majesty," he boomed in stentorian tones, "Queen Rhianna!" He stepped back with a polished bow and stood at attention. Eva jumped to her feet, then knelt and lowered her head as the queen entered.

Eva heard the door close behind the bailiff. She waited.

Finally the sound of the queen's slippered feet crossing the thick carpet whispered across the room. "Rise, child," the queen's cool, silvery voice commanded. "Come, sit here next to me."

"Thank you, Your Majesty," Eva said as she perched on the edge of the divan where the queen sat. "I am so grateful, Your Majesty, for this audience. I am desperate, and have no one else to turn to."

"I have taken a personal and active interest in your welfare from the start, my dear," the queen said with an angelic smile. "Your time in Riardan has not been a particularly peaceful one, and this last fortnight must have been deeply troubling for you."

"Majesty," sobbed Eva, not having to fake the tears, "I feel so lost. Talak has been so good to me, and he has protected me just as you ordered him to do. I can't understand why he would be arrested on the basis of a single comment made by an infatuated girl like me."

"Perhaps there is more evidence against him than you are aware of. Have you considered that?"

"No, Your Majesty, but I am absolutely certain he hasn't committed treason." Eva fell to her knees, her head nearly touching the floor. "I beg you to disband this very unfair tribunal and set him free."

"As powerful as I am, child, I could not do what you ask. Even I can't disregard the laws relating to this complaint. The balance between the clans and Our throne is delicate and must be respected." The queen touched Eva's arm, infinitely sympathetic.

"Come, come, now. Sit up here."

Eva shakily returned to her seat on the divan, wiping her eyes. The queen's beatific smile, at once distant and caring, was perfect. "But surely, Your Majesty," Eva sniffled. "After so many centuries of faithful service you could—"

"Do not presume to lecture me on my responsibilities, child!" she snapped. Her smile evaporated and danger blazed from her eyes. "I could have you thrown into prison for your affront to Our Sovereign Majesty."

The queen's smile blossomed again, seraphic but helpless. "You must trust me in this, my dear," she said. "You are not the only one who loves Talak so. We already miss his wise counsel and loyal service. If there is anything We can do to guide these events to his advantage and freedom, We shall do it."

Eva slowly dried her eyes with a handkerchief. "Thank you, Your Majesty. I know you will help him if you can."

"Go home, child, and concentrate on your suitors. The sooner you choose a husband, the better off Our realm will be. In fact," the queen added, "if you could arrive at your choice sooner than the formal date, it would be a great service to Us. We would be"—she paused for emphasis—"extremely grateful."

Eva nodded and knelt again. "I will do my best, Your Majesty. Thank you for your guidance."

The queen stood, and Eva dropped her head. She heard the door open and then click shut. When she looked up, she was alone.

After a moment a page appeared and guided her back to where Yurud was waiting by her carriage. Her stomach twisted when she saw him, not because she didn't like or trust him, but because it should have been Talak there, ready to take her home.

Before her carriage landed, she saw another one, shaped like a boat with a beautifully carved horse's head on the prow, resting on the grass and glowing in the midday sun. Tekko's. With Kernan relaxing beside it.

Yurud had to hurry to follow Eva up the steps. The door opened, and Rachel stood waiting for them. "Tekko is in the drawing room, Lady Eva," she said softly. "He says it's urgent but won't say more."

"Allow me to accompany you, milady," Yurud said. "Just to be—"

"Thank you, but that won't be necessary. Tekko and I will be in the water lily garden. Please make sure no one, not even staff, comes near while we are talking. And if you can shroud our conversation in privacy, please do that." She kept getting painful reminders of how much she had taken for granted Talak's meticulous skill and oversight.

"Of course, milady, consider it done."

It wasn't social polish that made Eva greet Tekko with a rush of warmth, but relief in seeing a friend. "It's awfully good to see a trustworthy face, Tekko," she said as she reached up to give him a warm hug.

"I realize this is outside of protocol, Lady Eva," he said, visibly flustered. "But I have something I must discuss with you in utmost privacy."

"Of course." She took his burly arm. "Let's walk in the garden. It's been sealed away from uninvited ears."

They strolled through large glass doors and across a broad stone patio to step down onto the path that led to the lily ponds. They stood on the arch of a small stone bridge for a while, watching the multicolored carp swim languidly toward them, expecting to be fed.

Tekko gently smothered Eva's hand with his. "This is delicate, per-haps dangerous, but honor requires," he began. "I'll speak plainly, as I do best with that. I hope you will believe that I'm telling the truth."

He looked Eva in the eye. "I want you to know I had nothing to do with this business concerning Talak. I want you to understand that I wasn't being possessive when I asked you about him in Pandrakis, when you told me in good faith he was your lover. It was clear that you care deeply for him, and I certainly would not conspire to have him arrested on these trumped-up charges to get rid of him." Tekko took a deep breath. "I believed you when you agreed that you would have my children." He blushed scarlet. "Assuming, of course, that you were to choose me for your husband." He looked away, still a bright red.

"It never occurred to me that you might be involved." Puzzled, Eva turned to gaze into Tekko's eyes in complete frankness. "Did I do something that made you believe it might have?"

"No. Not at all." He shook his head emphatically. "But a member of the Pandraki envoy to court had a nasty argument with Talak the morning you left for Riardan. I've just learned that he has put his name forward as a judge on the tribunal that will hear the case against Talak. He's also filed testimony in the case stating that Talak swore against the throne in their argument."

Tekko grimaced, baring his teeth with outrage. "But one of my people overheard the whole argument and reported it to me. I pres-sured him to make sure that he was telling the truth, and I'm satisfied he is." He glowered at the fish below them. "Talak said no such thing to Haran bron Sarkscun. The Pandraki man in question. Bron Sarkscun is lying."

Warmth flooded Eva's heart, and she squeezed his arm affectionately. "Thank you for your forthrightness, Tekko. I know that's one of your many strengths. For my part, I can tell you that the Athat Ambassador also will likely introduce false evidence against Talak. But I still don't understand. Why is this delicate?"

He jerked his head back toward her, looking shocked, but his face quickly softened. "The ways we protect our honor may still be strange to you, Lady Eva. Simply put, your relationship with Talak was part of my relationship with you. Anyone harming him in a way that harms you attacks my honor as your suitor and protector. Even if the harm comes from one of my own clan. Or yours."

He shrugged. "It probably seems silly to you, but it is of great consequence to me. Should Talak be convicted falsely, I would feel obliged to...acquit myself honorably." He patted her hand and beamed at her. "Best not to say more about that. Just wanted you to know I'm not involved in Talak's arrest, but am affected. In my own way."

He looked around, as if noticing where he was for the first time. "And now, milady, I would be honored if you would show me the rest of this lovely garden. A fine refuge from city life, I'm sure. Myself, I can't think clearly without being near something green and growing."

Chapter Thirty-Eight

Eva shifted restlessly in her seat, battling the nervous tension that jangled every nerve in her back, legs, and arms. The air in the courtroom already seemed stuffy to her, and they hadn't even begun the actual trial. The tribunal's whole morning session had been taken up with the naming of the officers, their swearing in, and tedious explanations of the process about to begin. She realized most people already knew to avoid the first session—this afternoon there were far fewer open seats than earlier in the day. Somehow the tension had only built as the dull introductory formalities dragged on. She itched to get this started.

She scanned the large square courtroom and its gallery, which ran several rows deep along three sides in a U, open to the end where the judges sat. She'd been surprised and relieved to see that both Salar and Tekko were in attendance, sitting on opposite galleries, perpendicular to the judges' bench. They were there again now. At least she wasn't completely alone.

Down on the main floor with Eva sat those with more direct connection to the case and who might be called to testify. She didn't recognize anyone around her.

On a high dais bordered by an ornate polished wood railing sat three imposing chairs behind a long enclosed table. There was no prisoner's dock. She'd asked someone about that, and they had told her the prisoner was unlikely to appear at any point during the trial. Talak would have no chance to face his accusers. That was no surprise, Eva thought. They wouldn't dare let him.

Finally, it seemed that everything was ready, and the queen's appointed judges filed in. Haran, the Pandraki official with whom Talak had argued, had been appointed, along with Welryck, Athat's Ambassador. It seemed inconceivable to Eva that men who had lodged the complaint against Talak should be allowed to sit in judgment, but no one else seemed to be surprised. The third judge was an official from Clan Occitanto, but even if he voted innocent, one vote against the other two hardly mattered. This was just a formality.

Eva fought down a wave of nausea, terrified for Talak and furious that these pet dogs of the queen would do for her what she had failed to accomplish herself. Her lip curled as she remembered the queen's angelic smile as she urged Eva to trust her.

She wanted to bolt. But she had to see this through, to an end which right now looked inevitable. She folded her summons to testify and tucked it back in her cloak.

First to testify was some minor official who swore under solemn oath—what a laugh that was—that the brief about to be entered as evidence was a true transcription of testimony given by Haran when he entered his complaint against Talak. The testimony was read by a clerk of the court in a bored voice. It described behavior and language that she knew Talak would never have used. It was a pack of lies, but all Eva could do was sit quietly, seething with frustration and outrage.

At one point she looked up into the gallery at Tekko. He sat with his arms folded across his chest, face impassive. When he caught her gaze, he lifted his eyebrows but gave nothing away except that he'd caught her glance.

Then came an assistant to Welryck bron Ryckmet, who read a long list of events and statements that Welryck had received from an unspecified informer. As soon as he began rattling through his list, it became clear that these could have come from none other than Efron. If this man's testimony was true—and there was certainly no guarantee that it was—it confirmed that Efron had been reporting to Welryck from the time Eva had arrived, long before he'd become ambassador.

The clammy sweat of fear tickled Eva's neck. There were two more days of testimony, but the trial was already over. Yet she would not give up hope. She would think of something that could shine some light on this smug deceit.

Then Eva was summoned to testify. She forced herself to stand and walk in firm steps to the witness stand. She nodded her head to the panel of judges and then looked out on the sea of faces, all staring at her. Their collective focused attention was like a body blow. She looked up into the gallery, seeking out Salar and Tekko. Who else was a friend in all this crowd? Anyone? Even if there were, she was certain that they were outnumbered by her enemies. And Talak's.

She was sworn in, promising on her loyalty to the throne and Queen Rihanna to tell the truth. It was all she could do to keep from laughing at how alien any real concept of the truth actually was to this kangaroo court, to say nothing of justice. They both had been banished when the judges had been appointed by the queen.

"Lady Eva," Haran began. "Are you a loyal subject of Queen Rhianna?"

"I am."

"Has the accused ever said or done anything in your presence that could be construed as treason?"

She could play this game as well as any of the other straight-faced liars in this crowd. She squared her shoulders and stared back at him. "Absolutely not. He has repeatedly risked his own life to carry out the mission he received from Her Majesty to protect me."

A few murmurs and whispers sounded behind her. She kept her gaze on Haran, who was clearly undeterred.

"Did you recently say, in front of witnesses, that you and the accused were totally devoted to each other?"

"In the context of my bedroom, which is where that comment was made, yes. But that has nothing to do with—"

"Just answer the question please, Lady Eva."

"I am answering the question, you bloated old toad! I am giving you the context of my remark, which shows the real meaning of what I said."

A rustle of amusement skittered through the room, and Haran's face turned purple. He signaled to the bailiff, who pounded his staff on the floor until order had returned.

Haran leaned forward. "You would do well to treat this tribunal with proper respect, young lady," he said with a menacing sneer. "It represents the full dignity of Her Sovereign Majesty Queen Rhianna. I am certain you would not enjoy feeling her punishment for your impudence."

"Your Honor," Eva said in a voice sharp with sarcasm, "if your interest is in the truth, then the factors surrounding my statement are of great significance. However, if you wish to banish the truth from these proceedings, then by all means stay fixed on the statement itself and avoid its actual meaning."

Again the courtroom broke into muted laughter, louder and more open than before. And again the bailiff's staff pounded the floor until silence returned.

"The witness is dismissed with a formal warning for contempt against the throne," Haran announced, his voice unsteady. It was clear he was both angry and embarrassed. "This tribunal is adjourned and will resume session tomorrow." The bailiff pounded his staff. People rose and began to file out of the room.

Eva couldn't wait to get home. She had a new task for Rachel, and she needed her to get on it right away.

Chapter
Thirty-Nine

E va settled in her courtroom chair. This was it. The third day of testimony, the day of the verdict. Her whole chest ached with the blatant and shabby injustice of the trial, knowing there was nothing she could do to change its course. Yesterday had been taken up with a long line of witnesses, each describing some minor interaction with Talak that contained laughably insubstantial nuances—which were then twisted or inflated into supposed evidence in support of a charge of treason.

As she had so often in the past two days, Eva scanned the gallery to find Salar and Tekko. Seeing them already seated in their places from yesterday, she felt a whisper of relief. They hadn't missed a single session.

Once more the bailiff marched in and announced the arrival of the judges. The three men filed in and took their seats amidst the hushed buzz of the crowd.

Haran bron Sarkscun had aggressively dominated the proceedings and had raised most of the questions from the bench. Bron Ryckmet had piped up only to support some misinterpretation of the evidence. But Lariel, the judge from Occitanto, had thoughtfully probed various pieces of testimony—enough to make it clear that he had serious doubts about Talak's guilt. More than once his line of questioning had been cut short by harsh whispers from the other two, serving only to emphasize the grim inevitability of Talak's conviction.

Eva took a deep breath, exhaling slowly. Everyone waited as the three judges conferred. When they were finished, Haran signaled to the bailiff, who pounded the floor for order in the court.

Haran cleared his throat. "We have heard all the scheduled evidence," he intoned. "If there is further testimony to be heard, please stand to be recognized by the court."

Eva jumped to her feet. No one else moved. Haran made an elaborate show of scanning the room. "There being no further offered testimony to be heard in this matter," he said, staring directly at Eva, "the hearing of this case is completed. The judges will now record their votes as to the verdict."

The bailiff marched to the center of the room and struck the floor with his staff. "Lariel bron Oste of Clan Occitanto," he declaimed, "how vote you, my lord?"

Lariel leaned forward slightly and addressed the assemblage in a clear voice. "Not guilty."

"Welryck bron Ryckmet of Clan Athat, how vote you, my lord?"

Welryck wore the satisfied look of a man who had just completed his favorite repast. Holding Eva's gaze, he announced in a voice full of gloating, "Guilty as charged."

A third time the bailiff called out in his orator's voice, "Haran bron Sarkscun of Clan Pandrakis, how vote you, my lord?"

Haran took a moment to adjust his robe of office before he looked up and declared, "Guilty as charged."

Whispered comments skittered about the room until the bailiff rapped the floor to restore quiet. "My lords, are you ready to pronounce sentence upon the guilt—"

"We are," announced Haran, so eager to speak that he cut off the last syllable of the bailiff's question. "The traitor is to be flogged and beaten for seven days. He will then be castrated, stripped of all magic, and imprisoned in a geas that will render his practice of any magical art impossible for the rest of his traitorous life."

Eva couldn't breathe. Like Efron. Torture and humiliation heaped upon this unspeakable travesty. She sat paralyzed, unable to cry, unable to rage, unable to move. Slowly the room emptied, but she sat inert, not caring that everyone else was gone. She couldn't think of anywhere she wanted to go.

Even in her darkest imaginings, she had never contemplated this kind of brutality. At the very least, Talak deserved a swift and honorable death. Instead, he would be beaten, stripped of his magic, and—oh, god. She couldn't even think about the rest.

She started when a hand touched her shoulder. She looked up to see Salar and Tekko standing next to her.

"I'm so sorry," Salar said. "This was a gross miscarriage of justice against a man who I'm convinced is innocent."

"I also am sorry," Tekko said. "In addition to the miscarriage of justice itself, a member of my clan was the lead dog in this shameful pack." He turned quickly to Salar. "And I exclude Lariel from these comments, Salar. It was clear from the first that he struggled for justice in a battle he couldn't win."

Salar nodded, not taking his eyes from Eva. "No offense taken."

"Thank you both. I don't know how—" Eva began to sob and tears stung her eyes. "How I would've managed so far without the two of you."

"If there is anything either of us can do, Lady Eva, please do not hesitate to ask," Salar murmured. "Anything."

"Exactly," Tekko said. "I'm ashamed to say that there is nothing I can do to help save Talak. He's beyond reach now." He paused, frowning. "However, there are other things. Things I can do. Must be done. There will be at least a trace of honor in this business, I promise you."

They helped her up, and the three of them walked slowly out of the courtroom. The yard around the courthouse was already empty. The sun shone brightly on the perfectly maintained gardens. Eva closed her eyes against the hideous contrast.

"Would you like us to accompany you home?" Salar asked. "Either, or both?"

"No. Thanks, though. I need a little time to myself, to sort things out a bit." She did have somewhere to go, after all.

She smiled grimly. "And do a little long-overdue housecleaning." She had a house manager to fire and wanted to check on Rachel's progress in the project she had given her. "Perhaps tomorrow, though?"

They both nodded their promise. She hugged each of them and then hurried to her carriage, where Yurud waited to take her home.

Chapter Forty

E va was out of the carriage and striding toward the front door before Yurud could even get out. One of the new guards opened the door as she stormed in. "Bring Efron here to me," she ordered. "And don't worry about being gentle."

She turned to Rachel. "Summon the staff. All of them. I want them to witness this."

All the servants had gathered by the time Efron, with a guard holding each arm, was marched into the front hall. "No, hold him fast," she instructed the guards as Efron tried to jerk free. "He is my prisoner."

She surveyed the group. "Today," she began, and her voice faltered. She swallowed, and cleared her throat. "Today, Talak was convicted of treason against Queen Rhianna." She stared hard at Efron before continuing. "The testimony against him was insubstantial, to say the least, but deliberately twisted to appear seditious. Some of that testimony came directly from within this household, through an unnamed informer."

Shocked murmurs spread through the group.

"The treacherous informer," Eva said, turning again to Efron, "reported to our ambassador a conversation which had occurred between

Celine and me, but was witnessed by someone who had entered my chambers unannounced and uninvited."

She fisted her hands against her hips to stop herself from crossing the short distance between them and striking him. "Efron, since you were that unannounced, uninvited intruder, and the only one who could have reported that conversation, perhaps you can tell us all how that information ended up in the ambassador's hands."

"Milady," Efron said in his usual oily voice, "in fact that report could have reached the ambassador through Celine and not me."

So startled by his bald-faced gall, Eva almost laughed. Then her fury took over. "How dare you insult my intelligence, as well as my faithful servant Celine?" she shouted. Her whole body shook with rage.

"That conversation wasn't the only one reported to the ambassador. There were others, and Celine wasn't present in some of them. The only common presence in all of them," she said, fighting the tightness in her throat, "was you. You slimy worm."

She covered her eyes with her hands for a moment, unable to look at him. Taking a deep breath, she pulled her hands away, forcing herself to face him again. "Talak never had the chance to face his accusers," she growled, "but I am giving you that chance. Efron, I accuse you of this treachery."

Eva shook her head vehemently. "I trusted you! Talak urged me to dismiss you long ago, and I refused, believing...believing I don't know what, but never believing that you were an informer worm in the heart of my own home!"

She stepped forward to stand directly in front of him. "What do you have to say for yourself?"

He spat in her face, and a collective gasp erupted. One of the guards kicked the back of Efron's knees, driving him to kneel. Shocked at being contaminated, Eva carefully wiped her cheek on her sleeve.

"You can't touch me," Efron gloated, pushing again to his feet. "I have the protection of Ambassador bron Ryckmet. Dismiss me if you wish, but you can't harm me."

"Ah," an old woman's voice, sharp and triumphant, came from the back. Everyone turned to see Ernesta hobble forward, leaning on her cane. "Lady Eva might not be able to give you what you deserve, but Talak arranged for me to be here to act on her behalf. His, too." She stared up at Efron, her frail body shaking. "Do you recognize me, Efron?"

Efron squirmed violently in the grip of the guards, trying to back away. "Keep this hag away from me!" he cried, his eyes bulging with terror. "Keep her away!"

The old woman stood in front of him, not moving. "She was only thirteen, you monster. My granddaughter Jara, only a child when you stole her innocence."

"She wanted me!" Efron gurgled.

"Liar! You ripped her innocence from her!" the woman screeched. "You took what you wanted. And then," she moaned, "to keep her from speaking out against you, you killed her." With surprising speed, she swiped at Efron's face, slicing open one puffy cheek with the small knife that glittered in her hand. Then she spat at him.

"I spit in your face, you pig—just as you did on the Lady Eva." She closed her eyes and tilted her head skyward, as if in prayer, dropping the knife on the floor in a clatter. "Justice! You poisoned my

Jara—with the very same poison that now spreads through your veins."

His eyes bright with panic, Efron shrieked, twisting to escape the grip of the guards. Ernesta pointed a gnarled finger at him and cackled. "Justice! Finally! I have lived for this moment for over thirty years." She looked around, as if just noticing she wasn't alone. "My poor, lovely Jara is finally avenged, and I am finished." She turned and hobbled slowly toward the door.

"Someone go take care of her," Eva commanded, hearing her own voice through a fog of shock. "She remains a protected part of this household as long as she wishes."

Efron whimpered. He began to wheeze and groan, sagging against the guards.

The room began to turn slowly around Eva. "Someone, please," she said, and immediately Yurud was at her side. She leaned on him gratefully and took deep breaths to steady herself.

Efron's body spasmed, and his eyes rolled backward. A thin gray line of spittle trickled from the corner of his mouth. He convulsed, face ghastly dark, mouth contorted and gaping, wild and barely conscious. The guards let him drop to the floor and stepped back. The only sound in the room was his inarticulate gagging.

Eva couldn't look away, at once horrified and fascinated, holding on to Yurud's arm as she watched Efron die.

Some time after the body stopped twitching—Eva had no idea how long it had been—she looked at one of the guards. "Is he dead?"

The guard knelt and pressed his fingers against Efron's neck. "There is no pulse, milady."

She watched the corpse a moment longer, half afraid it might start moving again. No, it was over. She sagged against Yurud, who squeezed her arm gently in reassurance. She took a deep breath and let it out heavily.

"Then draw up a report of his death—have it witnessed. Rachel, you oversee the details. Send the document and the body to Ambassador bron Ryckmet. They belong to him, and he can do what he likes with them."

She turned to Yurud. "Thank you for keeping me upright. I assume you can ship the body back to the ambassador?"

"Certainly. I'll use a small kitchen barge, and send notice of its approach."

"Good." She raised her voice to address the group. "Well, I hadn't intended this to be Efron's execution, but I can't say I regret it. He deserved worse, as far as I'm concerned. If anyone wishes to voice an objection concerning Efron's treatment, please say so now. I promise there will be no retribution."

No one made the slightest gesture or sound.

"Please also know that I will not tolerate an informer in my house. If you are supplying others with news of what occurs here in my home, this is your only chance to leave without punishment. If you wish to be released from my service now, for whatever reason, no questions asked, you must leave now. And I mean right now. I'll be taking steps to assure that this,"—she gestured at Efron's body—"this kind of violation of my home never happens again."

She scanned the group. "Those of you who choose to stay, please return to your duties, with my sincere thanks."

Chapter
Forty-One

O ver breakfast, Eva pondered her situation. Efron's violent demise was certain to increase the tension—perhaps even outright animosity—between the ambassador and herself. He would come after her, she had no doubt. A husband would protect her from her own clan. Salar and Tekko would be here this afternoon, and she'd talk to them about bron Ryckmet.

The queen wanted her to choose a husband ahead of schedule, but right now it seemed that she needed both of them just to stay alive.

Whether it was because they didn't want to be associated with Talak, or whether they just didn't care, neither Graf nor Kevs had attended the trial at all, so she had no qualms about eliminating them as candidates. She was being backed into a corner, and it made her angry.

Part of her didn't want to deal with this mess any further. Talak had already set up her escape. Before anyone could figure out what had happened, she could be through the portal to Italy to live out the rest of her life there in comfort. No, not just comfort. Spectacular wealth. A villa, which, knowing Talak, had to be furnished with impeccable taste. Two apartments, and twenty-five million euros in tax-free cash.

But she couldn't do that. Not yet, anyway. Not while Talak was alive. Not while there was the slightest chance that she could save him. She knew him well enough to know that if the queen's sentence was carried out, he would kill himself at the first opportunity, making his own exit with honor. So no, no exit for her until Talak was gone. Not until the last candle of hope had been snuffed.

She rose from the table and stared down at the gardens below. So long as she was here, she would fight for Talak. And while she didn't understand yet how it could be used effectively, the evidence that he had given her had to be her primary focus. They were dangerously powerful documents, and she would figure out how to use them, even if it meant being charged with treason herself. She owed this queen no loyalty at all.

Eva entered her study to find Rachel already at her desk with piles of documents arranged around her. "Are you making progress?" she asked.

"Yes," Rachel said looking up, "it's intricate work, but a pattern is emerging. Her majesty makes Lady Macbeth look like a saint."

"You know Shakespeare?" Eva asked. "I'm surprised. I thought the Lower World was considered inferior in every respect except as a convenient kind of gene pool."

Rachel grinned. "To hear some people talk, like our treacherous ambassador, one would think that to be true. But many royals brought books, paintings, and musical instruments, even repertoire with them when they arrived. There's even a central library in the palace, although most of it was kept by the newcomers in their own homes."

"I had no idea."

"The fact is, our culture treats artists as trades-people, except in the rarest circumstances. Yet many of us find inspiration in what has made its way here from the Lower World."

"Interesting." Eva pulled up a chair next to Rachel. "So tell me what we have here."

"First off, we're lucky that Talak was so meticulous—and explic-it—in keeping these records." Rachel gestured to the arc of piled documents around her. "Without his level of detail we'd never be able to make sense of this."

She rubbed her eyes. "I catalogued all the documents to begin with and made a note of the date and victim, along with the queen's given reasoning for having him or her removed." She scrunched up her face in disgust. "Her majesty does not require a very significant reason to have someone eliminated."

Eva wasn't surprised. "So the stacks are by date?"

"No. Actually, the stacks are by clan of the victim. It seems to me that if we organize the documents that way, we can create a body of information specific to each clan, with cross-reference to any clan that might have been framed for the murder."

"Perfect!" Eva exclaimed. "Once we know what we've got, I bet we'll also see how to use the information."

"I'm afraid, Lady Eva," Rachel said, staring at the stacks, "we have only a few days before Talak's...sentence is carried out. I don't know if we have time."

Eva put a hand on Rachel's shoulder, trying to reassure them both. "We have to have time," she said, feeling a new and terrible urgency. "How can I help?"

275

Tekko reached across the table and helped himself to a mound of thirds. "This is delicious, Lady Eva," he said happily. "Your chef is excellent." With a good-natured wink at Salar, he added, "Perhaps you can convince her to come with you to Pandrakis as part of your trousseau."

"The last thing you need, Tekko, is another cook preparing food for you," Salar said drily. "By the time you are fifty your staff will have to roll you down the hall to the dinner table."

Salar stretched contentedly and clasped his hands behind his head. They sat at a table on Eva's terrace, basking in the early afternoon sun and surrounded by the remains of an unhurried meal enjoyed in each other's company.

"That is, of course, another reason why the Lady Eva will ultimately choose me. We stay lean in Occitanto." He winked back at Tekko, just as broadly. "For the very best of reasons."

"Perhaps," Tekko mumbled around a mouthful of food, apparently completely unconcerned. "By the way, if you haven't received the news already, Lady Eva, you will hear it soon."

He swallowed and scrubbed his mouth with his napkin. "Haran bron Sarkscun and Welryck bron Ryckmet were found dead this morning. In a forested park near Castle Riardan. Nasty business. Hung by their heels from a tree branch, with their throats cut. Just like butchered pigs. Can't imagine how that happened. They were supposed to be so well guarded."

Stunned, Eva slowly put down her wine glass. She knew she should feel horrified, but she didn't. She wasn't thrilled at the news, but did she object? Was she angry? Absolutely not. She looked first at Salar, who simply shrugged, and then fixed Tekko with a stare.

"I hope," she said carefully, "that the queen does not decide to hunt down and punish their killer. Or killers. Perhaps she will treat this sad event as one of the many run-of-the-mill political murders that characterize our tranquil life in Riardan."

"Doubt they can find the slightest clue, milady," Tekko said. "This villain was crafty, and apparently left no trace of his identity at all."

"Even if they knew for certain who had done this terrible thing," Salar added, "I doubt the queen can afford to mount a formal prosecution. Her very public position on the tribunal those two headed up is deep disappointment at the verdict against her loyal subject Talak."

He lifted his glass to Tekko and Eva in a playful salute. "In fact, I'll wager that most people assume that it was the queen's own assassins getting even with them for that verdict."

"Indeed." Tekko sighed heavily, as if burdened with a great sadness. "I can't imagine why they would both be wandering around in the public woods in the middle of the night. Dangerous things, forests, if you don't know what you're doing in them."

"But let's talk of happier things," Salar exclaimed, shaking his head. "This is too beautiful a day to dwell on the death of two villains at the hand of a third."

Salar's remark caught Tekko in mid-swallow. Wineglass still at his lips, Tekko gagged as he struggled not to laugh, and wiped his mouth with the back of his hand. "Indeed. Much too fine a day. On to happier things, then."

Eva stared at them both. She had real allies, and right now that was a huge relief. Overnight, one or both of them had probably exacted a hefty measure of Riardan-style justice on Talak's behalf. And she realized she didn't want to know more. "Agreed," she said, lifting her glass. "Happier things."

The double doors to the patio swung open, and Rachel hurried toward the threesome, looking agitated. She curtsied and handed Eva a letter. "Pardon the intrusion, milady," she said, her face flushed. "But it's from the queen, just arrived. A summons."

Chapter
Forty-Two

"I need something from you," the queen began without preamble. Eva had just sat on the bench of the grotto in the queen's walled garden. "This unfortunate incident with two of the tribunal judges has put me in a very awkward position."

Eva watched her fidget with the cuff of her gown and realized that the queen was nervous. Her whole demeanor was anxious, perhaps even afraid. Yes, she would have to be frightened if here in her private sanctuary she kept casting glances over her shoulder or scanning the garden, as if expecting to see some approaching threat.

"Of course, Your Majesty," Eva replied. "Whatever I can do—"

She didn't wait for Eva to finish. "I want you to announce your choice of husband soon. The day after tomorrow would be ideal." She smiled. Eva was sure it was an attempt to look friendly, but it came across painfully hollow.

"It sounds cynical of me, perhaps," she continued, "but I need an important and especially festive event to distract the court's attention from the deaths of those two awful men."

Eva nodded. The woman had brass, that's for sure.

"Rumors are flying that it was I who ordered their death." She sighed like a martyr waiting for her own execution. "I am, of course, terribly disappointed—no, shocked—at the tribunal's verdict, but I must yield to the law set in place to govern such things, even if I don't approve of the outcome."

Perhaps this was her best opportunity to see if the queen would change her mind, given these new developments. "Can't you just pardon Talak?" Eva begged. "You would get your faithful magician back and a horrible miscarriage of justice would be righted, all in a single act."

"No, child, that is the very last thing I can do." She sighed again as if on the verge of tears. "My pardon would simply give more credence to the rumor that I had ordered the killing of your ambassador and Haran bron Sarkscun in the first place."

She leaned forward and grasped Eva's forearm. Eva hadn't noticed before how long the queen's nails were. And sharp.

"There are so many plots against me already, and if people believe that I had anything to do with these deaths, I would become terribly vulnerable."

"Your Majesty," Eva said, smiling inwardly at the harsh honesty of her reply, "it will be my honor to make sure that you are not wrongly accused."

The queen's face brightened, but without warmth—it glittered with a reptilian satisfaction. "Thank you my child," she said. "I will make sure you receive ample reward for your loyal service."

"Majesty, the best reward I could hope for is Talak's pardon. Are you certain there is nothing you can do to save him?"

The queen's face hardened instantly, and her voice became sharpened steel. "I have explained myself to you more than is my habit, and certainly more than is my obligation. You must take my word for it that if I could save Talak I would. After all, I have far more to lose with his demise than you do. Unfortunately, saving him is beyond even my power to do." She shook her head slowly, and her voice softened into resignation. "No, I'm afraid there is nothing anyone can do to save him now."

She patted Eva's hand. "Besides, he's just a magician. He was a valiant servant, to be sure, but there are always more."

The queen stood, straightening her robes, and Eva jumped to her feet to kneel. Rhianna hurriedly scanned her garden again before stepping out of the grotto. "You must excuse me now, child, for I have a great many things to attend to. I will publish the date for your Ceremony of Choosing as we have agreed." She smiled, satisfied and cold. "I'm sure you have many things to take care of before then yourself."

"Indeed I have, Your Majesty," Eva said as she lowered her head. "I—" Eva began, but stopped as she looked up. As she had before, the queen had already turned away, headed for the garden gate. Eva stood and watched her go.

Only a magician. That's all she thought of him. She shook her head, incredulous. Talak was just a servant—disposable, easily replaced by another. If Talak had only known how cheaply the queen valued his loyalty and devotion to her throne.

But the queen was right. Eva had plenty of things to take care of—finding a way to save Talak was at the top of the list. She strode toward the guarded exit.

Chapter
Forty-Three

On the trip home, Eva became steadily angrier at the queen's disregard for Talak's life. She'd never imagined that Rihanna had thought of him as just a chattel, easily replaced, and the more Eva thought of how meticulously and passionately Talak had served, the more furious she became. He had served with honor, and the queen had thrown him away without hesitation.

"Call ahead to Rachel, please," she said to Yurud. "I want her to help me right away." He nodded. If he had to do anything external to make the connection, she couldn't see what it was. Eva had been relieved when he'd been able to form a telepathic link with Rachel as Talak had. It made everything so much easier.

When they landed, Rachel was waiting for them and approached, beaming. "I've finished our project, milady," she said with obvious satisfaction. "I look forward to briefing you at your convenience."

Eva nodded her thanks to Yurud and headed for the house with Rachel by her side. "Let's do that right now," she said. "I'm definitely in the mood to hear of success."

Once they were settled in Eva's study, Rachel outlined succinctly how the queen had used Talak as her assassin to keep four powerful clans at each other's throats. The essence of it lay in two pages of summary that Rachel had drawn up. As Eva read, an idea began to formulate. If each of these clans knew what the queen had been doing...

"Thank you so much, Rachel," Eva said. "This is more compelling a picture than I had hoped for. How difficult would it be to make more copies of your summary and whatever other documents might be necessary to support it?" A grim satisfaction spread through Eva's heart. "I'm thinking that each of these clans might be very interested to learn about these events."

"A day at most, Lady Eva," Rachel replied. "It's all organized already, so it would be easy to copy." Eva could tell that she wanted to say more, so she looked up and raised her eyebrows.

"It's such volatile information, milady. It would be almost as dangerous for the one disseminating it as for...the one whose actions these documents reveal."

"I know, and thank you for your concern." She wanted to add that she didn't yet know exactly how to orchestrate what she had in mind. But she could feel in her bones that something—some way—was possible. She just had to figure it out.

"Is there anyone you would trust enough to let them help you in making the copies?"

"Absolutely not, milady. I'll be glad to do it all."

Eva placed a hand on Rachel's shoulder in genuine affection. "Thank you so much." She paced to the window. "Before you begin, though, I need you to send messages to Salar and to Tekko, letting them know that the queen has moved up my Ceremony of Choosing to the day after tomorrow, and that I would like to meet with them together late tomorrow morning."

283

Rachel nodded and reached for Eva's stationery. Eva left quietly and went to find Yurud. "How quickly can you get me to Albessind?"

"If milady does not mind a little discomfort," he replied, "I can have you there in under two hours."

"Good. Notify them that we're coming, and arrange for whatever we'll need for an overnight there. Plan for our return early in the morning."

While Yurud hurried off, Eva went to the kitchen to arrange for some packed food. She suddenly felt very hungry, but she couldn't delay. She could eat en route, unless the discomfort Yurud had warned against was so severe that it banished her appetite.

Eva strolled through the terraced gardens high above the river Achthon, breathing in the evening air and the rich fragrance of the night-blooming flowers. Every now and then she heard a cow bell from the farm on the far side of the water. She'd been right to come here to think. She gathered her shawl more closely around her and sat on a wooden bench, staring out across the landscape until the stars and a half moon were the only illumination. The river was black and silver, the trees on its banks merely black shapes against the slightly less dark fields. The windows of the farmhouse on the other side glowed a warm, cheerful yellow.

A flash of envy took Eva's heart. The people inside that cozy house were more fortunate than she was. They weren't torn apart by court intrigue, they didn't risk betrayal every time they relied on someone. Their lives... She shook her head, embarrassed at her self-pity. She knew very well that those farmhouse lights looked perfect only from a distance, and inside they shone on at least as much bitter hardship as happiness.

In the meantime, she had work to do. She needed to come up with a plan, and quickly. Only a day remained before she had to choose a husband, and then she'd no longer be free to act unilaterally. Whatever she did after that would be officially tied to another clan's will and reputation. Much more cumbersome. And dangerous.

She was sure that somewhere in the tangle of her knowledge was a way to force the queen to release Talak, and maybe even... No, she was getting ahead of herself. She couldn't keep focusing on the goal. She needed to concentrate on how to get there. She had to think outside the box. Eva regretted not having asked Hulvis about some possible appeal of Talak's horrible sentence, even if the verdict couldn't be overturned and the queen wasn't willing to pardon him.

Then Eva stopped breathing. Outside the box—of course! The answer had been staring her in the face all along. Hulvis had already given her the strategy! Adrenaline fired her blood. So dangerous. But it might work. Now all she needed to do was to figure out how to implement it without getting herself killed.

Then again, Talak had saved her life several times at the risk of his own. Did she love him enough to give up her life trying to save him? Yes. She did. The answer came simply, without fanfare, like a dragonfly landing on reeds by the river. And now that she knew that, the plan was obvious.

Elated and terrified, Eva strode back to the house and marched straight into the library. She lit a lamp and sat in front of her mother's portrait until she was perfectly calm. "Madris," she whispered,

"Mother. Share your wisdom with me, your knowledge of this world. Help me find a way through this. For love. For justice, and for Albessind."

The silence of the library folded back in upon her, and she extinguished the lamp. In the moonlight the portrait seemed to take depth as Madris leaned out to her, smiling. Eva sat basking in her mother's presence until some trick of light made the painting look flat again.

Satisfied, she rose and climbed the stairs to her apartment. There, she paced quietly as she pondered how the pieces of her plan might fit together. As the moon arced from one window to the next and finally set in the gray light before dawn, she mapped out her strategy.

Finally Eva sank into an overstuffed chair and dozed for a little while, content with her plan, fragile and dangerous as it was.

They'd left Albessind just after sunrise. As they sped back toward Riardan, Eva stepped carefully through each phase of her plan. It was far from foolproof. In fact, she gave it about a forty percent chance of success, and that was being optimistic. Still, there was really nothing else she could do except disappear through Talak's escape route and leave him to his fate, and that was no option at all.

"Please let Rachel know we're coming," she said to Yurud. "Have Celine ready a bath and some fresh clothes. And maybe a little food. Are you hungry? I am."

Yurud nodded, and after a moment's silence he answered, "Rachel says that both Salar and Tekko have confirmed their meeting with you, and everything else will be waiting for your arrival."

Eva relaxed back in her seat, feeling surprisingly calm. She'd done everything she could at this point. "Thank you," she said, watching the countryside scroll past below her.

She felt a little giddy. What was life worth if she didn't do what she knew had to be done? The rest was just existence. As beautiful as the world might be, abandoning love to stay alive in it would turn paradise into a wasteland.

She turned to Yurud. "Can we go any faster?"

He grinned like a teenager behind the wheel of his dad's muscle car and hunched forward. "As milady wishes."

The burst of acceleration pushed Eva back into the seat and Yurud howled like a wolf into the rushing air.

Once she had bathed, changed, and eaten, Eva met with Rachel and Yurud. She felt obliged to warn them without giving away her plan, give them a chance to distance themselves from her before she went into action. They deserved to know that if this plan failed, her head would not be the only one that rolled.

"Absolutely not, milady," Yurud swore emphatically. "Talak is both my mentor and my friend, and I welcome this opportunity, no matter how dangerous it is."

Rachel shook her head. "I passed that point of choice some time ago, milady. And I don't regret leaving it behind."

"Very well," Eva said, "and thank you. I'm really touched that you would cast your lot with me in this gamble. Now if I can get Salar and Tekko on board, we'll have a fighting chance, even if the odds are lousy."

When they arrived, Eva led the two men up to her study and seated them away from her desk, which was covered in the stacked copies Rachel had completed.

"I'm going to ask you both for more than I have any right to ask," she began. "And it's dangerous. Deadly dangerous."

Tekko and Salar glanced at each other and then back at her, their faces guarded.

"I'm about to do something terribly foolhardy tomorrow," she continued, watching them carefully. Nothing too negative so far. "Something I'm quite sure that neither of you will like, particularly. My problem is I can't pull it off without your help."

"Difficult position to be in, Lady Eva," Tekko said thoughtfully. At least he was smiling.

Salar seemed more cautious. "Of course, I'll be glad to help any way I can. But as disposed as I am to help, Lady Eva," Salar said carefully, "I must be clear there are limits to what I will do—nothing that would hurt my family, for example, or expose them to danger."

Tekko nodded gravely. "Same here."

"I understand," Eva said, with her heart in her throat, "and I can't pretend that this isn't dangerous. I won't lie to you. It could well be beyond what you can commit to. And I don't object to those very honorable limits, no matter what happens."

She took a deep breath. "If my plan works—and there's no guarantee that it will—I believe I can unmask the one or ones behind the murder of your relatives, Salar, and behind the attack on us in Pandrakis."

"That dispels some of my caution, then," Salar said. "But what do you want?"

She knelt in front of them. "I'm begging you—for your joint protection tomorrow and probably for the day after." She smiled gently. "After that, it probably won't matter one way or the other."

Tekko stood and drew Eva to stand. "No need to beg, Lady Eva," he said gruffly. "You aren't the only one who's been thinking about how to deal with this mess."

"You think the same man is behind both attacks?" Salar sounded dubious.

She sat and in turn looked each of them in the eye. "Yes, the same man—or woman," Eva said, emphasizing the last word. She watched it register in both men.

"But the risk is high," she continued. "Even with what protection you can give me, I might not live to see next week. And if I'm taken out, then any number of people associated with me could also have been put in great jeopardy."

Salar frowned and looked around. "I think it's best for all of us if you don't say any more, milady, even here in the safety of your own home," he said. "As Tekko already mentioned, we've been thinking about this too. I have an idea of what you intend to do tomorrow, and if I'm right, then yes, it's incredibly risky. But let's not speak of details. I'd rather not know more, at this point."

He glanced at Tekko, who nodded. "Still, we'll support you as best we can."

"Even if I need armed protection at the Ceremony of Choosing tomorrow?" she asked. She had to know.

"Even then," Salar said calmly. "We'll be ready, if it means getting to the ones who have been using our courtship as a stage for murder.

I'm ready to take my hair down from its warrior knot. Even if I can't support you fully, I will protect you as much as I possibly can."

"I can't ask for more than that, and I thank you from the bottom of my heart," Eva's voice broke with gratitude. "You two must be as crazy as I am."

"Well, not quite that crazy, Lady Eva," Tekko rumbled. "But close enough. Crazy enough to hope you can do what you must tomorrow."

Chapter Forty-Four

Since it was forbidden for her to bring an armed escort into court, Eva left her guards at the carriage and led her small entourage—consisting of Yurud, Hulvis, and Rachel—across the entry hall of Castle Riardan on a carpet of silver and midnight blue.

"Her majesty has laid out the royal carpet of welcome, milady," Hulvis gurgled under his breath. "Reserved for the most important delegations to court." He was obviously impressed.

Eva acknowledged his observation with a curt nod. That would certainly be in keeping with the queen's plan to use this event as a distraction from her political troubles. And how like the her to roll out a carpet of official welcome and honor for the arrival of a person she had only recently attempted to kill.

Well, this is it, Eva told herself as she approached the oak doors, which slowly began to swing open. She squared her shoulders and banished her butterflies.

All or nothing at all.

They stepped into the intense color and energy of the court. As it had every time before, the charged atmosphere struck Eva as if it were physical. The throne was empty, as she knew it would be. Immediately in front of the empty throne and one step down on the wide dais sat three officials in royal robes. Magistrates, Hulvis had called them, representing the queen.

At floor level and at right angles to the magistrates sat an ornate chair which Eva knew was for her. Opposite her chair, also at right angles to the magistrates and no more than twenty feet distant, were four others. In each of them sat one of her suitors, dressed in the traditional groom's white trousers and belted tunic. In wide arcs facing the throne sat the crowd of spectators.

The suitors stood—as did everyone else—when Eva entered. Polite applause broke out, which continued until she had knelt before the empty throne, curtsied to the queen's magistrates, and seated herself in her chair.

She tugged lightly at Hulvis's sleeve. "Is this customary?"

"Not at all, milady," he gushed in a whisper. "Usually there is only one. The queen has afforded you the greatest honor possible, short of those she bestows upon the ambassadors themselves. By seating three magistrates, she indicates to all that she has taken personal concern and pleasure in your ceremony. It is a profound honor!"

Eva scanned the crowd. Fanning out behind the four suitors' chairs sat rows of representatives from each of their clans. Easily half of the entire court was here. Eva had hoped for fewer, thinking that a larger audience increased the risk to her plan, but there was nothing she could do about that now.

She nodded her head and smiled in greeting to each of the suitors. Tekko winked, Salar nodded gravely, but Kevs and Graf both looked resigned and bored. With good reason, Eva thought. According to all reported rumors, everyone was already convinced that her choice would be between Tekko and Salar.

A herald stepped forward, announcing the beginning of the ceremony. He saluted the clan ambassadors present, then everyone else, and delivered the queen's greetings. He then introduced the magistrates and described the protocols that Eva's period of courtship should have followed, but which were shortened at the request of her majesty. People began to get restless halfway through his opening remarks, and Eva couldn't blame them. She knew, however, that very soon they'd get more excitement than they expected.

When finally the herald had finished, he turned to Eva and bowed his head. "Lady Eva bryl Madris, this ceremony has been convened to witness your choice of husband. Whom, now, do you choose?"

The room buzzed briefly and then fell silent.

"Before I begin," Eva said, clearing her throat, "I require the presence of the magician Talak dun Rashbon dun Brekst."

Shocked, even angry chatter rippled across the room, and for a moment Eva's courage faltered. The obvious disapproval of clan officials and courtiers alike was more intimidating than she had imagined it would be. It was too late, though, she knew. She'd already crossed the threshold of no return.

She stood, steeling herself, and addressed the magistrates on the dais. "I was told that I am empowered to have any person present at this ceremony that I choose. Is that not true?"

While the crowd buzzed with speculation and objections, the magistrates bent their heads together and conferred. In a moment they straightened, and the middle one nodded. "It is true." He turned to the herald. "Summon the prisoner Talak dun Rashbon."

"This is an outrage!" exploded one of the men in the Morindiere contingent, standing up behind Graf. "Unacceptable!"

Eva stared him down. "It is not meant as an outrage, sir." Surely it is a small thing that I wish him to be present and witness my choice of husband. It was he who kept me alive to see this ceremony. Surely you can't object to that."

The man sat, looking angry and embarrassed.

In a surprisingly few moments, two guards and a magician frog-marched Talak into the room. He was clad only in a ragged cloth that someone had tied around his waist. His arms, chest, and back—his whole body—was covered with bloody welts.

Eva's heart lurched in her chest.

"Yurud, is he...all right?" she whispered.

"Yes, milady," Yurud whispered in her ear. "He has been beaten as prescribed in his sentence, but his captors have added their own range of punishments. I am amazed he is alive."

She addressed the magistrates again. "I ask that the spells that prevent the prisoner from moving or speaking be suspended for the duration of this ceremony. I have no objection if the spells preventing his use of magic remain in place."

Again the courtroom exploded into speculation, dismay, and mounting outrage. Above the din, Eva declared, "My lord magistrates, it is fully within my right to ask him a question, and if I do I will require an answer."

Again the magistrates conferred, and again they signaled to Talak's captors to unbind him as requested. The guards stood back, and the magician began to speak and gesture. As soon as the spell-restraints were lifted, Talak collapsed on the floor. The buzz in the room swelled to an uproar.

"Bring a chair so he can sit!" Eva shouted. "And for mercy's sake, give him water!" Someone brought a chair and placed it next to Talak. He groaned as he rolled onto his stomach, then struggled to his hands and knees. He clawed at the seat of the chair, then its back, as he slowly dragged himself to his feet. He paused, leaning over the chair, coughing and gasping at the effort, his face twisted in pain.

"Please sit, Talak," Eva said. It took all her self-control not to run to him.

"I will stand, milady," he croaked. With excruciating care, he steadied himself against the chair, then let it go with a trembling hand—proud, defiant.

"Can you communicate with him, Yurud?" she whispered.

"A little. He is very weak, and it is hard to hear beyond his pain... He says...to save yourself. Don't use the box. Whatever that means."

Chapter Forty-Five

Eva gazed at Talak, then smiled and shook her head. She stood and bowed to the magistrates. "I thank you for honoring my request, my lords. I am ready to proceed. If the herald could call for quiet..."

One of the magistrates signaled, and the herald's voice thundered out. "Quiet, please! The ceremony shall proceed, ladies and gentlemen! Quiet please!"

When the tumult subsided, Eva turned to the four suitors in their chairs. "I thank you each for your attention, your hospitality, and your generosity. I am honored by your offers of marriage. You are all fine men, and I wish each of you a long and happy life, filled with many healthy children. I also wish you love."

Unexpected tears welled in her eyes, and she let them fall without any attempt to wipe them away. "Although I understand that love is not a priority for you in marriage, it remains paramount for me."

She took a deep breath. "Therefore, I choose Talak dun Rashbon dun Brekst as my husband." She heard a gasp behind her. Out of the corner of her eye she saw Hulvis crumple in a dead faint, heard him hit the floor. The room exploded in a clamor of shocked voices. She looked at Talak and smiled through her tears. He grabbed the back of the chair, shaking his head no—slowly, as if giving up. He fell to his knees, clutching the chair.

"You mock our clan, choosing a convicted traitor over our suitor!" A man behind Kevs bellowed. "This is an unbearable insult!"

Without a word, Tekko and Salar strode to Eva's side, flanking her, arms folded across their chests. A hush of amazement fell over the assemblage.

"I mock no one, my lord." Eva felt a ferocity rise in her that she had never felt before. "I mean your clan no disrespect. I mean no one disrespect, but I will marry the man I love."

"But he's a convicted traitor!" the man exclaimed.

"His trial was a filthy joke and you know it," Eva snapped, "an embarrassment to honest men and women everywhere." She put her hands on her hips and widened her stance, ready for a fight. "You know he was wrongly convicted by two men with their own villainous agendas."

Over the rising hubbub of the crowd she declared, "You already know there was more justice in their punishment than there was in their behavior at the trial."

The head magistrate stood, looking aghast. "Lady Eva, do you understand that your choice disqualifies you from royal succession, strips you of your inherited authority, and banishes you from the realm?"

"Yes, milord, I do. Again, I mean no disrespect, but all I've wanted since I arrived was to return home."

Another magistrate spoke, as if he couldn't believe her first answer. "Is that really what you wish, to throw away your unquestioned power and privilege here?"

She squared her shoulders, feeling a new kind of power flowing through her. "Yes. I want Talak to be set free and allowed to live in the Lower World without threat or interference from this realm."

The magistrate bent to confer with the other two. "Such a decision must be brought before the queen for her permission."

Eva knew Rhianna would never agree. It was time to risk everything. "My lord magistrates," she declared firmly, "with all due respect, the queen no longer has a say in this."

The stunned silence in the room was sudden and absolute. Nothing moved, as if everyone were holding their breath. Eva signaled to Rachel, who approached with the bundle and the box. Eva took the box and raised it above her head, ignoring Talak's look of horror.

"From the moment I was brought here, I have wanted to return to my home. Queen Rhianna forbade that. She had her reasons, and I have since learned what they are. She wanted me as bait in a scheme to stir enmity among your clans—to keep you weak through feuds that she herself conceived and fostered."

A voice from somewhere in the crowd shouted, "You speak treason!"

A volcano of rage and defiance boiled up from Eva's core, the sum of all her frustration and anger. "The truth is never treason!" she shouted. "I am no traitor. I have been a loyal subject. I have no interest in upsetting or usurping Rhianna's throne. All I want is to be allowed to leave with the man I've chosen as my husband."

She wheeled to address the wide sea of faces. "You are all welcome to this kingdom exactly as it is, if that's what you want!"

She lowered the box and cracked it open. She saw Talak's head drop. "But I give you proof that the queen conspired to have me killed in

Pandrakis and make it look like Morindiere was behind my death." She reached in and grasped the severed hand. It felt unpleasantly like plastic—cold, not completely firm, and lighter than she expected.

Eva held it up for all to see. The crowd gasped. "This is the hand of the man who died trying to kill me. He was standing beside the body of an archer from Morindiere, readying it to be planted nearby in Pandraki forest." She paused to draw another deep breath. "You may recognize the ring."

A flash of scarlet light arced across the room, igniting the dead man's hand. The fire enveloped Eva's hand, burning her, but she couldn't seem to let go.

When she could finally move her hand again, she let the blackened hand, still wearing the queen's ring, fall to the floor. Tekko lunged from his seat to snatch it up as Eva cried out in pain.

"What magician attacks Lady Eva, and on whose authority?" Salar shouted. He motioned to Yurud. "Can you tell?"

Yurud pointed out the magician, and Salar shouted again, "Seize that man! He's violated our highest law by attacking one of royal blood and by doing it in this place of guaranteed safety." Men from both Pandrakis and Occitanto rushed to obey.

Eva's burned hand was throbbing so much she couldn't manage the knot tying the bundle of documents. "Rachel, open the package and distribute the copies to the ambassadors. Hurry."

She turned to the crowd again, clutching her hand to her chest, and spoke through the pain. "I'm distributing accounts of murders ordered by the queen for the explicit purpose of keeping your clans fighting each other. You will see that for decades, feuds among you have been falsely initiated and fueled. What you decide to do about that is up to you, but if the queen treats the lives of your clansmen as disposable commodities to preserve her own security, what might she do to your people next? Look what she did to Talak! She abandoned him to villains, in spite of hundreds of years of his loyal service. Who might be next?"

She doubled over in a wave of pain, groaning. Clenching her jaw, she forced herself to stand upright, lifting her burned hand above her head. "So no, I'm not being disloyal. It is her majesty who has shown utter contempt for loyalty."

She beckoned to Yurud. When he leaned close, she grabbed him with her good hand and whispered, "Let me lean on you. Are the clans sending messages back to their homelands? Do you think they are mobilizing their forces?"

"There is a surge of telepathic communication, milady. However, there is no way for me to know what is being said."

Salar and Tekko returned to their contingents to examine the evidence with the others. The silence was terrible, disturbed only by the rustle of papers as clan officers shuffled through her documents.

She turned to the magistrates. "Restore and release Talak. Please. Let us go, before this gets further out of hand."

But before the magistrates could move, four ambassadors stepped forward. "My lord magistrates," the ambassador from Occitanto said, "we hereby suspend this ceremony. We will take the Lady Eva and her chosen husband into protective custody while we examine this evidence further. In the meantime, we have placed our standing armies on full alert as a precaution against...precipitous action by her majesty."

At this, two more ambassadors joined the group. "If it proves true that her majesty has acted as described, it is in direct contravention of the Pact of the Clans that governs us all. Please notify the queen that she will receive our delegation soon."

Tekko strode to Talak and signaled to his comrades to join him. They grabbed the magician who had accompanied Talak from the dungeon. Salar stepped forward to Eva, and several of Occitanto's men followed him. "We will escort you both to safety, milady," he said. "We are all safer if we keep you separate for the time being."

"Please, Salar, let me at least touch him before—"

"No! It's not possible, Eva. Trust me," he said, his voice decisive and harsh. "You gambled your life—and the lives of several others, including Tekko's and mine—and won, at least for the moment. But don't push right now. This is far from over."

He laughed, softening, shaking his head in disbelief. "You're astonishingly brave—or mad, probably both—but if the Clans reject your evidence, we all could still end up in prison very shortly."

He took a firm grip of her elbow and nodded to his men, who formed a circle around them. "Right now we've got to get you both out of the city if we're to have any chance at all."

Chapter Forty-Six

"How is your hand feeling?" Salar joined Eva, who stood gazing out the high-vaulted windows of her apartment overlooking the gracious streets of Occitanto. "Our healer says there should be no permanent damage."

"It still hurts, but not all the time. Kind of like a regular burn—sometimes quiet, and sometimes on fire going all the way up my arm." She looked up at Salar. He'd taken his hair out of the warrior's knot he'd worn since her deadly first visit weeks ago.

"You look good with your hair loose again. I'm glad you're satisfied your search is over. How is Talak?"

"It took the combined work of several magicians to remove the imprisoning spells, but they've been lifted. Yurud and Talak now work together on his healing." Salar paused. "He was beaten brutally. Broken bones. Serious internal damage."

Eva remembered his groan as he pulled himself upright, refusing to sit, and shuddered, imagining the kind of pain he must have fought through just to stand.

She looked out the window again. "Occitanto really is a beautiful city."

"And to think it could have been yours," Salar said with a melodramatic sigh.

Eva turned to him, ashamed at his reminder. "I'm really sorry."

His voice became serious again. "I am not a frivolous man, and I do understand about love, regardless of our culture. I have to tell you..." He put a hand on her shoulder. "I admire your courage more than I can say. I hope I find a wife with a fraction of yours."

Eva laughed, close to tears. She had disrupted so many lives. "I hope you don't bear me any ill will for the way I...I can't begin to thank you and Tekko for the risks you took." A heavy wave of fatigue broke over her. She sank into a chair and massaged her eyes, ignoring the rising pain in her arm. She forced her eyes open. "I'll always be grateful. Thank you."

"Eva," he said, kneeling. "I...care for you deeply. Far more than formal interest. Knowing what I do now, I can't honestly say I'd do it all over again, but I certainly have no regrets."

She tried to lighten the serious moment. "Just Eva?" she feigned insult. "No 'Lady Eva' anymore?"

But Salar's face grew more serious still. "No, I'm afraid it's just Eva, now. You've been stripped of clan standing." His smile was wistful. "One of the many things you've given up with your choice of husband."

She was surprised that the demotion stung a little. Privileged status had been easy to get used to. "Do I need to call you Lord Salar?"

"Technically. But,"—he shook his head, grinning,—"I think we can overlook that requirement." He stood and went again to the window.

"When do you think I'll be allowed to return to my house?"

"In Riardan? You can never go back—you are banished forever from the city. Your house has been repossessed by Clan Athat."

He stared out the window a while before continuing. "I checked. The place is already empty, and your belongings have been shipped to Albessind under Yurud's and Rachel's supervision." He turned to her with an encouraging smile, leaning against the casement. "Albessind is still yours, as it belonged to your mother. Athat officials can't do anything about that, although some have called for its seizure."

The jolt of surprise was worse than the actual loss. Of course. The house in Riardan had never been hers, it was only afforded her by the clan.

"What about my staff?"

"They've been disbanded."

That hurt more than losing the house. Rachel and Celine, Yurud, others. "I want to pay them all a year's salary. Some I want to take care of longer. Can they go to Albessind if they want to?"

"Yes, if they want."

"Will you let them all know that?"

Salar nodded, crisp and businesslike. "Certainly."

"Thank you so much." More lives she'd disrupted. She wanted to change the subject. "What about the larger turmoil—the clans and the queen?"

"The queen is restricted to the castle. All kinds of evidence has come up that corroborates yours. Frankly, I do not expect her to live out the week. Every clan has now endorsed the Provisional Council and no one dares speak out on her behalf."

Eva imagined Rhianna—her mother's murderer—prisoner in her own castle, waiting for news of her fate, and shivered, chilled. Just like Talak and herself.

"What about Talak and me?"

"That's still being debated, although I expect you'll get what you asked for—exile, rather than execution."

Salar sat in a chair next to hers and took her good hand in his. "I don't know if you were fully aware, but you had serious enemies within Athat. Some of them really do not want to see you live. I suspect they were your mother's enemies before they became yours, especially the bron Ryckmet faction. I think you are actually better off returning to the Lower World than trying to live among those vipers."

Eva shivered. "Oh." That made perfect sense. Someone had tried to kill her in Virginia, before she even knew what was going on. Talak had always said the attempt came from relatives. And then the next attempt on her first official event months ago—the welcome dinner scandal that had opened the door to bron Ryckmet's ascent to the ambassadorship. Lifetimes ago, now.

"I'm not surprised. I never really felt much connection with anyone in my own clan."

"The good news is that most other clan representatives have no problem with letting you go, as you've asked. Athat can't afford to press too hard, or they will risk isolation in the new Coalition." Salar's lip curled. "That would be a serious tactical error on their part."

"Coalition? What's that?"

"There will be a new Council of the Clans, and some new governing charter, yet to be defined. Probably still with some kind of monarchy, but not one occupied by lineage. More democratic, probably elected. Hopefully with less room for betrayal and murder."

"Can I send a message to Talak?"

Salar shook his head and got up to pace. "No. You're officially under house arrest and can't communicate with anyone." He turned, caught her eye and winked. "Although, if I were to find a scrap of paper on the floor, I'm sure no one could object if I put it in my pocket."

"So we can't see each other until this is all decided?" Eva ached at the prospect. "What if these deliberations stretch out into weeks?"

"I don't think the Provisional Council will take much longer before passing resolution on your situation. Personally, I think the house arrest is unnecessary, but for me to violate it would jeopardize Occitanto's role in the new clan agreement we are trying to forge." He shook his head. "I can't risk that."

He strolled to the window and his voice dropped, as if he were talking to himself. "That said, you might leave the windows of your apartment ajar one warm night. The ones that open to the balcony. Let me see when it might be good weather for you to do that."

Eva jumped up from the chair and embraced Salar, ignoring the pain in her hand as she hugged him tight. "Thank you so much, Salar! I already owe you so much more than I can repay."

Salar peeled Eva away gently, firmly. "Please, I—I suffer when we embrace." He touched her cheek. "I can make no promises, but let me see what I can do."

Chapter Forty–Seven

E va surveyed her room and shivered with anticipation. Although she'd checked it all at least a dozen times, it had to be perfect. Besides, fussing made waiting easier—a little.

The soft lights were right, the silver platter of fresh fruit waited for him, as did the bed, turned down and littered with petals of fragrant flowers. She'd set the doors to her balcony ajar, and the warm evening breeze flowed in, rich with the scent of night-blooming jasmine. She laughed at herself for being so nervous, but she couldn't help it. And she didn't care if she was being silly.

It had been less than two weeks since she and Talak were together, but it seemed like years. She pulled the soft shawl tighter around her shoulders, not for warmth but for comfort, and looked around the room yet again.

There was a soft noise, no more than a whisper, at the balcony door. She spun around, and there he was. She couldn't find her voice, couldn't even say his name, but instead burst into tears and ran to him, burying her face against his chest, clinging to him as if he might suddenly be snatched away again.

Eventually some words came. "Oh," she sobbed. "Oh..."

Talak buried his lips in her hair and made a soft, sweet hushing sound, wrapping his arms around her, pulling her to him, filling her hair with kisses. For a long time they stood unmoving, just being together again, letting the reality sink in without help of words, without motion, with nothing but the feel of their bodies pressed together again.

Eva drew her head back a little and gazed into Talak's eyes, parting her lips, tears streaming down her cheeks. With infinite tenderness, he lowered his mouth to meet hers. She sobbed again as their tongues met. The electrifying wonder of his kiss filled her, took her soaring.

Reluctantly she drew away to see him better. She ran her hands in caresses over his face, his arms, his chest. "Your injuries...are you healing? Are you okay?"

"More than okay, my love," he murmured as he scooped her off her feet and carried her to the bed. "Your touch cures my deepest ache, but your kiss creates it all over again."

Eva trailed another strawberry along Talak's lips. He growled softly and took it in along with her fingers. "I have to go," he mumbled before pulling away from her touch. "We mustn't trade carelessly on our hosts' generosity and goodwill."

"I know." Eva sighed. "Salar says it shouldn't be much longer."

"That's Tekko's impression, too. Their decision on what to do about us has been sidelined by the queen's suicide."

The relaxed glow in Eva's body vanished, replaced by the old tension of intrigue. "Oh," was all she could say. Deep down she felt no anger. There was justice in it. Her mother's killer dead by her own hand. How appropriate. "When?"

"Yesterday." Talak rolled out of bed and bent to pick his clothes off the floor. "Salar will probably fill you in tomorrow when he comes back to Occitanto. They've had constant sessions since, even called a late-night session tonight."

She watched him dress, missing him already, hating that he couldn't stay. "How did you find out?"

He crawled back onto the bed half-dressed and kissed her playfully. "I still have a few contacts on the outside, as they say in Lower World crime movies," he said, grinning. "Yurud is very well connected."

"Good." She pulled him down for a long kiss. "As long as I'm very well connected with you. I like it way too much to let that connection go."

"Stop doing that." Talak laughed. "You're making it hard for me to leave." He grimaced as he stood and fastened his trousers awkwardly. "In fact, you're just plain making it hard."

He shrugged on his shirt, blew her a kiss, and then he was gone.

Eva fell back against the cushions and closed her eyes, refocusing on the wild and sinuous fire of their loving.

After a while, she got up and put the platter of fruit on a table, closed the balcony doors, and put out the lights, then crawled back into bed. She brushed a crushed flower petal across her lips. Sleep, whenever it might come, would be very good.

Chapter
Forty-Eight

"Rise, Eva bryl Madris, and hear the decision of the Council of Clans."

Eva stood. The last time she'd stood in this courtroom was at Talak's trial. This time there were half a dozen chairs in the judges' box, all occupied. Below them stood the man who was speaking. She had no idea who he was. He lifted a piece of paper and began to read.

"Article One. You are convicted of high treason against the throne, and sentenced to death," he began. Eva's heart clenched in shock. What had happened? She looked at Salar, but he just shook his head slightly.

The spokesman continued reading. "By order of the Provisional Council, your sentence of death is hereby suspended, to be carried out only upon your entrance into Riardan City. This sentence is permanent and irrevocable.

"Article Two. Your choice of husband is confirmed, and you are hereby relieved of your standing as a member of Clan Athat's royal lineage, with all its privileges and responsibilities.

"Article Three. You shall retain possession of your personal estate of Albessind. You and your husband will be allowed to visit said estate four times a year for purposes of supervision of the property's operation, each visit to last no longer than one month."

He looked up from the paper and fixed Eva with a stern eye. "Any overt attempt by you or your husband to influence the governance of this realm will be cause to lift the suspension of your sentence contained in Article One.

"Article Four. It is hereby declared that Talak dun Rashbon dun Brekst is no longer eligible to hold title to property in this realm. Your deed to property previously held by him is ruled to be invalid. You will convey said title to a citizen eligible to own property within seven days, or said property will be seized and disposed of by this Council.

"Article Five. You are hereby granted a period of two weeks to dispose of property, satisfy debts, hire staff, and prepare for your exile. Any matters pertaining to your presence in this realm still outstanding at that time will be resolved by this council, and all decisions shall be final, without further recourse."

The spokesman looked up again. "Do you accept the dictates of these articles without reservation and willingly swear to such acceptance?"

Eva knew there was no alternative, so she simply said, "I accept."

"Then sign this document, which shall be witnessed and duly executed, according to the authority of the council."

Eva signed, others witnessed, and she was brusquely escorted from the courthouse by armed guards.

Yurud was waiting by her carriage.

She looked around, knowing this was the last time she would see this city, dominated by Castle Riardan. She felt nothing but contentment at the thought.

They had won. This was the beginning of her new life with Talak. She could see her family again. "Take me to Albessind, please," she instructed Yurud, tears of joy welling in her eyes.

Chapter
Forty-Nine

Tekko reverently caressed a graceful silver hunting horn—Talak's gratitude gift—then lifted it in salute as Talak climbed onto the barge readied for San Vito. He turned to Eva with a boyish, almost bashful smile.

"Lady Eva," Tekko said clearing his throat, "and I deliberately use the title you will always have in my heart. I have a small gift for you as you head into your new life." He gazed at her earnestly. "I hope you will remember me as a loving brother rather than an unsuccessful suitor. And I look forward to when our paths might cross again."

He drew a marvelously wrought brooch from his cloak and cradled it in his big hand. "I would be honored if you wore it from time to time."

"It's beautiful, Tekko!" Eva exclaimed. She took it, but held onto his hand, matching his sincerity. "I look forward to a lifetime of friendship between us. You stood by me and took risks beyond any obligation, and I will always be grateful. Always."

She let go of his hand with a squeeze. "And I look forward to becoming friends with your wife and children as well."

He bent down to give her a peck on the cheek. "Soon enough, milady. Soon enough. I look forward to that too." He cradled the hunting horn in the crook of his elbow and jumped aboard his long boat-shaped carriage with the horse's head prow. His magician gestured, and they rose into the air. He gave a blast of the horn as they sped away.

Eva held the brooch in both hands until Tekko was no more than a black speck in the sky. Then, sighing tenderly, she tucked it into a pocket.

A breeze came up from the river, sweet and cool. She looked across the river to the farms below. The line of dots in the hay field told her they had already started harvesting the first cut. It promised to be a good year.

"I'll be back by supper," Talak called out from the barge. Eva waved and watched as the last load of the belongings they wanted to take with them lifted and headed out over the river, gaining speed as it went.

To Italy and back before sundown. It still felt unreal to her. She was going home. Well, to a new home, to be sure, but at least it was the world she was familiar with. She knew she'd come back to Albessind often, but now she was going home. Finally.

She looked down at her hand, at the square-cut emerald and diamond ring Salar had given her earlier that morning. Their farewell had been more poignant. She knew he felt strongly for her, perhaps even loved her, and she admired him deeply.

Eva had tried to apologize for asking so much of him and giving so little back, but he had stopped her with a gentle finger placed over her lips. "No regrets, Lady Eva," he'd said in a voice no more than a whisper. "None. And you will always be Lady Eva to me. I hope we will have many opportunities to look back on these days and lift a glass of wine, laughing and shaking our heads at how we leaped so madly into the jaws of danger—and survived."

She hugged herself as she turned and walked back to the manor. Rachel and Page had already gone on to Italy, and Eva was thrilled that they had wanted to come. She'd invited Celine, too, but she'd declined, saying this was the world she knew, and she was content in it. Still, she had happily relocated to Albessind with her entire family. "We'll all be waiting to take care of you when we can, milady," she'd said, brushing tears from her eyes. "You and your little ones, too, when they come."

Yurud had already moved his parents into Talak's former home, as well as new staff. Without even having to discuss it, both she and Talak knew he was the right one to have title to the place. He'd been agog when Talak had shown him its most important magical features, including the secret portal that led directly to San Vito.

Talak had selected two particularly appropriate objets d'art as gifts for Salar, but had left almost everything else in the house as it was for Yurud. Eva's paintings and a few other things were already at the villa.

She closed her eyes, lifting her face to the sun, happy and at peace. Talak would be home by supper. They would spend one more night in Albessind, and leave for Italy in the morning.

Talak had suggested engaging Yurud as manager of Albessind and its holdings, and Eva had agreed with relief. He was the obvious choice. She looked across the river to the village and the surrounding farms, knowing Albessind would be in good hands in their months-long absences. When they'd offered him the position, Yurud had laughed and accepted gratefully, saying they'd most certainly rescued him from having to work for some clan lord whose ethics he might not share.

Eva turned slowly toward the house, utterly content.

Before she could reach the door, Yurud came around the corner, a scowl on his face as he rolled his sleeves down over muddy forearms.

"Anything wrong?" she asked.

"I'm afraid we've let the food gardens run a bit wild in all the political excitement, milady. Nothing we can't repair, but it will take time and work."

"What about hiring... what did Talak call them... a nature witch? Tekko told me they do that often in Pandrakis."

Yurud looked thoughtful. "Yes, I suppose we could. I hadn't thought of that. They're a strange lot. Keep to themselves most of the time." He brightened, nodding vigorously. "Yes, I think a garden witch is a very good idea. I'll find one, although I have no idea how to contact them, exactly."

"Do you want Talak to do that? He seems familiar with them."

Yurud wiped beads of sweat from his forehead with a grimy sleeve. "That would be ideal, thank you." He laughed, cheerful again. "He can surprise me with his choice."

Curious about what happens next?

Here are the opening pages of
The Garden Witch

The Garden Witch
Prologue

Lira refused to be bitter as she prepared for death. Ashamed, of course, and achingly sad. So, so tired. The bare stone walls of her dungeon cell were as gray and hopeless as she felt. She was grateful there was no mirror to confirm it. She already knew what she looked like, though — what she was — a husk. A nearly empty vessel, no longer fit for its real purpose. Just as it should be. This was the inevitable culmination of her choices, made nearly a year ago.

Her connection to the flow of the great balance was dying, and when it did, so would she. Over and over, she had violated her bond to the balance of nature, and with each violation, her connection waned. That was the price she paid to save her daughter.

He'd offered her a deal: for her daughter's life, she would steal dragon-line fire from the flow of nature to power an artificial gate between the worlds. Her lips twisted in disdain. It was obscene. It would never work like the natural ones that held Riardan and the Lower World together, two halves of one living whole.

His gate might work for a while, but the great balance would never allow the relationship between the worlds to be so disrupted for long. Knowing that brought her comfort, knowing the aberration she had forfeited her life for would eventually fail.

From the moment he had offered his poisoned contract, she knew she'd agree without hesitation. Did she love her daughter more than her oath to serve the great balance? Yes, she had. Did. That was the true root of her crime. She'd sacrificed a life of integrity for her daughter's safety. Perhaps a stronger nature witch would have refused. Far too late to fix that. Those choices had been made, and there was no way to undo them now.

Lira stood and placed her hands flat on her belly, lifting her face toward the sky far above the stones of her cell, reaching through her feet to the fires far below.

"Come, river of nature—" her voice broke. "Fill me one last time, I beg you. Take me, reclaim me, let me be compost for the sacred wheel of the seasons."

She opened her arms, feeling the remaining slender threads of the glory, the belonging, the *meaning* of all she had betrayed. And still it came to her, diminished, poignant, a glimpse of what she once knew, touching and filling her with its magic, its beauty. She thought she felt her Book spark in acknowledgment of what she was doing, and she smiled at the dungeon walls.

"Take me," she whispered. "End my selfishness. Take what little of me is left, and let me melt into your wise flow, become all I am once again."

The magic of all nature answered, winding around and through her, comforting her, lifting her up tenderly. Like a wounded animal

319

rescued, she thought. She sighed contentedly. That's exactly what she was. She gasped with gratitude as the flow of nature reclaimed her and flowed on.

The Garden Witch

Chapter One

All around her the life of the garden sang. Delen lay flat on her stomach between the vegetable rows, eyes closed, letting the heavy afternoon sun press her body down against the warm dark loam. This was perfect. Right where she belonged, she was doing the work she was meant to do. She rested her cheek on the dirt, cherishing the moist grit against her skin and the soil's ripe fragrance. Even if she didn't have a Book of Seasons, she'd do everything she could to see Albessind's gardens thrive under her care.

She opened one eye. In her line of sight, the generations-old espaliers of mulberry bushes spread high against the stone wall dividing garden from forest. Their thick, gnarled limbs spread in a living fan against the weathered yellow blocks, open as a lover to the sunlight.

Their leaves no longer curled inward, sick and dusty white, hiding from the life around them. Her remedy for blight had finally worked, once she began painting the trunk and branches with it as well as the leaves.

Yes, Albessind was a great improvement over her last position. The rocky, wounded soil of the Durn estate up in Kotor-Brod had been so polluted with the noise of greed and generations of family strife it had been difficult to hear the earth's voices at all.

She hadn't even had a decent chance to make friends with the orchard trees before she'd been dismissed from service and sent away. Men were so arrogant sometimes, presuming to take a woman as if it was their right. People must have thought she'd spat in old Lord Durn's face, he was so angry—just because she wouldn't let his whiny teenage son under her skirts. All she'd done was say no. She'd even been polite about it.

Still, it proved Auntie Bran was right. Delen held no status, and had none of the magical power that came with having a Book. Too many times to count, even on Delen's last visit, Auntie had warned her that men would think her unusually beautiful, that her beauty would be a burden she'd have to carry with great caution until merciful age lifted it from her. That men wanted power, either over a woman's body, or over her magic, and that the only path for someone of her calling was solitude.

Delen didn't mind solitude at all. She'd had lovers here and there, but in all her twenty-three winters she'd never met a man she desired enough to give up much of anything in order to keep him as a permanent partner. Even if she didn't have a Book of Seasons she treasured what magic she had, and she would hang on to it. Her magic would always be her real lover, the only one she'd ever need.

She curled her fingers around the base of her spinach plants in a caress and closed her eyes, sending her inner sight down, down into the lightless earth. Below the soil's surface the roots branched and re-branched, reaching out in living threads until they were delicate as a spider's web, more beautiful than the finest lace.

The root maggots were back again, chewing away. The charm she'd set had seemed to work for a while. Why hadn't it held? What was she missing? The answer to that was painfully easy—almost everything. She knew too little to do this garden job well. Auntie, even with her limited magic, could probably do better. At least she had long years of experience to draw on. Auntie. She choked back a sob.

Auntie was dying, and Delen was helpless to prevent it. Fear so familiar it almost had a name slithered into her, cold and slimy around her stomach. She couldn't bear to lose Auntie, but didn't know how to save her.

The warm soil beneath her called to her. *Remember.* She sent her listening down into the earth, to hear the slow music pulsing below her, deeper down than the river bed at the bottom of the hill a quarter mile away, a comforting, fecund mother's song—unhurried, content, unimaginably powerful. With a ragged sigh she let it flow up into every part of her until her bones vibrated to it, and sang its ageless song. She would find a better cure for the maggots soon. She wished she had someone to teach her. Then she wouldn't have to guess.

"Hoyoo! Delen!"

She lifted her head, twisting around enough to see Cook standing at the garden gate, hands fisted on her hips. Delen pushed herself up, peeved at being yanked from her solace. Some indoor people seemed to always carry a cloud of ragged urgency that made it hard even to think around them. Cook was like that.

"Get in here right now, young lady. Master Yurud has arrived and staff are already gathered in the great hall to greet him."

Oh. She was in trouble now. She'd forgotten that Mistress Eva's personal representative, Albessind's manager, was coming today, first time since her arrival. "I was encouraging the spinach, ma'am, and lost track of time." Delen hoisted her skirts and hurried down the long rows of vegetables.

"I don't know what I'm going to do with you," Cook said, wiping her glistening brow with her apron. "This is no way to make a proper first impression. And look at you, dirt all over you and no time to wash! Well, you'll just have to present yourself as you are, as poorly as that reflects on the rest of us." Cook turned and lumbered back toward the house as fast as her ample body could move. Delen followed, whispering a quick *back soon* to the cherry tree and flowering vines near the garden gate as she passed.

Delen took her place at the very end of the greeting line as befit her rank, acknowledging Cook's scolding eye with a bob of her head, straightening her apron as best she could. Light filtered through the high arched windows, casting soft shadows behind the line of servants onto the marble floor. Dull indoor light, stripped of time, motion and weather.

Mirren, the house manager, dressed as always in her severe gray dress and starched white apron, stood next to Master Yurud, making the introductions. Still ten staff away from Delen, they currently spoke with Celine, Mistress Eva's personal maid—a warm, round, generous-hearted woman whose cheeks always glowed as if she had just taken pies out of a hot oven.

Neither Mirren nor Master Yurud gave any sign they were in a hurry or even that they had noticed her late arrival. Delen pursed her lips. She would have had plenty of time to make herself more presentable. Maybe she could cast a harmless glamour on herself to make her appear properly tidy. No, it wasn't worth the effort. She'd done nothing wrong. She'd been doing her job. Surely they would understand that.

Celine let out a whoop of laughter at something Master Yurud said, putting her hand to her mouth too late to stifle the sound. As he stepped away from Celine he bent close to her ear and she laughed again.

Delen nearly laughed aloud with her, but remembered not to just in time. She liked Celine. She'd been Mistress Eva's personal maid in Riardan the capital, and had moved here after Eva's exile. In fact, Delen had come to Albessind only a short time after Celine and her family. More than anyone else, she had welcomed Delen with open arms, with such comforting warmth it had made her ache for her own mother, so many years gone. She smoothed the collar of her smock and pushed her hair back over her shoulders. And waited.

As Mirren and Master Yurud came closer, she could feel his energy—lively, kind, intelligent. And charged with magic. So he was a magician. No doubt a rote magician who relied on spells, what Auntie Bran scornfully called a will magician.

They outnumbered nature witches like herself by far, and Auntie said they always seemed to end up in the important positions, too. Like manager of the rich estate of Albessind.

Delen glanced furtively at the man, and a shiver of curiosity skittered between her shoulder blades. She'd never met a rote magician before. Auntie always said they were worse than clan aristocrats in their arrogance. It would be interesting to see what he was like.

Master Yurud made his way slowly down the line. He took his time conversing with Cook, and out of the corner of her eye Delen watched the interchange carefully. Why had such a young man been given this powerful position? He was tall and alarmingly good looking, with an angular, expressive face. He was probably quite used to getting his way all the time.

For a moment she resented his effortless, affable charm. In addition to his choice of magic, his youth and looks were two more reasons to be wary of him. But at least he'd tied his hair, the color of dark honey, at the nape of his neck instead of winding it into something more formal. At least he wasn't pretentious. Her resentment melted away.

"And this, Master Yurud," Cook said in a voice laced with apology, "is Delen, the new garden witch. I apologize for her unkempt condition, I do."

"I suppose our garden witch was busy in the garden," Master Yurud said with warm humor in his voice. "I'm glad to see you enjoy your work so." He gently brushed some dirt from her cheek.

"Don't touch me!" Delen recoiled, defending herself against the casual, uninvited familiarity. How dare he? She backed away, breaking the greeting line. The words were out before she could think. She shouldn't have said that so loud, though—it had sounded like a challenge. Too late. His green eyes widened, and gasps rippled all the way up the line. Mirren's mouth fell open.

"You impudent girl—" Mirren began, but Yurud raised his hand to stop her.

"Don't, Mirren, please. She's completely right. I was in the wrong."

It was Delen's turn to be shocked. She'd never have expected him to admit his trespass openly, let alone come to her defense. Maybe he wasn't as predatory as the brat who had got her sent away from her last position. That would be a relief.

"I apologize for taking such liberty, Delen," he said, his eyes gazing earnestly into hers. "Touching you like that—I wasn't thinking, and I admire you for speaking up. I should have shown you more respect."

Respect for a mere garden witch from the rote magician with charge over the great house of Albessind, its village and all the tenant farms? Delen studied Yurud's open face, looking for sarcasm, unable to find even a trace. She couldn't help but smile, feeling more timid than she wanted to. "Thank you for understanding. I shouldn't have said it so harshly, though. That was wrong, too, and I apologize for it."

For a suspended moment nothing moved. Master Yurud stared at her, his lips parted as if he were going to say something, and she stared back, held by a pleasant agitation, awkward and warm, rising in her body as she did. She shouldn't feel like this. He had nice eyes. So green, and deep. It seemed no one even breathed.

Finally Mirren cleared her throat and broke the spell. "Master Yurud, that constitutes our entire household staff." She scowled at Delen. "At present."

She turned, leading him across the hall. "If you'll come with me to the library, I'll show you the house books of account." As soon as the heavy library doors had swung shut the greeting line broke, melting away as servants headed in different directions, back to regular duties.

Only Cook remained, standing next to Delen, frowning, fists again on her hips. "I wouldn't be surprised if Mistress Mirren doesn't send you packing by sundown. I hope she doesn't, but if you want to keep your position here you're going to have to learn to treat your betters with more respect than you did just now."

Delen gazed at Cook, feeling sorry for her. Cook didn't even use her real name, only her title. If she had ever held any power of her own, she had given it up, probably long ago. It seemed she didn't mind the loss, though. She seemed content to think of herself only as a function of the house.

"Better is as better does, Cook," she replied quietly, hoping she sounded strong. "That's what my Auntie Bran always taught me." She curtseyed again and turned away, eager for the tranquil refuge of her garden.

A sharp worry gnawed at her as she gazed down the long rows. What if Mirren did decide to send her away because of what she'd done? Without a Book the work she could get was scarce.

But if she had one! Then...what would it be like to be a full nature witch with a Book of her own? She'd be free. Powerful as the earth's slow music beneath her. She'd heal Auntie, and many others. She'd be free to help where she chose, full of the wisdom of plants and animals, of the weather, and the pure elements themselves.

Delen set to work on the beans with a sigh, chilled at the possibility of being dismissed again. Rote magicians ran everything for the clans royal. He could have fired her on the spot and no one would have thought twice about it. What had she been thinking, to be so rude—and in front of the whole staff, too? These gardens were a pleasure to care for. Who would make the right poultice for the mulberries if the blight returned next spring?

No. She'd been right to stand up for herself. But she also needed to keep this position. Why couldn't she have been more polite to him?

Auntie relied on her completely now, weak as she was, even for the food Delen sometimes could bring from the kitchen. She needed to stay here, for Auntie's sake as well as her own.

The Garden Witch
Chapter Two

The cherry tree outside the garden gate whispered along its roots, running its message through the soil into Delen's feet. A man approached, with friendly intent. It was probably Master Yurud—no one else but Cook would have reason to come here. But why would he? To dismiss her? Surely he would have Mirren do that. Besides, the cherry tree had felt his intention as friendly. Even so, her heart began to race. He could easily send her away without being hostile.

She glanced at the sky. The afternoon had slipped away while she worked, and now the sun hung only a little above the forest to the west. She continued tying bean vines to the new stakes. Even if he was Mistress Eva's personal representative, she was still in charge here. At least for the moment.

The sound of his footsteps stopped a polite distance behind her. "Let me hold the plant while you tie it up."

Yes, Master Yurud. Again, a stir quickened her body. He had a voice like warm summer wind.

He cleared his throat. "After you've finished here, perhaps you could give me a tour of the gardens. I know a little about nature magic, but I've never met anyone working as a garden witch before. I'd like to understand more of what you do."

Delen turned to greet him with a diffident curtsey. His hair had much more chestnut in it than had shown indoors. "My work is pretty simple. Mostly, I listen. To the plants, the weather, the forest, the river, the earth. I ask for help when it feels like something is out of balance, and try to understand the answers. I talk to the plants a lot. They like that."

He laughed. He seemed far too relaxed to be here to dismiss her. That was a hopeful sign. "I'm certain there's more to your work than that."

"Yes, but that's what it boils down to, though. Mostly." Oh. She needed to acknowledge his offer. She couldn't afford to insult him again. "I'd welcome your help, and will be glad to show you my gardens afterward." She saw her claim register in a twitch of his eyebrows, and it seemed he wrestled down a smile. She pretended she hadn't noticed. She pushed a loose strand of hair behind her ear and pointed to the other side of the row.

"If you get on that side and hold, I can tie from over here." She watched him lift the sprawling vine with both hands, feeling the care flowing from him. That was a nice surprise. Auntie Bran had always said rote magicians cared little for the natural world or its seasons, but this one showed some respect for living things. She drew a soft strip of boiled flax stem from her apron pocket and tied the vine to its pole.

They worked together smoothly, without much need for words. It was a pleasant feeling. At the end of the row Delen straightened and smiled at him. "I can show you the gardens now, if you still have time."

"I'd like to," he said, squinting briefly at the sun. "We have plenty of time before dark."

He turned to her, his face serious. "Besides, I want to apologize to you again, while my insult is fresh. You were right to rebuke me, even though I meant no harm."

Delen blushed and looked down. "But I was in the wrong, too, Master Yurud. I should have shown more respect, given your station."

She looked up. His eyes were intent upon her—dark, captivating green. She had to explain. "I was sent away from my last position because the Clan-lord's youngest son tried to take me and I refused. I'm sensitive about being touched without permission." She hoped she didn't sound pathetic and weak. "I can't afford to be sent away again."

She watched a thought shadow pass behind his eyes. "Ah. I understand better now." He opened his mouth as if to say more, but he looked away for a moment. "That's an outrage," he said, his voice flat and hard. He turned to her again, his cheeks flushed. "An outrage. I personally guarantee you that will never happen while you are here at Albessind, and I'm sorry to have seemed like I might be another with similar intent. I just wanted to brush away... I have no excuse. I just didn't think."

"Thank you for saying that." So he wasn't angry—that was a relief. She checked her hair for bits of leaf, in case she'd picked up more. "Perhaps that is a difference between our craft and yours, Master Yurud. We almost always have leaves in our hair and dirt under our fingernails." She pointed to the gate. "I'll take you to the fruit orchard first."

On the other side of the beans, Yurud fell in step beside her. "Our traditions certainly have reputations of being different. I'm intrigued."

"You won't be offended if I speak plainly?"

Yurud laughed. "I seem to have survived your plain speaking so far. I'm pretty secure in my craft and its role in the welfare of Riardan, so please—speak as plainly as you wish."

Delen glanced at him, jealous of his confidence. Very well. She would speak plainly. "My Auntie Bran calls your rote tradition will magic, because you are governed only by your will, which you use to bend the world to your purpose. She says you cast whatever rote spell you wish whenever it pleases you, with results anyone can predict. In contrast, we who practice nature magic are obliged to work according to the elements and seasons, because the power we wield is not ours. It belongs to the forces of nature. We borrow it when they are willing to lend it, and channel it through our casting. The result is not always so predictable, because the casting must always serve the balance of nature before it serves us. Then the power we called returns to the flow of nature when the working is done."

Yurud looked thoughtful as they passed through the gate. "Hmm. Not sure that's completely fair to us, or even accurate, but your aunt may have a point. Anyway, it's a fascinating argument." He tilted his head toward the path before them. "Lead on."

Just beyond the garden wall Delen paused at a vine covered in delicate white star-shaped flowers with unusually long corollas. "These have the most delicious nectar in the neck," she said, picking one. On impulse, she spun a small glamour over it, nothing so obvious or aggressive as an attraction spell, just a small bias to make him more inclined to protect her should Mirren still want to let her go. Good. He didn't notice her use of magic. She'd strengthen the glamour with a second casting, if he took another one.

She offered him the flower. "Just hold it on your tongue and let the nectar leak out. That's what I do," she said plucking one for herself. "You don't have to eat the flower, but I love to. The petals add spice to the nectar's sweetness." She watched Yurud put it in his mouth.

"Mmm, that's remarkable. The bees must love these. Thank you." He frowned and passed a hand over his eyes, as if the light was suddenly too bright for him.

"Another?"

"Please. I've never tasted anything like them."

By the time they resumed their walk to the orchard, she had given him two more.

After a little silence, Yurud spoke again. "I'd like to revisit the differences you see between your magic and mine sometime, maybe with my mentor who has knowledge of both traditions." He grimaced. "And with a referee. Your aunt doesn't seem to think much of us."

Delen laughed to cover her surprise at how open-minded he seemed. And he had a sense of humor, too. "I'm just telling you what I've been taught. Auntie thinks rote magicians are all selfish, arrogant and dangerous. She has her reasons." She hesitated over a confession. "Although you're the first I've actually talked to myself."

He cocked his head at her and smiled playfully. "I have my work cut out for me then, don't I?"

His smile made her shiver. He was too charming. She didn't dare answer or she'd start flirting. Instead, she pointed to the first trees of the orchard. "We have apples, pears and cherries here, about a dozen of each, and figs down the slope, closer to the river. We use or preserve most of what we produce, and trade or sell the rest. I think the coming crop will be good. All the signs so far are strong."

Yurud stared up into an apple tree. "Have you had any teachers other than your aunt?"

The familiar shame welled up, bitter in her mouth. "I should have learned from my mother, but—" she wondered how dangerous it might be to admit her true weakness. No, she'd not disclose that she had no Book of Seasons of her own, and therefore wasn't fully able to do her job here. Even worse, it meant she had little hope of learning how to cure Auntie Bran—that too soon Delen would be utterly alone and without family or even a single ally. "—my mother disappeared. Taken prisoner, Auntie says, when I was but six. I can't remember much of what she was like." That would have to be enough. It was a relief when he nodded but didn't press for more.

"This is the path that leads to the lower orchard," she said. "Mind the stone steps, they'll be a bit slick after the rain."

"I'm sorry about your mother," Yurud said, his voice surprisingly tender. Then he tilted his head as if he'd just heard a strange noise. "But surely there's been no rain. The sky's been clear all day."

Delen smiled, hoping not to seem smug. "Not down there. The conditions were favorable today, so I asked the river mist for a good soaking this morning, just for this bottom part of the orchard. Figs need more water than the other trees. The rain was a little slower in coming than I'd hoped. It's just finished."

Yurud stopped on the first flagstone with naked surprise across his face. "Weather control is high level work. I had no idea you were so accomplished."

How Delen wished that were true. She shook her head. "I can't control the weather. I just invited rain to come, and this time it said yes. Sometimes it says no." She didn't dare reveal how painfully unfinished her magic really was. On the other hand, she couldn't afford to have Yurud think she was too powerful, perhaps even a potential threat.

"Auntie Bran says she has nothing left to teach me, but I know I have much more to learn. I know I have ability, but no teacher to take me deeper."

"Hmm." Yurud's face brightened. "I might be able to help with that."

Delen tensed. What did he want, behind that quick and far-too-generous offer? "That's good of you, but I don't want to learn your kind of magic." She hoped he wouldn't be too insulted.

"No, I wasn't thinking that at all." He turned to her, looking at her as if she were a puzzle he couldn't solve yet. "I would never try to force my craft on you, but a couple of possibilities occur to me." He fondled one of the fleshy fig leaves on a branch in front of him. "One is studying with a renowned nature witch up in Pandrakis. Albessind has a strong relationship with one of the Clan-lords there." The leaf snapped between his fingers. "I could—"

"Be careful," Delen interrupted. "Don't get any of that fresh sap on your skin, it's a harsh irritant."

"Thanks for the warning." He held on to the leaf, clearly unconcerned. "I could arrange to speak with Mistress Talwyn in Pandrakis, if you like, to see if she'd take you on as an advanced student."

"Oh," was all she could say. To have a chance of real training dropped in her lap so easily, after years of aching hope—it was too much. He had to expect something in return.

"And I think you should join the Magician's Guild," Yurud went on, his voice bright, words coming faster. "It recently formed under order of the new Council of the Clans. We've been assigned some very important work, and I think you could help us. I'd be glad to sponsor your application for entry."

"Why would you do that?"

Yurud's eyebrows shot up. "Why would I not? Doing either would benefit Albessind, and I for one would take pleasure in seeing you come into your full potential."

Delen looked at him sideways, unnerved. "You would? But I'm just the garden witch, who stood at the very end of your greeting line today."

He shook his head. "I understand that. But I have nothing to gain from preserving your lack of knowledge or skill. Quite the contrary. It's clear you have significant natural ability."

"But what would you gain if I became more skilled?"

He looked puzzled for a moment, then spread his arms and laughed. "What can I say? I like having powerful friends." He sobered and rubbed the back of his neck. "I keep getting the feeling you think there's a dark motive behind my offer. You should know that I don't hold the same low opinion of nature magic as many of my colleagues do. Is it really so hard to think my help might be free of some secret trap?"

The glamour had obviously taken, but Delen still couldn't bring herself to trust him. "Auntie Bran says most men are interested only in power they themselves can wield, take or use. It's happened to both of us. Most of my experience confirms that."

"Well, that stings." Yurud scowled at his hands. Maybe he'd touched some fig sap after all. "I admit that might well be true of some men. But please don't condemn all of us as if we were like that." He turned to her and grinned. "Some of us are pretty decent people in spite of our tragically male flaws."

Delen laughed against her better judgment. He was easy to laugh with. She wished the real issue was just a question of decent intention. "Don't you want more power?"

"Of course I do," he said without a trace of hesitation or apology in his voice. "I've been called ambitious more than once. I'm hungry for more skill and more knowledge. I even want the increased recognition among my peers which would come with all that." He gazed at her and paused. "But never at the expense of others. Especially you."

"So you would help me, and I wouldn't be obligated to you somehow?"

Yurud screwed up his mouth, looking frustrated. "No obligation at all outside of our professional relationship. We do both work for the same employer, after all."

Magical collaboration with a man was exactly what Auntie had warned her against for years. "In a very different capacity," she said. She ached to say yes, but his offer seemed too perfect, and the difference between their ability to say no was too great.

"Yes, in very different capacity. But I don't think you're listening to what I'm saying. We can work together to benefit Albessind. And you could help the cause of nature magic in the guild."

So tempting. So dangerous. She couldn't find the right answer.

He held up his hands, as if giving up. "Look, I will never coerce you to do anything. I promise. I'm not a predator. I've offered you my help. You decide whether or not to take it." He turned and started walking back toward the house.

She had to say something. "Yes," she called out, her heart pounding. "Thank you." The words slid out too easily. She hoped she didn't sound desperate. "Especially learning from Mistress Talwyn. But I'm afraid of joining the guild."

Yurud turned back to her, looking surprised. "Afraid? Of what?"

She caught up with him, and they started up the hill together. How could she tell him that she wasn't skilled enough to join the guild, and every hostile rote magician would see it immediately? "It's too dangerous. Auntie Bran says—"

Yurud's snort startled her. His irritation was obvious, but what could she do? All she had was what she'd been taught, and she would never apologize for that. "Auntie Bran says lightning never strikes cabbages."

He stopped mid-stride. "Cabbages?" He shook his head. "Really?"

"It's an old saying from the Lower World. A revolution somewhere, long ago. It makes perfect sense to me."

"You'll be fine. And you'll have my support as your sponsor. I don't offer that lightly. My reputation would be on the line, too."

"I need to talk it over with—"

"Auntie Bran." He seemed more resigned than disapproving now. "I understand. Just let me know what you decide."

"May I take leave to visit her tonight? I'll come back with my answer."

He gave her a curt, businesslike nod. "I'll let Mirren know you'll be gone for a couple of days. Will that be enough time?"

"More than enough. I need only one."

Delen missed their earlier relaxed banter as they climbed the slope. Still, his offer was a reason to hope, finally, for a Book of her own. And soon! Before, she'd had only wishes. She forced herself to seem calm.

As they headed back in the direction of the walled garden and the house, she pointed out features she thought would interest him: the woodlot, the herb garden, the patch of lavender to be sold in dried bundles at the village market, and finally the improved mulberries and even the struggling spinach.

As they paused by the garden gate, she made her best curtsey. "Thank you, Master Yurud. I hope you enjoyed seeing the gardens. I'm grateful for your interest in helping me learn, I really am. I hope you can sense my gratitude in spite of my caution."

He studied her in silence a moment, as if trying to read something behind her eyes. "The gardens are lovely, and interesting, but not near as much as the one who cares for them. Let me know your decision concerning my offers, once you've discussed them with your aunt." He gave her a little smile and turned to stride toward the house.

Delen watched him walk away, wondering if she'd made a mistake in challenging his motives so openly. No, if she'd been too harsh the glamour should soften any negative impact. He'd even thought her lovely and interesting. But the glamour wouldn't hold forever. She would take care to be more diplomatic in future.

She touched the pouch at her belt, where her flying feather and other charm-objects lay. After sunset she would fly to Auntie. In the meantime the garden called for more attention.

The Garden Witch
Chapter Three

Y urud leaned back against his office door, grateful to be where he could be alone and regroup. His nerves fizzed from his time with Delen. He was in trouble, that much was painfully clear. He glanced at his desk. A silver tray bearing today's messages had arrived while he'd been making a fool of himself in the vegetable garden.

He riffled through them, checking the seals. All from the Guild. He was in no mood to wade into its squabbles at the moment, which surprised him. Usually he leapt into them hungrily as a wolf into a pen of piglets.

The ink on the charter forming the Guild and appointing him as its first Chair was barely dry. Only days after his appointment the Council had ordered the membership to solve the problem of the unstable gates. In the ensuing five months they'd accomplished almost nothing except to form competing factions within the membership. No one seemed the least interested in solving the problem put in front of them. Unless they got credit for the solution while making sure no one else did, of course.

The Council didn't care about Guild factions. They had plenty of their own factions to worry about. More importantly, the Council would run out of patience with them if they didn't deliver a practical solution soon.

The next Seeding was scheduled to occur in the spring. The clan houses selected to take part would be announced soon. It would be the first since Queen Rhianna's demise, and the Council couldn't afford to tell three dozen aristocratic families they'd been awarded the coveted rights to travel to the Lower World to breed, only to have their chosen representatives die in a malfunctioning gate. The Guild would never survive that catastrophe, either. Heads would roll. Possibly his.

The Albessind farm ledgers Mirren had given him sat on the desk, waiting for his review. One each for River Farm, Spring Farm, and High Meadow. He knew so little about farming, and now he was responsible for three of them in addition to the great house and the village itself. A wormy little voice wondered if he was in over his head. No. He was young and lacked decades of experience, true enough, but he'd been chosen by the Council to chair the new Guild precisely because he didn't have decades of political baggage, and he'd been chosen by Lady Eva and Talak to manage Albessind's holdings on her behalf. He'd prove to them all they'd chosen well.

But his barely controlled attraction to the garden witch was a complication. Delen was beautiful, no one would dare say otherwise, but he'd dallied with beautiful women before, never once feeling this, this, what was it, even? This staggering, consuming longing. Fascination. She was altogether disorienting. Maybe even dangerous.

It wasn't just her pluck or her physical beauty, though. Something about her magic, too. Just watching her as she stood in the garden, she'd seemed so vast and mysterious, so *planted*, far, far beyond his reach. Her feet seemed to sink deep into the soil, her hair spread out into the sky, her body...

He barked out a laugh. Good thing she had no idea how unnecessary her little attraction charm on the flowers had been. She'd already bewitched him without their help. He snorted at the thought, but it was true. He was utterly bewitched. He'd dispelled her charm immediately, of course, without effort. But as they tied up the beans together he'd felt her magic swirling around him, calling to him, as if it might draw him into some mystery he'd never known before.

Yes, his fascination with Albessind's garden witch meant trouble. But for reasons he chose not to examine, he found he didn't care as much as he should.

He had plenty of work to distract him from daydreams. With fresh resolve he sat at his desk and sliced open the seal on the first message.

Author's Note

Thank you for choosing to read my book. I hope you were moved and satisfied.

Word of mouth is powerful!

When a reader leaves a review on Amazon (and elsewhere!) to let others know they enjoyed the book and why, they are helping an author like me—more than you might imagine.

I hope you'll consider leaving a review for Last Lady. My Amazon Author Page (amazon.com/stores/Lloyd-A.-Meeker/author/B008F C5VF4) provides a path to all my books where you can post your review. Thank you!

While you're there, I hope you'll take a look to see if any of my other stories might be of interest to you.

I love to hear directly from readers, too. I can be reached at stories @lloydmeeker.com or through my website (lloydmeeker.com). I hope you'll subscribe to my low-key newsletter, which should come to you every four to six weeks. That way you'll hear about new developments before non-subscribers.

Thank you for spending this time with me, and until our paths merge again I wish you a good and fulfilling journey.

About the Author

Having led what can only be described as an irregular life, Lloyd A. Meeker can honestly say he's grateful for all of it, and he's got stories to tell.

Born and raised in an intentional community in rural Colorado, he's been a minister, a light aircraft pilot, an office worker, a janitor, a drinker, and a software developer on his way to writing novels. A Dodgers fan and three-time cancer survivor, he's practiced and taught subtle energy healing all his adult life. He's sung in church and rainbow choirs, and currently channels his passion for music into learning the octave mandolin. He and his husband met in 2002, and live in Montpellier, France.

His titles include Traveling Light, Russ Morgan, PI, and Stone and Shell. His novel The Companion was a finalist in the 2015 Lambda Literary Awards.

www.ingramcontent.com/pod-product-compliance
Lightning Source LLC
Chambersburg PA
CBHW020354260626
47156CB00007B/2110

* 9 7 8 1 9 3 9 0 9 2 1 2 0 *